GRACE

GRACE

Jane

Roberts

Wood

DUTTON

DUTTON
Published by the Penguin Group
Penguin Putnam Inc., 375 Hudson Street, New York, New York 10014, U.S.A.
Penguin Books Ltd, 27 Wrights Lane, London W8 5TZ, England
Penguin Books Australia Ltd, Ringwood, Victoria, Australia
Penguin Books Canada Ltd, 10 Alcorn Avenue,
Toronto, Ontario, Canada M4V 3B2
Penguin Books (N.Z.) Ltd, 182–190 Wairau Road, Auckland 10, New Zealand

Penguin Books Ltd, Registered Offices: Harmondsworth, Middlesex, England

Published by Dutton, a member of Penguin Putnam Inc.

First Printing, May, 2001
1   3   5   7   9   10   8   6   4   2

 REGISTERED TRADEMARK—MARCA REGISTRADA

LIBRARY OF CONGRESS CATALOGING-IN-PUBLICATION DATA
Wood, Jane Roberts.
Grace / Jane Roberts Wood.
p.   cm.
ISBN 0-525-94602-0 (alk. paper)
1. World War, 1939–1945—Texas, East—Fiction.   2. Neighborhood—Fiction.
3. Texas, East—Fiction.   I. Title.
PS3573.O5945   G7   2001
813'.54—dc21
00-050336

Printed in the United States of America
Set in Galliard
Designed by Julian Hamer

PUBLISHER'S NOTE
This book is a work of fiction. Names, characters, places, and incidents
are either the product of the author's imagination or are used fictitiously,
and any resemblance to actual persons, living or dead, business
establishments, events, or locales is entirely coincidental.

Portions of this book originally appeared in
The Pawn Review and the *Southwest Review.*

This book is printed on acid-free paper. ∞

For
Annabel, Thomas, Alex, Catherine Jane,
Victoria, Clinton, and Charles.
With love, Jane

AUTHOR'S NOTE

For their careful listening and perceptive comments
during the writing of this book, my thanks to
Jeannie Davis and Nancy Jones Castilla.
And for his expert and generous help and advice,
I also wish to thank Paxton Moore.

GRACE

Prologue

COLD Springs is an East Texas town of forty thousand inhabitants or so. It was named by the earliest settlers, long before the Civil War, who, when they saw the lake and found the spring that fed it, rested under oak and linden trees in full leaf, and marveled at the greenness, at everything surgent with spring, said: *"Here. Here is where we will cast our lot."* The next wave, most from Tennessee, Mississippi, Alabama, Georgia, the Carolinas, a few from Virginia, was swept here by the aftermath of the Civil War when GONE TO TEXAS was crudely scratched on shattered doors all over those states. The last immigrants, and by far the largest number, have come from the North to work in the defense plant and the prison and the army supply depot. They have come to a town whose inhabitants (not counting the soldiers of two wars or the sons sent off to Princeton) have seldom traveled far from Cold Springs—a mere handful to Europe and several dozen families to New York during the 1939 World's Fair.

It is a town where people boast about being southern, although few would attempt to define the term. "A proud way of looking at the past," ventures the history teacher at Cold Springs Junior College. "Nonsense," replies the government teacher, a cynic marking time until his draft number is called.

"What do we have to be so proud of? It's all hot air. Hot air nurtured by a defeated people."

But the word *southern* conveys more to the people here than a lost cause, a romantic past. It is a state of mind and a way of life. It means fine linens and good cooking and a courteous way of speaking. It means close family ties and good breeding and respectability. This last most of all.

And *northern?* This from a biology professor at the college: "Well, they're just different."

"How? In what way?" Again the government teacher, now poised to report to Fort Belvoir in Virginia.

"In every way!" they chorus.

The newcomers, desiring nice kitchens, are hurriedly building nondescript, rather shabby houses in the far north part of town. The natives live in the older sections where the streets are numbered and thus named: First Street, Second Street, Third Street, and so on, through Twenty-ninth Street. The streets that run north and south have names that are only slightly more imaginative: Pine, Elm, Olive, Wood. The town is not zoned, for this is the South, and who ever heard of zoning in the South! Zoning implies snobbery. And unfairness. Still, all these new people, so many of them, moving in. It was better before the War. Everything was better.

Four houses, as distinctively different as are those who live in them, sit on the 900 block of Pine Street. The Moore house, built just after the Civil War, rising slightly above the others, once stood alone, the only house on the block. But three generations ago the property on the south end was sold, and then— who knows when?—a little miserly scrap at the north end of the block was sold by an improvident, careless ancestor. The Moore house is a nice old Georgian with its hip roof of tin over shingles, its plastered walls and simple, elegant cornices. The only ornate thing about the house is its entrance with the marble steps leading to a carved mahogany door. The house is well kept. You have to say that for Robert Moore. Half the time some worker is over there, painting, repairing, replacing, propping up the old house. It, the Moore house, is clearly Robert's house, for what did his Yankee wife bring to the marriage? Nothing that anyone can touch or polish or hold up to the light. But Robert is crazy about his wife. That counts for something! And Robert's old aunties, the Little Brontës the town affectionately calls them, have nothing but good to say about Barbara. It is a fact that the whole town, having grown used to her ways, is markedly charitable toward her.

Although the Moores have come down in the world, it is only a monetary decline. There is still family—the two aunts, who are beyond reproach, and Robert Moore's ancestors—a great-grandfather who had been a Texas congressman and a great-great aunt who had become the fifty-three-year-old bride of a man who had once been the governor of Texas.

Although the Balderidge house is on the north corner, right next to the Moores', it is firmly separated from their house because it faces Ninth Street rather than Pine, and it is separated by the thick and ancient crepe myrtle hedges that surround it. It is even further separated, irrevocably separated, by the lack of family and money and education of those who live in it. This house—unpainted, unrepaired, *unloved*—has four small rooms and a front porch furnished only with a rush-bottom rocking chair, it, too, unpainted. It is here that Mrs. Balderidge sits and talks, sometimes quite angrily, to people no one can see. From her rocking chair, she can look across the street and see the row of houses the church rents to the "coloreds." Those houses—identical, two rooms, junk pine—that have never known a coat of paint, sit behind an open drainage ditch.

Grace Gillian's house sits on the south side of the Moores'. And what she's done to that house since Bucy Gillian left her! First, painted it turquoise, a ridiculous color. Hardly respectable. Then moved her stove and refrigerator upstairs, moved the whole kitchen upstairs! Who knows how much that cost! The very next year, she closed in the long, narrow, upstairs porch (calls it "the gallery"), and put her dining table and chairs up there. That's where she spends her time. But the town understand the roots of all this. Grace is a Cold Springs girl, the daughter of Molly and James O'Brian, and so all this decorating foolishness is just that wild Irish streak that runs in the O'Brian blood. And, thank goodness, the front of the house, a simple, two-story clapboard, looks the way it has always looked, except for its turquoise color and the dark green (so dark it looks black) front door.

The Appleby house on the south corner, right next to Grace's, was built before the First World War. John Appleby bought it in the thirties when he, invited by a cousin to join his law firm, came to Cold Springs from North Carolina. It is a restrained, old Victorian—modest gingerbread trim along the eaves and gables, a steep roof, floor-to-ceiling windows, a simple front door, robust porch posts and a generous porch that sweeps across the front of the house. What with Anna being sick so long, John has not kept it up. And who could blame him? The green shutters need retouching, and in the back, the white paint just above the kitchen door has begun to peel.

The people in Cold Springs do not enjoy change. Things on the 900 block of Pine have gone along for years just the same, but now everything is changing. It's the War. Changing everything. Changing everybody.

Part

ONE

Chapter 1

· *1* ·

GRACE Gillian kneels before her hyacinth bed, her bare fingers raking the accumulation of decaying leaves from around the plants. She has long since shucked off her gardening gloves. She loves the feel of the earth's awakening, the humid, fertile smell of it.

Grace is thirty-eight years old. Slender. High cheekbones. Generous mouth. Dark brown hair, almost auburn with the russet highlights around her face. But it is her eyes, soft gray eyes tilting up at the corners, that one remembers. When she reads a poem she loves or when a student makes a perceptive comment, her face lights up and her eyes become radiantly blue. But she does not know she is beautiful. And, although her name is Grace, neither does she think of herself in metaphysical terms, such as, *state of.* When she thinks of herself at all, it is in sensible, nearly mundane terms—teacher, gardener, friend. But she is neither sensible nor mundane. And on this day, as she rakes the sodden leaves from the hyacinth bed, she is thinking of John, whom she loves beyond the telling. *My true, pure love. A love not fueled by desire.* This is what she believes. She feels she has long since turned away from desire.

The pecan trees, arching high over her and over her turquoise-colored house, have not yet leafed out. Nor has the elm by the front door. But the magnificent live oak is in full leaf. And a single wild plum and a domestic peach in the northwest corner of her garden are dizzily in bloom, infusing the blue air and the yellow grass with the colors and scents of spring.

A song from the kitchen radio drifts out into her garden. "I'll be seeing you in all the old familiar places," Jo Stafford sings tenderly. Since the War, all the songs are heartrending to Grace. Looking closely at the hyacinth buds, she can faintly discern the color—purple or white—each will become. Colors of mourning.

She, Grace, although not in mourning, is deeply sad. Anna, her next-door neighbor, is sick. Sick to death. When she thinks it again, *sick to death,* the phrase takes on its literal meaning. Anna is sick, and in a day or two she will go to her death. And then John will leave. He has told her this. "If something happens to Anna"—*if* not *when* said carefully—"I'm going to get into this War." Raising an eyebrow, he smiled. "I'll probably end up with a desk job. But if they'll have me, I'm going." Remembering, her eyes fill, and she sits back on her heels and with the sleeve of her sweater wipes the perspiration and tears from her face.

It's true that the tide has turned. Yesterday the Allies bombed industrial targets in a town called Brunswick, deep inside France. The Allies are winning. Everybody knows the War will soon be over. Farmers meeting on muddy, country roads trade shots of whiskey and hope through windows of pickup trucks: "This time next year, my boy will be home, helping me get the fields ready for cotton." Then, unable to voice the unthinkable, they add, "if the creek don't rise," or "if nothing don't happen." Women, boldly tempting the gods, lean from under hair dryers at Chic-les-Dolls Beauty Salon: "I didn't have the heart to put up a tree last Christmas. But this year we've already picked out the biggest one on the place!" So! It was agreed. Probably by September. Certainly no later than Christmas. All the sons and lovers and husbands—just boys, so young—will be coming home.

Young, until lately. Now they are calling up men as old as forty-five for active duty. And all over town, men even older are trying to get into the War. Some are fathers, desperately trying to follow their young sons—living, dead or missing-in-action sons—into battle. Everybody longs to play some part, however small, in the great and terrible—made unbelievably romantic by Hollywood—War.

Now a small gray spider, its filament of newly spun web invisible, appears before Grace's eyes. She moves her finger through the air above it, finds silken thread and deposits the wiggling spider on a hyacinth. By Christmas. *Maybe by Thanksgiving,* she tells herself, getting up, stretching.

In her kitchen, she fills the soup kettle with water, drops in cubes of beef (two red points, but never mind, she can get more from her washwoman), adds fresh vegetables, a can of tomatoes, garlic, a dollop of vinegar. She rolls oregano in her fingers, sniffs it, drops it in. Adds thyme. Rosemary. A witches' brew. Then she takes a bottle of red wine from the cupboard.

She has bathed and, dressing, got as far as her slip and stockings when Amelia calls. "Heard anything? From the hospital?"

"No."

"Call me."

"I'm fine."

And in the space between Amelia's question and her reassurance, she sees the evening, imagines it stretching before her—she, sitting with John while he eats, talking quietly about her garden and the good news from the European front, and John, comforted by the news and the soup, gradually relaxing, able to get through another night, another day.

After the briefest pause, "Good-bye," Amelia says.

Within the strong bonds of friendship between these two East Texas women there are carefully drawn boundaries that must not be breached. When Bucy left, Amelia had asked,

"What would have happened if John had come to your door first? A blind date? Do you suppose—?"

Plucking a grocery list from the kitchen table and Amelia's questions from the air, "Let's go to the grocery store. Get our shopping done early," Grace had said quickly, strengthening a barrier, redrawing a line. But in the small neighborhood grocery (bread on one side of the aisle and canned goods on the other), Grace had imagined an eighteen-year-old girl, herself, in a white dress, running to answer the doorbell, opening the door to John—tall, blue-eyed, dark. And John, laughing, teasing, "I'm selling magazines, ma'am. Can I interest you in a *McCall's*? *Redbook*? In me?" And she, recognizing (a preternatural recognition) that here—in his arms, this!—is home, would have stepped through the doorway into John's arms. And in that single golden moment, she would have fallen in love with John, rather than slowly, sensibly (she tells herself this), through the long years.

"Grace, four cans of asparagus! I didn't think you liked canned asparagus," Amelia had exclaimed, calling her back. And she, astonished by her asparagus-filled basket, had laughed, "What could I be thinking of!"

John, that's what! Amelia had told herself. And since Grace's husband had gotten on a train and gone to New York with never a word to Grace or anybody else, Amelia kept her thoughts—*always impossible, completely inappropriate*—about her best friend's marriage to herself.

However, Amelia feels free to give certain kinds of advice: "Grace, you ought to get out more." She says this frequently.

But where in an East Texas town does an abandoned wife go? Grace wonders. Although she is not expected to climb upon a funeral pyre, she is psychologically shielded by the mystery of abandonment, the *awfulness* of it. For why would a man do that? Cold Springs asks. Just up and leave his wife! And one so pretty!

But Grace keeps her counsel about the *whys* of her husband's leaving, and John is there, next door. She is consoled by John's presence in the house next door, comforted by long summer evenings overhung by pewter-colored skies and John's telling of this or that trial and laughing at his own foibles, solaced by autumn's ripeness followed by the smell of pines drummed into the cold, crisp air by winter rains and the three of them before a bright fire in the Appleby dining room and, now, a new spring with the hyacinths and daffodils, the plum and peach trees once more in flower.

Listening to the evening news, Grace hears that guerrillas have killed four hundred Nazis near Mount Olympus in Greece and that the Germans in retaliation have shot 317 citizens at Messina. And our boys are still on the beach at Anzio, desperately fighting to gain a foothold. *Oh, God, this horrible war. Let it be over soon,* she prays.

When the soup is done, she goes outside to watch for John. She sits under the oak tree in the swing that John, under Anna's close direction, had hung for her. Clouds have rolled in, big cumulus clouds, the lowest one darkening, and it is this cloud, growing ever darker as it sweeps across the sky, that brings the wind. Thunder rumbles distantly. Over her head the huge branches of the oak lift and sway, propelling her back to her childhood. As a little girl, on just such a day, she would climb up into a tree as high as she dared, reveling in the wind that tossed the branches about.

She stands and, hands on her hips, gauges the height and the distance between the swaying branches. *Could she climb this tree? Now? Maybe.* Kicking off her shoes, she puts a foot on the swing, holds the chain by which it hangs, and then, grasping the highest limb she can reach, she sets her foot upon a strong, thick limb and pulls herself up. Turning to sit snugly against the trunk, she is immediately caught up in the revelous frenzy of the leaves.

Watching the branches tossing in wild abandon all around her, she thinks: *If he were to see me now, what might he say?*

"Move over. I'm coming up there with you." Or *holding up his arms: "Jump! Come on! I'll catch you."*

She stays in the tree until she hears the phone, runs to answer it. John is calling from the hospital, his words so closed off, so choked by grief, she barely recognizes him. "The doctor says Anna will die tonight." His voice, sandpaper tearing, coming harshly from his throat: "Grace, could you—?"

"I'll come, John. I'll come right down," she says, but when she gets to the hospital, John has gone.

She sits outside Anna's door, knowing her friend is on her last journey. She listens to the staccato sounds of the crisply ticking clock, watches the sun dapple the brown linoleum floor. *"Glory be to God for dappled things."* She thinks of apples at the A&P and oranges. Lemons. Traps! Her mind veers away from Anna, trapped by death, on the other side of the shiny gray door.

Sometime later—who knows how long?—the nurse appears. Her look sweeps the waiting room. "Where is Mr. Appleby?"

"I don't know."

"Mr. Appleby's been drinking."

"Mr. Appleby's been suffering."

There is no compassion in the nurse's voice. "Mrs. Appleby is dead."

"I'll tell him."

Both houses are dark when she turns into her drive. She calls Amelia.

"Poor thing," Amelia says. "Two years is too long for anyone to suffer. How's John?"

"He's anesthetizing himself right now, or was. I'll take over some soup when he comes home."

When John has not returned by nine o'clock, she takes a tray—the soup, hot cornbread, fruit cocktail—to the gallery table. She eats slowly, listening for the sound of John's car in the drive.

When he has not come by eleven (*Is he at the hospital? At the funeral home?*), Grace puts on her gown and goes through the house turning out lights. Downstairs, a plaintive *meow* at the back door reminds her she has not fed Cal. She unhooks the back screen door, and although it is dark, some movement of shadows signals John's presence.

"John?"

"Here, Grace, I'm out here in the swing."

She slips on her robe and pads barefoot out to the backyard.

"Anna died," he says dully.

"I know."

"Sit down, Grace. Keep me company."

She sits by him. From time to time he starts the swing, and they move back and forth, or he reaches over and picks up a glass and drinks before carefully setting it down again.

"Anna," he says hoarsely. "She was never happy. I never made her happy."

"I don't know if you can make someone . . ."

"Don't, Grace. Don't analyze this with fancy logic. It won't help."

He leans down, picks up his glass and holds it in both hands. "Sorry. But . . . need to say this. Need to face it. My wife was never happy. She lived all those years and was *never* happy. When I married her, this little slip of a girl, eyes sad as a dove's call, 'You'll be happy with me,' I told her. But, oh, Jesus!"

John is past tipsy. He is drunk. Tomorrow, will he remember what he is saying to her now? Will he be sorry? Will she?

"John."

"Hush. Hush, Miss Gillian. Oh, Miss Gillian. Hey, you know that poem? That crazy love song. You read it to me one day. Mr. T. S. Eliot wrote it, and God, I loved that poem! 'I have heard the mermaids singing . . . I do not think that they will sing to me.' Remember those lines? Well, Anna had. She had heard them. She knew they were out there, sunning on rocks far out in the sea. Listening to the songs of whales. And singing their mermaid songs. But they never sang to her. They only made her sad."

John. Always steady. Sound. And yet, this lovely poetic side, sending an unexpected note of pleasure down her spine.

He sips from his glass. She looks up at the sky. Not a star in it, not even the moon.

"Anna knew she was missing the fullness of life. Grace, old friend, do you know how sad that makes me? She went round, worried, trying so hard all the time to be happy."

"There were times when she seemed—"

"Seemed. Seemed!" His voice is scornful. He turns in the swing, grasps her shoulders. "Grace, you're happy. What makes you happy? Your silly garden? Your silly cat? Your silly turquoise house? Your silly . . ."

"Husband?"

"Sorry, Grace. Sorry. No right. Have no right."

"What you just said. That's what's silly! My cat's not silly. Nor my garden. Nor my husband."

"Bucy. Well, I never understood how you and he . . . Sorry. No business. But got to say one more thing. About Anna. I never made her happy. And, son of a bitch that I am, after a while, I stopped trying."

Feeling soft fur twining around her leg, she picks up her yellow cat. "John, it's misting. Let's go in. I'll feed you and Cal."

"No, no soup. Soup's for tomorrow. Come on," taking her hand, stumbling over a small wisteria bush, "I'll walk you home." He looks up at the sky. "Where are the blasted stars? Every blasted one of them has disappeared." Carefully holding his drink up, as if toasting the missing stars, he turns in a clumsy circle.

She takes his arm. "I think I'd better walk you home."

"No. No, Miss Gillian. Escort you to your kitchen steps."

At the foot of the steps he stumbles again, and she turns and brushes his face. Then he is in her arms and she in his, and nothing, not Anna's death, or old voices, not God himself can still the passion that sweeps them from the steps to her bed. He, made so by Anna's long illness, is as starved as she. Their lovemaking is fierce, passionate. Deeply satisfying. Afterwards, lying in his arms, tears run down her face.

"John." She sighs, a deep contented sigh. Words gather: *I love you. I have always loved you.*

But, "God," he says and is asleep.

Lying there, by his side, she wonders if some part of her has always known this would happen, that one day he would be her lover. Tomorrow she will tell him she loves him. She shifts her body so that it follows the contours of his and sleeps.

She wakes, is instantly awake, before daylight, and before she opens her eyes, smooths the empty pillow, she knows that he has gone.

When the sun rises, the house next door begins to stir. Cars come and go, doors open and close, muted voices sift into the bedroom. She does not see John. In the full light of day, in the full realization of his loss, she does not want to see him. It is too soon.

· 2 ·

ON Monday Amelia calls. "The funeral's at eleven. I'll pick you up at ten-thirty."

Grace makes coffee and takes it to her bedroom. Looking into the mirror, she feels vaguely surprised that she looks just the same. Dazed, drenched by the memory of lovemaking, she bathes leisurely, bends to shake her breasts into a bra, slips on a navy blue dress, coils her hair in a bun at the nape of her neck, puts back the veil of her small hat and puts it on, gathers up gloves and purse. In the kitchen, she feeds Cal, pours more coffee and slips bread into the toaster.

Frowning, she is unable to believe that Anna will never again be at the table, in front of the fireplace, in Grace's swing.

How astonishing death is! she thinks. *How sad!* She was fond of Anna, but who would believe it now?

And how hungry all this love and grief has made her. When the toaster clicks, she butters the toast, smears blackberry jam on it and eats.

Amelia is all business when Grace gets into the car. "Hard luck. Poor Anna. But now John can get some rest. Going to work every day. Coming home to a sick wife. Ed said this morning that if that happened to him, he'd shoot himself. He's meeting us at the church. He's one of the pallbearers. And, oh, the funniest thing. When Ed went over there . . . Grace?" Having pulled up to a red light, Amelia is looking intently at her neck. "Grace?" she says again.

"I'm listening. Ed is a pallbearer, and what was the funniest thing?"

"Grace, I could swear that is a love bite on your neck. I could swear it is!"

Grace fumbles with the white collar of her dress. "Amelia, for goodness' sakes! We're going to a funeral."

"I know. I know where we're going."

"What about Ed? The funniest thing. You were telling me."

Having dared such a comment only because she recognizes the impossibility of lovemaking for Grace, at least so recently as to leave a bruise, Amelia again turns her attention to the road. "Well, Ed went over there this morning (I'm surprised you didn't see him), and just as he was driving up that woman that everybody says is crazy was hurrying away from the front door. She left a bunch of jonquils and a note that said, 'We are sorry.' John was touched. Ed said he really appreciated it."

"Her name is Balderidge. Her daughter, Dixie, a really bright girl, is one of my students."

"What about her father? Do you know him?"

"No. I don't know one thing about them, except that they live in that pitiful little house at the end of our alley."

"What about her mother? Who was she?"

"You mean before her marriage? Oh, Amelia, I don't keep up with all that. You know I don't. But I don't think she's from around here."

The parking lot at the church is almost full. The Moores arrive just as they do. Bobby is driving his mother. His father is, doubtless, also a pallbearer. Bobby hops out of the car and opens the door for his mother. Cold Springs, mildly criticizing, says that Barbara Moore is a little too reserved even for a Yankee. But, they add, as if in mitigation, she wears her clothes well. Today she wears a black linen dress, short sleeved, and a natural-colored straw hat with a black silk band. She is tall. Slender. The simplicity of her dress causes Grace to consider removing the veil from her own hat. As Bobby and his mother walk quickly into the church, the solemnity of his expression seems all wrong for the slight vulnerability of his body. *So young, too young for war. The problem with his eye will keep him out,* Grace tells herself, comforted by the thought.

Grace and Amelia, these two friends who have known each other since kindergarten, go in solemnly. In all their lives there have been so few funerals. Amelia's mother this past year. Grace's parents five years earlier. And so few of the funerals have touched them. But now, there's the War. Now the young men. Boys, still so young, whom Grace has taught two, three years earlier. She sits in the church, remembering them, silently calling their names, seeing their faces. Lawrence Shelborne. Redheaded with freckles and shy. Steve Bryce. Tall, high-tempered, responsive. Bob Wood. Handsome. Brilliant. A wonderful laugh. She begins to weep. It is all so terrible.

Amelia reaches over and pats her knee. "Don't cry," she murmurs. "Don't cry." But she, too, is weeping.

Afterwards, they stand, firmly singing, as the cortege leaves the church. Grace does not look at John, although she knows the moment he passes the pew where she stands.

*   *   *

A day after the funeral Grace sits in her gallery looking out into the treetops, all bare except for the live oak. She thinks: *He won't come today, not so soon. He'll be in and out of the house, taking care of all the things that one must when someone dies. But tomorrow he will come. He will be wearing his blue shirt, the color of his eyes, and he will follow me up the stairs. Together we will sit on my blue-and-white sofa, and I will say, "I believe I have always loved you." He will be surprised. He will say nothing for, of course, he has not loved me. Or he might say, "Grace, that night was wonderful. I'll never forget it." And then I will say, "I believe I have always loved you."*

It is all there before her—his voice, the touch of his hand, the easy grace with which he will take coffee from her hand, settle into the wicker chair or on the sofa beside her. He will say, *"Grace, I've always wondered . . ."*

But here her imagination fails. Leaning forward, she straightens the magazines on the low table in front of the sofa and then fills the blue bowl on the dining table with apples.

By Friday afternoon she is sure he will come. Filled with energy, she goes out into the garden and breaks off branches of wild plum and peach blossoms and puts them in a terra-cotta vase on the floor by the sofa. She makes a pitcher of lemonade, gets out tall glasses, chips ice. Looking at her watch, she is surprised to see that it's not yet five o'clock. Knowing John likes iced coffee in the spring, she makes a pot and sets it, steaming, in the icebox to chill.

This smell of coffee, the flowering blossoms, even the apples, give her house a wonderfully expectant, breathless air. Is this what she loves? she wonders, thinking vaguely of Bucy. Is this what she needs? The waiting? The anticipation?

Sitting beside John in the swing that night, she had caught his scent—faint, like newly turned earth. And when he had brushed against her, she had eagerly welcomed his mouth on hers and, as filled with urgency as he, had led him to her bed.

Spring is meant for love and for lovemaking. The thought comes swiftly, causing such delight that she rises and hurries downstairs, certain that he has come, and is surprised to see his empty drive.

He does not come on Saturday. When he comes (as she has known he would come), it is Sunday afternoon, a time reserved for visiting old ladies and newcomers. He comes in suit and tie, comes formally to the front door.

Knowing he has taken advantage of Grace's loneliness, of her impulsive and generous nature, John is filled with remorse. He has done what no gentleman would do. Ever. Never mind the coarseness of the barbershop and golf links comments he has heard about Grace since Bucy left, comments most often focusing on her breasts, for Grace does have the most wonderful, generous breasts. But then, he has always liked small breasts. Anna's. A wave of self-pity sweeps over him so that he hesitates before knocking. He has prepared an apology, made no less sincere by its carefully practiced nature, and he stands on the doorstep, marshaling his thoughts.

When Grace opens the door, her expression is, at first, totally blank. Then her eyes open wide, and she steps backward into the shadows of the entrance hall. Her face, bare of the bright lipstick she usually wears, together with her bare feet, makes her seem so completely vulnerable that he experiences another wave of remorse.

He leans forward and carefully kisses her cheek. "Grace, about the other night. It was an accident. I'm sorry it happened." As he kisses her and begins to speak, he notices a faint flush rising on her cheeks. His voice remains firm: "I'm embarrassed. It was a terrible accident. I had too much to drink. And, oh, Lord, I don't know what to say. Grace, I am so sorry!" He notices her gray eyes narrowing, and curiously, they seem to be growing darker. He is glad he has his apology firmly in mind. "It was Anna's being so sick for so long, and I was godalmighty

tired, and that's no excuse." He hears his voice rising and wonders why he is speaking as if to the deaf. He winces. Anna always
said that at times his voice was a poor imitation of Kaltenborn's.
He plunges ahead at almost a whisper: "I wouldn't hurt you
for the world." Now her eyes flash so alarmingly that it is a
minute before he can summon the rest of his apology: "Can you
forgive me?"

Grace cannot believe it! Such words—*sorry, embarrassed, an
accident*—to use about the wonder of their lovemaking. "Are
you finished? Anything more?" she asks.

Feeling dizzy now, for support he puts one hand on the
door frame, leans against it and continues with what he has
planned to say. "That's exactly how I feel," he says, briefly realizing (another wave of dizziness) this non sequitur is what he
had planned to say after she had said (as he had been sure she
would say), "Well, John. What happened doesn't change our
friendship."

It has not gone as he has planned. Grace has not been at all
receptive. He is not even sure that she is listening. He doggedly
continues: "Another reason I came over is to tell you that I've
been in touch with Washington. With Guy Latham. We were in
school together. He's a general now, and he says—"

"You can go straight to hell, John Appleby," she says.

Robotlike, he mentally continues his prepared remarks even
after Grace has slammed the door in his face.

Chapter 2

ROBERT Alexander Moore V, called Cinco by his friends and Bobby by his family, sits on the back steps of his house. Bobby is seventeen and, even with a lazy eye, can see well enough. He is planning to run away and join the navy. And another thing: He is planning to ask Dixie Balderidge to the Silver Key Gypsy Dance. He can't tell his folks about that, either.

The War is driving everybody crazy. Everybody but Dixie's mother, who was crazy *before* the Japs bombed Pearl Harbor. Last week after meeting Dixie in the Applebys' old carriage house—she had to climb out a window to meet him—it was about to storm, so he had cut across the backyards. With Mrs. Appleby real sick in the hospital, *real sick,* the Appleby house was dark almost all the time, and it was safe to cut across. Mrs. Appleby didn't like kids cutting across her yard—*wearing a trail,* she called it. But cutting across, he had seen a dark blue something, like a scrap of night sky, up in a tree. Going close, he saw it was his English teacher! "Hello, Bobby," she said, just as calm. "Hello, Bobby." Like that.

What with all the thunder and lightning, he said, "Mrs. Gillian, aren't you afraid you might get struck by lightning?"

She sat up straight and crossed her bare feet at the ankles.

"It's unlikely. And I've always enjoyed being out in the weather. It's exhilarating, Bobby."

Well, every boy in high school wants to help Mrs. Gillian, her husband just walking out on her like that, but he couldn't think of what to say next and went on home. He had not mentioned seeing Mrs. Gillian in the tree, because his father would say something dumb like, "I never knew an English teacher who wasn't frivolous." And then he would have gone on about frivolous English teachers all through supper, knowing Bobby's mother likes to read poetry and stuff like *The Red Badge of Courage*.

This morning he has come outside to wait for the new maid to come and cook his breakfast. He is trying to muster the courage to ask Dixie to the dance, a thing infinitely harder than joining the navy. But it is this last, his plan to tell her about the navy, that makes him pretty sure she will say yes. Voted the most popular girl in the junior class, Dixie is real popular with the boys. Real popular. But his telling her about joining the armed services will do the trick. When the Weatherly twins joined, every girl in high school stayed home for two weeks, hoping one of them would come over to say good-bye. He might ask Dixie tonight.

Bobby likes everything about Dixie. He likes her long brown hair and her glasses, thick as Coke bottles, that perch high on her nose. He likes the way her lips curl this way and that when she reads her poems to him. And her breasts underneath her sweaters. He thinks of touching them, longs to touch them, wondering if they'd feel like Jell-O. Or a loaf of warm bread just off the bread delivery truck. Studying in the old Appleby carriage house, he's been getting closer and closer to touching them, his hand sneaking farther and farther up under her sweater, inching up, until she giggles, "Oh, Bobby," and moves his hand. But sometimes it's quite a while before she notices where his hand is heading.

From Celia's radio in her room right above his head, B. G.

(he calls Benny Goodman "B. G.") swings into "Bye, Bye, Baby." Frank Sinatra, this skinny little guy about his own size, is singing. The girls are crazy about The Voice, as they call him. "Seems kinda tough now," Sinatra sings, and Bobby can feel his arm around Dixie, gliding with her across the floor, Dixie following so lightly it's like he's dancing by himself. "To say good-bye this way," Sinatra croons, and a quick movement, almost but not quite a step forward and back, "But papa's gotta be rough now," and he releases Dixie, whirling her off, her red skirt and brown hair flying, "So he can be sweet to you another day," and a quick two-step to catch her, and hands on her waist, he swings her between his legs, widespread, and then out and up as the applause begins.

He's getting hungry, but when he hears the whistling, he thinks it is the iceman whistling; but no, it is the new maid. Barefoot, swinging her shoes in her right hand, she seems to sway, rather than walk, up the winding drive. Wearing a blue cotton dress, the sun glistening on her gold earrings and gold necklace, she whistles right up to the steps. When she smiles down at him, the star-shaped gold filling in her front tooth shines like a jewel. Unexpected.

"You Bobby," she says. "Well, I'm yore mama's new maid."

Sitting beside him, she brushes the dust off her feet and slips them into her shoes. "Got to protect these shoes from road wear," she says. "Sold my last shoe stamps before I went to California to tell my honey good-bye. Rode all the way barefooted. Didn't put my shoes on till San Diego. Got off the train looking good. Sure did now." A note of pleasure in her voice, she fingers the necklace she wears. Then she puts her elbows on the step behind her and lifts her face to the sun. "I just about didn't come to work this morning. I'd rather a stayed home in my husband's arms, but he done left. On a ship. Going somewhere." The gold star, twinkling, belies the sadness in her voice.

He has no idea how to reply. He has never thought about a

maid being in her husband's arms or even considered that a maid might have a husband. If he has thought of a colored's sexuality at all, it is in the context of the movies: a cruel plantation owner having his way with a young colored girl, a faithful retainer saving a white girl from a carpetbagger. In his mind, maids seem no more than female eunuchs, but now here is his mother's new maid, talking about staying in the arms of her husband, *in bed* in the arms of her husband.

She does not seem to be in any hurry to cook breakfast, and there is nothing he can do but wait. Ordinarily, not even his father will ask a maid to perform a task. If he or his sister or even his father wants something done, one of them will tell his mother, and she will ask the maid to do it. After all, she is his mother's maid.

Throwing a quick glance her way, he sees within the mysterious confines of her blue dress the edge of a red brassiere and above it the curve of a dark breast. *Oh, Lord,* he thinks.

"What's your name?" he asks, dismayed by the squeak in his voice.

"Barbara."

"Why, that's my mother's name! Her name's Barbara!"

"No law against two," she says comfortably. "I'm Barbara Conner."

Another first. A maid with a last name.

"First name's Willie. Named after my daddy," she says. Standing up, stretching, she slowly raises her shoulders, rolls them back like a cat, revealing nipples the size of nickels. She smiles down at him.

Lord God! Does she know? Could she? He crosses his arms over his lap, leans forward.

"Well, I reckon I'll get on inside and heat up the stove, see if I can cook you some buttermilk pancakes. You reckon you all got the fixings for that?"

In a few minutes she has the stove going, the kitchen warm, the plates heating on the pilot light, and pretty soon she is placing a stack of pancakes and a pitcher of maple syrup on the table in front of him. Knowing before he takes a bite how good they are going to taste, he spreads the slowly melting butter over the pancakes and bathes them in maple syrup. She has retreated and stands, arms crossed, by the kitchen window. Outside on the steps, she had seemed small, but now he sees that she is tall, every bit as tall as his mother. She is also just as slender. At the sound of water running into the bathtub, she looks toward the ceiling. Her neck is unusually long, like a dancer's.

"Reckon that means somebody else will be down here pretty soon. Yore mama or yore daddy?"

"My mother doesn't eat breakfast. And you don't have to worry about Celia. When my father honks, she'll run down and grab a piece of toast so she can be out of the house and in the car before he honks again." The maid takes a plate from the stove and comes toward the table. *Will it seem like a correction, what he is about to tell her?* "My dad doesn't eat in the kitchen. He likes peace and quiet while he reads his paper."

"Reckon I'll just wait then. He can tell me what he wants."

"Celia, honey, turn off that radio." His father's voice, always gentle when he talks to Celia, floats down the stairs. Then, except for Celia's hurried footsteps and his father's more leisurely paced ones, all is quiet upstairs.

Two or three times a week Celia has a crisis. Over her hair: "I can't stand it!" she'll cry, this followed by his mother's voice as she takes the brush and persuades both Celia and her hair all is well. Or, "I haven't a thing to wear!" she'll wail, and his mother, cajoling, "What about my angora sweater with your blue skirt?"

Bobby butters another pancake. A mockingbird begins its extravagant song. He hears his father's footsteps coming down the stairs. Clean shaved and gray suited, his father comes briskly into the kitchen. Holding his jacket over his shoulder with his index finger, he sounds hopeful. "So, you're Mrs. Moore's new maid. What's your name?"

"Barbara." Her smile is wide; the gold star tooth glistens.

He frowns, tilts his head to the side. "Barbara," he says, puzzled. "But Mrs. Moore's name is Barbara." His frown deepens. "Well, she'll work all that out." A slight smile flickers at the corners of his mouth. "The truth is, I smelled those damn pancakes, and that got me up and going. You reckon you can cook up a stack for me?"

But the new maid is already pouring batter into one skillet, frying sausages in another and handing him a cup of coffee. "I be making apricot preserves to go with some homemade bread after while. Have it ready for your breakfast in the morning. Sure will now." Carrying a pot of coffee in one hand and the golden pancakes in the other, she pushes the swinging door between the kitchen and the dining room open with her hip.

"I'll just eat in here this morning. Keep Bobby company." His father rubs his hands together, pulls a chair away from the table.

She nods. "That way the pancakes still be hot when they gets to the table."

Suddenly the day is filled with possibility. The navy will take him. His mother will like living in the South. And Dixie Balderidge will be his date for the Silver Key Gypsy Dance!

· 2 ·

MARYANNE Balderidge sits in the darkness. She is not afraid of the voices. Even *his* voice, amidst the tumultuous cries of the many she hears, has lost its terror. The single cry that still moves her is that of the wounded young—a rabbit ripped by the talons of an owl, a mouse caught in a trap. The cry of a child. When she hears that, she dresses frantically, puts on her coat and, like a magnet, finds her way to Dixie, her baby, her child.

She strains to remember some time before the voices. There was *something* there in the time before. What was it? A brightness and the barking. Or a bottle? And the green? Yes, that was it. Before the voices, there was a bottle. And the green.

Her hands will not be still today. When Dixie comes from her room, she takes her mother's hands in hers, patting them, rubbing them, until they rest quietly in her mother's lap.

Once Dixie would plead, "Mama, get dressed." Or "Here, let me fix your hair like Ingrid Bergman's in *Casablanca*," and she'd do it in a roll around her mother's face. Now Dixie prays her mother will not get dressed, will not come looking for her.

That last time, she was sitting by Jack Pearce at the Strand when her mother came slowly down the aisle, wearing her moth-eaten fur coat (a fur coat in July!), calling "Dixie. Dixie, baby," coming closer and closer down the aisle, calling more loudly, "Dixie, baby, where are you?" so that Dixie sank low in her seat, guiltily, *cruelly* turning away from her mother.

It was Bobby Moore who got up from the seat behind her, whispering, "Here, Mrs. Balderidge. It's me. Bobby Moore. Come outside with me." And he led her mother out of the movie where she stood on the hot sidewalk, blinking and dazed by the hot sun, until Dixie followed, and together they brought her home.

When they were inside the house, Mrs. Balderidge sat in an old rocker and put her hand on her throat. Dixie bit her lip and looked about to cry. Nobody said anything, and Bobby decided he'd better leave. "Well," he said.

Mrs. Balderidge took her hand away from her throat and put it on the arm of her chair. She whispered, "Dixie, baby, play."

Dixie said, "Don't go, Bobby. Mama wants you to stay." She raised the lid of the piano bench and took out her sheet music and played boogie-woogie and "In the Mood" and

"String of Pearls" on the battered, old upright piano. Then she said: "Here's your favorite, Mama," and she played "Deep Purple" while Mrs. Balderidge frowned down at a tattered, brown rug.

Watching Dixie play, the way she sat at the piano, so straight in her tight, yellow sweater and plaid skirt and with her feet, in penny loafers and yellow socks, bouncing at the foot pedals, made his throat tight.

When Dixie stopped playing, she served brownies—dark, moist, sweet, with darker, sweeter chocolate icing—she had made for her father, and Cokes in tall, blue glasses with ice she wrapped in a cup towel and crushed with a pecan cracker.

Leaving, Bobby stood in front of Dixie's mother. "Thank you, Mrs. Balderidge." When she did not look up, he leaned forward. "The brownies were good, too."

Mrs. Balderidge cast a quick, bewildered look in his direction before returning her gaze to the rug. Tracing the thin, white scar that ran down the right side of her face, "It was stinging nettles did this," she said. "Or maybe it was a dog," she added, her voice uncertain as smoke.

Instantly, Dixie was between them, kneeling, taking her mother's hands in hers, patting them, rubbing them. "No, Mama. You remember. Daddy said it was barbed wire. A fence." Turning toward Bobby, "You'd better go now. Go on home," she said, drawing him outside.

On the porch, her arms crossed, Dixie said, "Sometimes she's better. It's when she tries to remember. It makes her a little crazy."

"What is it that she's trying to remember?"

"Oh, Bobby. I wish I knew."

Suddenly, Dixie leaned forward and kissed him full on the mouth. "She likes you, Bobby. I can tell."

Thinking about Dixie's warm mouth on his and wondering what Mrs. Balderidge was trying to remember, Bobby had walked down the alley past his backyard gate and past Mrs. Gil-

lian's and the Applebys' back gates. When he had walked
around the block to Dixie's house again, all the shades had
been lowered. He decided he'd wait to ask his father if he could
take the car to the dance. When he asked, his mother would
hug his father or take his hand to her lips and kiss it. "Robert?
Robert? Of course, Bobby may have the car," she'd urge until
his father agreed. But there would be all those questions about
his date for the dance.

· 3 ·

WHEN Bobby hears the whistling in the kitchen, he is instantly awake. Willie B. is whistling "Things Are Getting Better
All the Time." By the time the smell of bacon drifts up the
stairs, he's ready for school. His father is leaving for Chicago
this morning, and he will have the car, *practically* have it, all
week. This afternoon, he can take Celia home, hurry back and
pick up Dixie (Pearce has basketball practice, so she won't be
with him) on the way home. He can take her to Guy's for a
cold drink and peanuts. Then he could ask her to the dance. He
might do it.

On the way downstairs he stops by the open door of his parents' room.

"Good morning, Bobby," his mother says.

His mother, wearing a pink robe, sits on their old mahogany
sleigh bed watching his father pack. With her arms wrapped
around her knees, her thick, black braid pulled forward over
her shoulder, she looks younger. Shaking her head in amusement over his father's packing, she grins at Bobby. His father
prefers to pack himself, and if she would permit it, he would
like to pack for his wife. Her lighthearted approach to packing
unsettles him. When they travel together, she often has to shop

the very first day of their arrival—a toothbrush in Dallas, a pair of stockings in Austin, a nightgown in Memphis—for some article she has forgotten. When his mother mentioned the forgotten nightgown at the Memphis restaurant, his father, who had had two martinis before dinner, said, "You can forget the nightgown, as far as I'm concerned."

"Robert!" his mother had said, blushing so distinctly his father laughed.

Now Bobby and his mother smile at each other across the open suitcase. They watch as Mr. Robert Alexander Moore IV (at such times his mother calls his father this) takes a shirt from a hanger, buttons it, folds it and carefully places it in the suitcase. The leather of the suitcase is old and worn, but "Still better than anything you can buy nowadays," his father says.

His father compares the list he has taped to the inside lid of the suitcase with the contents. Satisfied, he snaps the suitcase closed, locks it and pockets the key. Only then does he turn to his son. "Good morning, Bobby." His father picks up the case, preparing to leave the room.

"Robert!" his mother calls. Her arms are open wide as Bobby turns to hurry downstairs to breakfast.

Things have been a lot better since Willie B. came to work for them. This is the name the family calls her.

"How did you decide to call her Willie B.?" his father had asked his mother.

"I asked her what she wanted us to call her. I thought perhaps Mrs. Conner."

"Mrs. Conner!"

"Robert, let's not even discuss it!" his mother said sharply. "I would have been happy to call her Mrs. Conner. But she prefers Willie B."

Things like that, *tiffs,* his mother calls them, are always popping up between his mother and his father. His father says their arguments (his father calls them *misunderstandings*) are caused by his mother's New York background.

This morning the kitchen is filled with the sound of Willie B. whisking egg whites into airy mounds for vanilla flavored custard and shucking sweet corn and filled, too, with the smell of bread baking in the oven. And the whistling. Usually, Willie B.'s whistling is the first thing he hears in the morning.

Now Bobby cruises through the kitchen, lifting the tops off pans to see what supper will bring. "Have you heard from—?" he begins. *What to call this man he imagines as always in her bed. Your soldier? Mr. Conner?*

Willie B. waits, hands on her hips.

"Your husband?" he finishes.

She beams and the gold star sparkles. "Yessir. Got a letter yesterday." She pats her apron pocket. "Read it so many times I knows it by heart. Want to hear it?"

When he nods, she says, "Now, Bobby, you set right down and eat your breakfast, and I'll say it for you." She pours his coffee. To be tougher, ready for the navy, he's been drinking it black. While he butters his toast, she places bacon, scrambled eggs and apricot preserves on his plate, all the while reciting in her soft, husky voice:

"My sweet woman. They give me a gun yesterday, a rifle. Before that I just been bringing supplies back and forth, back and forth. I reckon the white boys seen they need all the firepower they can get and they handed me this gun. 'Can you shoot?' the man said. I shot the limb off a tree and he nodded and left in his jeep. Some say we'll fight over here and some say across the river, but as for me I just wants to get home to you, my sweet honey."

She ruffles his hair. "You too young for the rest."

"Where do you think he is? Your husband?"

"It wouldn't do for me to know. Might let it slip."

"Walter Winchell said we bombed Berlin yesterday."

"I heard it. Wish we could bomb Hitler. That would put an

end to the old devil." She sits across from him, her chin in her hand, and smiles. Her tooth flashes. "How about that girl you so sweet on? You asked her yet?"

"I'm going to ask her this afternoon, I'm pretty sure."

"Now, Bobby, you go on and ask her. If she turn you down, ask somebody else. Don't be wasting the good times."

At the sound of his father's footsteps coming down, she gets up to pour his coffee, fix his plate. "They don't know yet," Bobby whispers.

She smiles widely, her gold tooth sparkling, and puts a finger to her lips. "You a rascal, Bobby."

By the time his father turns the corner onto Main Street, he has almost finished with his advice. "And don't ride all over Bowie County wasting gas and wearing out tires, Bobby. I know your mother's generous with the car, but we don't have a T Stamp. And don't worry your mother while I'm gone." His voice slows, deepens. "Son, remember that if something should ever happen to me, you'll have to be the man of the house."

"Dad, you're just going to Chicago." He hates this kind of talk.

"Well, you never know. No, don't come in the station. I can manage this bag. Celia doesn't want to be late to school."

Shaking hands with his father, he sees the small furrows across his brow, the wrinkles around his eyes. *He is getting old. He could drop dead in Chicago.* The thought causes him to throw his arms around his father's neck.

"Son, now, son," his father says, gently disengaging himself from Bobby's arms.

By the time Bobby pulls into a parking space at the high school, he has recovered from his embarrassment. He's pretty sure nobody saw him hug his father.

When he steps into the hall at the high school, the smells of chalk dust and sweat and cigarette smoke and perfume are so strong it takes a minute to get used to it. Everybody's hollering and hurrying to class, some running in the hall, risking a detention slip for that. Locker doors are opened and slammed shut. And now he smells whiskey. It's a heady smell. Schuster and Mobley have been bringing it to school. *Something is going to happen,* he tells himself then.

"Hey, Cinco!" Steve Schuster grabs his shoulder.

"Hey, man!"

Bobby is as tall as Steve but thin as a reed. Steve is big all over. And a brain. *And* captain of the football team. They are best friends, although neither knows exactly why.

They pass Mr. Lawson in the hall, who is standing with his arms crossed just outside his office door. His expression is always the same. Never changes. But he can swing into action. When Joe Boller and Tim Matthews somehow got a cow up three flights of stairs and into Mrs. Duck's classroom, Mr. Lawson had Joe and Tim in his office before they knew what had happened. Right away he knew who had done it! Schuster said army intelligence needed Mr. Lawson.

It's been crazy since the War. As soon as the seniors take off their graduation gowns, they are drafted. So, who cares whether they graduate or not? And not even Mr. Lawson would kick a senior out of school just before graduation. Not when he's headed off to the armed services to fight for his country and maybe die for it.

Taking his seat, third one, second row, in Mrs. Gillian's English class, right away, that's different, too. The class always smells like sweat. And perfume. All the girls wear perfume. Dixie wears Gardenia. But this morning Mrs. Gillian has opened the windows, so the room smells like pine trees and swimming holes. And ordinarily, Mrs. Gillian is marking papers at her desk, looking up now and then to smile as they come into the room. But now she stands with her back to the class, looking out the window. And her hair. Always done up in a tight roll, today it is loose, hanging down her back. When a breeze stirs, her gauzy dress, the color of butter, lifts and swirls so that it looks like she might float right out the open window. Bobby imagines his hands encircling her waist, anchoring her to the classroom floor.

When the tardy bell rings, she turns and gazes at the class with such a solemn look on her face that they wait, hardly breathing, expecting to hear her say that somebody they all know has been killed in action or that we've lost the Anzio beachhead. On Mondays she usually reads about the Anzio beachhead. A guy from Dallas is over there on the Anzio beachhead, and he writes about spring in Italy with farmers putting in crops under all the overhead barrage balloons.

She says, "I am going to read a poem to you. I am not sure what the poem means. I hope that you can tell me.

"The poem is called 'The Lady of Shalott,' " she says softly, and begins:

> *"On either side the river lie*
> *Long fields of barley and of rye.*
> *That clothe the wold and meet the sky;*
> *And through the field the road runs by*
> *To many-towered Camelot."*

As she reads, the morning sun comes through and shines on her almost-red hair and on her yellow dress that lifts and falls and blows forward again as her whispery voice sweeps out over the room:

> *"Willows whiten, aspens quiver*
> *Little breezes dusk and shiver."*

Her voice is breathless, excited, and her eyes are like sapphires as she reads on and on and the room is so quiet he can hear his heart beating. This lady she reads about, the Lady of Shalott, sees all kinds of people coming and going and there's a funeral and then she sees Sir Lancelot. When she's reading about him, about Sir Lancelot, Mrs. Gillian breathes so deep that her breasts rise and fall underneath her yellow dress, and now she's whispering the words and the words are a heart's cry and all he wants in the world is for the poem to be over, but the poem goes on and on.

She reads about this lady coming down from the tower and finding a boat and getting into the boat and dying, and now it seems like it's not Mrs. Gillian up there reading, but a stranger in a yellow dress with glittering eyes telling a story that hurts his heart. She tosses her hair back over her shoulders, and finally, she comes to the end of it:

> *"But Lancelot mused a little space;*
> *He said, 'She has a lovely face;*
> *God in his mercy lend her grace*
> *The Lady of Shalott.' "*

Then Mrs. Gillian sighs and closes the book.

The room is quiet like everybody is holding their breaths, and the sun is still shining on her hair and on her yellow dress, and in the still room her dress, blown by a breeze he can't feel, lifts and falls.

Then Steve looks over at him, raises his eyebrows in a "What's going on here?" look. Nobody moves until Mrs. Gillian pulls a pencil from over her ear and pushes it back again. Then she smiles, and right away it's the same Mrs. Gillian, the same old English class.

"Anyone? What is the poem about?" She looks toward Bobby.

He looks down, hoping she won't say his name.

"Jeff?" Jeff shakes his head, yawns, straightens the books on his desk. Mrs. Gillian looks at Steve, who grins, shrugs his shoulders. "Mary Jane?"

"It's sad. But I'm not sure what it means," Mary Jane says.

Mrs. Gillian looks around the room waiting for someone to answer. She waits like she has all the time in the world. He has seen her keep a class through the class break, waiting for them to gather their thoughts. He hates it when she does this. He raises his hand.

"Bobby?"

"There is this lady in a tower, and she sees Sir Lancelot. He rides off on his horse without telling her or telling anybody. And she comes down out of the tower to go and look for him. She probably wonders why he just up and left her without . . ."

Oh, God. Now he's done it. Made it sound like the poem is about Mr. Gillian leaving Mrs. Gillian.

"Go on," she says firmly.

". . . left without saying anything. Well, he will probably be sorry he up and left, her being a real nice lady."

Now he's made it worse. Betty Lou Culbertson, in the back of the room, giggles.

"Thank you, Bobby," she says. Then, "Class dismissed," and in the same breath, "Wait a minute, Bobby."

Leaving the room, Steve grins at him, gives him a *V* for victory sign.

She waits until the room is empty. Then she says, "Bobby, be proud of taking a chance. It's easy to be silent. Hear me?"

"Yes, ma'am," he says. Feeling pardoned, he hurries from the room.

After school he hurries to take Celia home. Then he drives slowly along Olive Street until he sees Dixie just ahead, her saddle shoes moving along, her pleated skirt swinging like she's keeping the beat to "Bye, Bye, Baby." Her hair hangs almost to her waist. (His father likes long hair, and in that way he is just like his father.) Sometimes she is with a bunch of girls or Jack Pearce. But today she is by herself!

"How about a ride?" He leans across and opens the car door.

She hops in, and he reaches across and pulls the door closed.

"I heard about Mrs. Gillian reading that poem."

He wants to tell her how it made him feel. Finally, he says, "Listening to it about wore me out."

Dixie laughs, and at the sound his spirits rise.

"I like Mrs. Gillian. I think she's swell."

"I like her, too. But that poem was real . . ."

"Sad?"

"Yeaw, I guess."

The car is hot. They roll down the windows so that the warm air blows into their faces. Dixie lifts her hair, piles it on top of her head.

At Guy's they order Dr Peppers. When their order comes, they take the drinks and the little paper cups of free peanuts out to the car. A few swallows and his is gone. Dixie is taking her time with hers. *Maybe tonight would be better. Not now. While they're studying, he could ask her. Or maybe Saturday would be better.*

He takes a deep breath, and the words just pop out: "How about going to the Gypsy Dance with me?"

Dixie takes another sip of her cold drink. Drawing her knees up on the seat, she turns toward him and leans cozily against the car door. Her right foot jiggles a little.

"Oh, Bobby. If Jack doesn't ask me, I'd love to go with you. And if he does, I want you to promise, *promise* me that you will dance at least three dances with me." She reaches over, pats his shoulder, allows her hand to rest there. "Will you? Promise?" She gives his shoulder a little squeeze.

"Sure, I will."

"Want to study tonight?"

"Sure," he says. "I'll meet you at nine o'clock."

They usually study together, using flashlights, in the Appleby's old carriage house. No one else ever goes there, as far as he can tell.

"One of these days someone is going to come out there and find us," Dixie says now.

Emboldened by having the use of the car, by thoughts of dancing with Dixie, "So, what if they do?" he says.

Dixie raises her eyebrows and giggles. "Well!" she says. "Listen to you!"

When he gets home, he noses around the kitchen, visiting with Willie B. He lifts the top off a pan, sticks his finger in the sauce and licks it.

Willie B. taps his hand with her stirring spoon. "You, Bobby! Get out of there!"

He grins. "All right. All right. Needs a little salt, Willie B."

She frowns, tastes. "Maybe. A pinch." Scattering the salt over the top of the sauce, she stirs, tastes, smiles with satisfaction.

He likes Willie B.'s smile. It's really nice with the gold star and all. He starts out the back door.

"You ask her yet?"

He stops.

"You did, didn't you?" Willie B. says, at the moment intent on crisscrossing dough over an apple pie. She looks approvingly at the pie. At Bobby. "Well, what did she say?"

"She's going with me if Jack Pearce doesn't ask her."

"What! Bobby, you crazy! Standing around waiting to be second choice. Why you didn't tell her you can't wait? You got to get it all lined up now. Why you didn't tell her that?"

"Well, I'm gonna dance three dances with her if she goes with Jack."

"That ain't good enough. You a good boy, Bobby. That girl with her little shaky hips and wearing those glasses, she'd be lucky to go out with you. And you from a fine family."

All this indignation, these vehemently expressed opinions, all on his side. "I'm gonna go outside to shoot some baskets," he says. Dribbling and shooting, he hits the basket four times in a row.

Chapter 3

· 1 ·

WHEN Bobby has the wreck, he is thinking about heroes. The paper has been full of heroes. Yesterday there was a story about a corporal who outwitted a Jap battalion by cutting their telephone wires. Another was about Emery Taylor, Bill Taylor's cousin, who bailed out of a Mustang at six thousand feet and knocked himself out against his own fighter. When he came to, he was hanging in a tree, just ten feet off the ground. Bobby looks forward to being a hero, which he will be the minute he joins the navy, at least in the eyes of Cold Springs.

Thinking about that makes him think about Dixie. She is going with him to the Gypsy Dance. Yesterday, Pearce walked Dixie home and told her he was taking Maudie Lewis to the dance. Said his mother made him ask her. Maudie's father owns the First National Bank of Hope and a rice plantation in Louisiana. Maudie is the kind of girl Bobby's father wants *him* to go out with. When Dixie told Bobby she was going to the dance with him, she said she was never going to speak to Jack Pearce again. Then she put her head on Bobby's shoulder and cried.

With all this on his mind, he doesn't see the black '37 Ford backing out. He hits it going thirty, whirling it around so that it faces the wrong direction. The right fender of his car crumples like tinfoil. A woman from Ashdown is driving the Ford, and she says why didn't he look where he was going and writes down his name and his father's name and their telephone number and where they live. When he tells her his father's name, she says, "Well, I'm sure Mr. Moore will do the right thing. We come in here regular from Ashdown." When Mr. Kennedy hears the crash, he comes out of his shoe store to see if anybody is hurt. Then he gets a mallet and knocks the fender away from the tire so Bobby can get the car home. Mr. Kennedy tells the Ashdown lady she might also have looked where she was backing. She says, "We don't do business with you." When Bobby gets the car home, his mother says, "Oh, Bobby. What bad luck. Your father's coming home today."

That afternoon, his mother walks to the train station to meet his father. "Bobby, I like to walk," she says. His mother is also the only mother in town who walks. "People always stop and offer me a ride," she says, laughing. "They think I've had car trouble."

They come home in a Yellow Cab. They are holding hands when they walk into the house. His father gives his mother a little hug and says, "Dear, does Willie B. know I'm home?"

"Yes, she does. And I'll just go see how supper's coming."

His father watches her leave the room with a big smile on his face, and Bobby knows it's going to be all right about the wreck.

Rubbing his hands, "Now, Bobby," his father says briskly, "your mother and I have talked about your little mishap. As she says, 'Nobody was hurt.' Still, it calls for an arrangement, a business deal between you and me, man to man. I expect you to pay for the repairs on both cars. Do you agree?"

"Yes, sir."

"You will get a job, part-time, until school is out." His father is barking out orders like a marine colonel or something. "When you have reimbursed me for the repairs, you may drive again."

"But, Dad, I have a date for the Gypsy Dance. I've already asked her."

"In that case," his father says, picking up the newspaper, settling into his easy chair, "you'd better not waste any time."

"Yes, sir."

Lowering the paper slightly, he says, "Son, there are Help Wanted signs all over town."

"What about a job at the store?"

"Out of the question. It wouldn't be fair to you or the other employees. Son, turn on the radio. It's about time for the news."

Willie B. pushes the swinging door open. "How you, Mr. Moore? Glad you got home safe and sound. That Chicago. Ain't nothing to fool around with. Got some mighty mean folks up there."

"Well, Willie B., I found it pleasant. A beautiful city."

"Uh-huh" she says. The *uh-huh*, the way she says it, means she doesn't agree with a word his father is saying.

Lowering the paper again, he says, "Willie B., you can go along home now. Just leave the supper on the stove."

"Mr. Moore, I needs to talk to Mrs. Moore about when I leaves."

Ignoring Willie B., his father raises the newspaper again. Then he lowers it so that only his eyes are visible. "Bobby, sit down. We'll listen to the news, and over supper you can tell us all about this young lady you will be escorting to the dance."

His heart sinks.

But halfway through supper his father has forgotten about his date, and Bobby begins to enjoy the meal—fried okra, corn on the cob and chicken-fried steak.

Celia finally comes to the table, all slumps and sighs because she had to walk home. She puts her elbow on the table and props her chin in her hand. Then she sighs, looks at her food, sighs again.

Their mother says, "Celia, sit up at the table. And, Celia, walking home, a little exercise, might be just what you need."

His father looks at Celia. "Baby, you are mighty quiet. A walk just might put some color in those pretty cheeks." Then he launches into a story about running into an old classmate in, of all places, Arthur's Restaurant in Chicago. "I had not seen Sam in years, but he knew me right away, came right over, and we had a drink and dinner together."

Celia, frowning, pulls her blond hair forward and begins to braid it.

"Celia, please," their mother says. "Not at the table."

"I know who Bobby's taking to the dance. Jack Pearce told me."

"Shut up, Celia!"

"Bobby!" his mother says, "I'll not have that kind of talk in this house."

"Sorry."

His father, feeling too good to reprimand anyone, takes a bite of steak, chews it with relish. "This must have cost a month's red points," he says. "But it's mighty good. Barbara, your maid is a mighty good cook." He puts his fork down. "Celia, Bobby will make his own announcement about the young lady he's taking to the dance."

His mother smiles. "Bobby?"

"I'm not real sure."

"Liar! Liar! Pants on fire!"

"Celia! I will not have this! What's gotten into you? For goodness' sake! Bobby can tell us when he's ready. Or he may choose not to discuss it with us at all."

"He's taking Dixie Balderidge, that's who. He's taking crazy Dixie to the dance 'cause Jack Pearce won't take her. He's sweet on her."

"Shut up, Celia," he shouts. Jumping up from the table, he turns over his chair, rights it and storms out of the room, out of the house.

He gets on his bicycle and, pedaling furiously, rides out to Cold Springs Park. *Celia has turned into a spoiled brat,* he tells himself. When she had rheumatic fever and Bobby was afraid she might die, he'd say anything, do anything to make her smile. But now. One of the best things about joining the navy will be getting away from Celia.

At breakfast the next morning his father carefully spoons blackberry jam onto his plate. "Willie B., the toast is a mite cold."

"Just take a minute, Mr. Moore. I'll make another piece."

"No. No use in wasting good bread and butter. Robert, don't slouch."

Robert. His father calls him Robert when he's mad. Straightening his shoulders, Bobby watches him cut his poached egg, well done, into a gridlike pattern, measure and cut a slice of butter, replace his knife, spear the butter with his fork, and place it dead center on the egg. He takes a bite, puts his fork down and raises his napkin to his lips. Then he turns toward his son.

"Robert, what are your plans for job hunting? Have you thought about it?"

"I thought I'd try the *Gazette.* Mrs. Gillian said—"

"Your mother doesn't want you to take a newspaper route. She feels you need your sleep. You'll have to find a job you can do after school."

"Dad, I'd like to write for the paper."

His father places his fork on the side of his plate and stares at him. "Son, what in the world would you have to write about? Just get a job."

Bobby knows what this is all about. His father is ticked off because he's taking Dixie to the dance. But he doesn't give a damn.

Pushing his chair back, he puts his napkin on the table. "Excuse me. And don't worry, Dad. I'll find a job."

*   *   *

In fifth period history, Bobby sees the small scrap of paper making its way down the aisle. Steve takes the note and, pretending to scratch his back, drops it on Bobby's desk. As he unfolds it, Dixie looks over her shoulder and smiles at him. He reads: *Come over tomorrow afternoon. Daddy's gone hunting. I bought some new records, and we can dance.* Dixie works at Woolworth's after school and has her own spending money.

He tears off a scrap of notebook paper and writes: *I'm not sure I can. I've got to find a job first.* He watches his note slowly pass from one hand to the next, moving only when Miss Speed's back is turned, watches until it is in Dixie's hand.

In last period study hall, he settles into his desk, grateful for an uninterrupted hour to sort it all out. He opens a book and stares at it. He would like to go over to Dixie's, but he doesn't know about dancing in front of her mother. Mrs. Balderidge is weird. How could anybody dance in front of her! But, oh, how Dixie can dance! Thinking of her saddle shoes moving light as a feather and her skirt swinging when she walks down the hall, his spirits rise. "Oh, kiss me once and kiss me twice and kiss me once again," her swinging skirt and light footsteps seem to say. Her favorite song is "It's Been a Long, Long Time."

But sometimes he can hardly look at Dixie's mother. And sometimes he can hardly *keep* from looking at her. Dresses with buttons missing. Pink straps showing. Bare, hairy legs. But even with all this, when she holds her head a certain way and smiles at Dixie, he can see she was pretty once. And when she lifts her hand to her thick hair and pushes it back, it, this gesture, is so like Dixie that he is filled with dismay and sorrow.

· 2 ·

MR. J. R. McMurray owns the paper and is financially sound. This is what his father always says. His father always calls Mr. McMurray by his full name. It's with the *Mr.* and the *J. R.* when he says *McMurray*, and he always adds the *financially sound.* Mr. J. R. McMurray is bald. His lips are always red and moist, like he's been drinking strawberry soda pop.

"Son, what in the world do you have to write about?" he growls now. Then he adds, "But, if you want a newspaper route, we can put you on as soon as Carl Wesley leaves for the army. Won't be long."

"Thank you, sir. I'd better look around. I need a job today."

He walks up Broad and down Main without seeing a single Help Wanted sign. *Where are all these Help Wanted signs, Dad?* He'd like to ask his father this right now. He decides to try Little Pig Branch. There are always Help Wanted signs in Little Pig Branch. It will chap his father, and realizing this, Bobby feels better. The pay is better in Little Pig Branch, but nobody wants to work there. It's a seedy part of town, where the stores—the liquor stores, a cleaners', two grocery stores, a single drugstore—are owned by men who keep their ownership a secret. Or try to. Little Pig Branch is next to Fourth Street. Fourth is where the women of ill repute, might as well say it, the *whores,* live. In the late afternoon, they appear on their little balconies, waiting for darkness and customers to come. Bobby and Steve have walked along Fourth Street. "Hey, honey, come on up!" the ladies called to them. And "Does your mama know where you are? What you got on your mind?" This followed by gales of laughter. *They sound happy,* he had thought when he heard them. No use in going to Fourth Street until you were eighteen or in the service. The town was strict about that. Last summer, Joe Shackleford, down from Tennessee visiting his cousins, managed to get into one of their little houses, but the woman threw him out. Joe was funny, telling about it. After he gets in the navy, Bobby will probably visit one of the Fourth Street ladies the first time he's home on leave.

By the time he walks to Little Pig Branch he is thirsty. He stops by Mr. Sandflat's drugstore. A girl named Maybeline from his history class is behind the soda fountain. She wears a white top and skirt, like a nurse's uniform, except for the spots of chocolate on the front of her shirt. He feels in his pockets, finds a quarter, sits at the counter and orders a chocolate soda.

Maybeline shoves the soda, full and overflowing, across the red countertop to him. "How you doing, Bobby?" she says.

"OK, Maybeline."

Maybeline has short blond hair and two black moles on her right cheek. But Maybeline is really stacked, so who cares about a couple of moles? She smokes on the way home from school, and everybody says she will go all the way with a football player. Steve is going to find out if it's true when they beat Arkansas.

She flips her hair up with her hand and smiles a big wide smile like she's glad to see him. He has never seen her smile. Smoking on the way home from school, she has always looked mad.

"What you doing in Little Pig Branch?" she says.

"Looking for a job."

"Mr. Sandflat's in his office. Up there." Maybeline waves toward an upstairs mezzanine railing that runs across the back of the store. Then she puts her elbows on the counter and leans against it. He notices that the top buttons of her blouse are unbuttoned. She smiles again and winks. "Ask him about a job."

Suddenly, he wants to impress her. "When I finish my soda, I will."

Straightening his shoulders, he clenches his fist to flex his arm muscle. He can handle working for Mr. Sandflat.

But the Sandflats are *really* weird. And Cold Springs is a town that has a lot of weird people. Dixie's mother. And Old Man Taylor, who's always drunk and passed out in the alley.

And there's the rabbi who, his mother says, has the most brilliant, compassionate eyes. And Gladys, who walks around the neighborhood at night and peeps into windows. Bobby's father says she's perfectly harmless. Just lonesome, his mother adds. But all the same, it's a shock to look out the dining room window and see her face pressed against the windowpane. One time, his mother went out to ask Gladys if she needed something, but as soon as the door opened, Gladys scurried away. And Mrs. Coleman, the banker's wife, takes things from stores without paying, just puts them in her coat or in her purse and walks out. Sometimes it's his father's store she's been in. Then his father has to call Mr. Coleman, who says, "Thank you, Robert. Just send me the bill."

But with all these weird people, the Sandflats are really weird. *Nobody* knows the Sandflats. On Sundays Mr. Sandflat drives Mrs. Sandflat and their daughter, Maxine, to the cafeteria and double-parks. Then he hobbles around on his little feet, made smaller by the rolls of flesh that hang around his ankles, and opens the door and reaches into the long black car and eases first Mrs. Sandflat out and then Maxine. By now the after-church cafeteria line is coiled inside and trailing out the door along the glass front of the building, sometimes reaching almost to the corner.

The Sandflats stand there, blinking, their mouths open, breathless from stepping up on the curb and walking the few steps from the car. When they catch their breath, they go inside the cafeteria to sit down and wait for the line to go down. Pretending not to see them, still Bobby sees Maxine's black hair that falls in coils to her waist, and as she passes, he smells the earthy odor of her body.

Now, he looks up toward Mr. Sandflat's office just behind the railing. Bobby's father says Mr. Sandflat's office is open so he can keep an eye on things. Mr. Sandflat's up there all right, keeping an eye on him and Maybeline. With Maybeline watching, he finishes his soda and climbs the narrow stairs to the office.

Bobby walks over to Mr. Sandflat's desk and stands right in front of Mr. Sandflat, who does not look up.

"Sir?" Bobby says. "Excuse me."

Mr. Sandflat slowly leans back in his swivel chair, the movement tilting his huge stomach upward. "Well, Mr. Robert Moore the Fifth. Good afternoon."

"Sir, I need a job. I was wondering if you have something I could do. Maybe delivering. Cleaning up. Unpacking boxes."

"Might. How much you figuring on?"

"I need to pay for some repairs on my dad's car and on another lady's."

"And that amount would be what?"

"I need about a hundred and twenty-nine dollars and fifty-two cents."

"About that, huh?" Mr. Sandflat eases one hip to the left, rolling his stomach that way, and his other hip to the right, his stomach rolling in *that* direction, and when he has got his stomach right in the middle, he crosses his hands over it. His gold belt buckle glitters through his fingers.

"That's a good bit of change." He chews his bottom lip, frowning. Finally, he unclasps his hands and pulls himself forward. "Well, son, there is something." He takes a cigar from his shirt pocket, clips it, lights it, takes a long drag, exhales and watches the smoke drift out over the drugstore. He looks at Bobby with eyes like coffee in sunshine. Then, talking fast, he says, "Maxine needs some help with her Latin. And if you could come out to the house a couple of evenings a week for a month, say on Mondays and Thursdays, I could see my way . . ."

Bobby's mind swings away, up and out of the drugstore to his Latin classroom. And to Maxine, somewhere in the back of that room. Maxine. Miss Dolby's star pupil. Maxine, who sits in an extra large desk in the back of the room. Most of the time nobody remembers she is there. But when nobody can translate a passage correctly, Miss Dolby says, "Maxine?" and Maxine's voice floats like smoke over the class. "I sing of the arms and the man," she recites, "And the hero who first from the shores of Troy . . ." Then the rest of the class, rescued by her bell-like voice floating over the room, can begin their struggle with the next passage.

"Well, Bobby," Mr. Sandflat says briskly, "you think it over. It's not a hard job. You'd be using your mind. You could pay for those repairs in a month. Or . . ." He stops again, sits forward in his swivel chair. "Tell you what. I'll just advance you that money now. A man doesn't need to be carrying a debt like that on his shoulders."

A vision of the evening swims before Bobby—the envelope filled with money by his father's plate, put there casually, as if he handles transactions like that every day of the year. His father astonished. His mother pleased. Even old Celia's mouth would drop open.

"I'll come tonight."

"Seven o'clock," Mr. Sandflat says, counting the money out in a neat stack on the desk.

But during supper the vision fades. He is not sure he can ever tell his family about his job. Churchill has made a speech, and the entire speech was on the news. Mr. Churchill said that the greatest hour of action is approaching.

"It's the invasion," his mother says. "He means the invasion. Oh, Robert, I'm so frightened."

She is so excited she can't talk about anything else. She loves Churchill, almost more than Roosevelt. All at once his job seems like nothing they would care about.

"Oh, Robert, isn't there something we can do? I know Mr. Churchill is talking about the invasion." Her eyes are alive with excitement and fear. "Doesn't it make you wish you were over there? *Doing* something?"

"Well, no," his father says matter-of-factly. "I'm doing what I can for the War right here in Cold Springs. All these men, jumping in when it's about over. A bunch of damn—excuse me, Barbara—fools. I heard this morning that John Appleby is going to Washington. Some general he knows. Now, I think that's a fool thing for a man to do."

"John Appleby's no fool. It might be just what John needs to do."

Jumping into the middle of it, Bobby says, "Seems like everybody from Texas is in Italy. That's what Mrs. Gillian said."

"Who? Mrs. Gillian! Why, that woman's liable to say anything."

"Robert!" his mother says, sharply. "Bobby, did she say who was in Italy?"

"Well, Wick Fowler for one."

"For christsake! Sorry, Barbara. Who's Wick Fowler?"

"Wick Fowler writes for the *Dallas Morning News*. He's in the same hospital as Ernie Pyle. Dear, you do know who Ernie Pyle is, don't you?"

"Now, Barbara."

"Mrs. Gillian reads the Dallas paper." Bobby says deliberately, knowing his father thinks it's unpatriotic to read anything but your hometown newspaper.

"The German troops are all over Hungary," Celia says, and after a minute, "Where's Hungary?"

Now his mother is back on Churchill. "I wish all of you had been here. They rebroadcast Mr. Churchill's entire speech. He said, 'Britain is no longer in mortal danger.' Think of it. Think of how they must feel in England hearing those words."

"Well, yes, Barbara. That's all very well. But what about Japan? We've still got to win a war with Japan."

"Excuse me," Bobby said, "I have to go. Dixie and I are going to study together."

He throws this out, knowing his father won't like it, but he cannot tell them where he is going. Not tonight. Before the words are out of his mouth, he is trotting through the kitchen and down the steps. Thankful for the gathering twilight, he gets his bicycle out of the garage, kicks the tires to see if they have enough air and rides out Pine Street toward Cold Springs

Park. It's already after seven, and he has only the vaguest idea where the Sandflats live, knows only that it is way out on Arkansas Lane. When he has turned left past the park, he starts to check the names on the mailboxes. The houses are farther apart, and the road narrows until, finally, he comes to a dead end. Thinking he has missed the house, he is about to go back when he sees it. It is set way back, a dark mass with what, at first, look like little towers all around it, but riding up the driveway, he sees the towers are only pine trees growing close around the house. There is no mailbox at the end of the drive, no lights come from inside the house, but there is a soft, luminous glow shining from behind, vaguely outlining the house.

He lays his bicycle down on thick tufts of grass and—oh, God!—how he wants to get back on his bicycle and get out of there. Only the thought of the money in his sweater drawer causes him to begin the long journey to the Sandflats'. As he moves carefully along the walk and eases up the porch steps, the only sound he hears is that of the wind in the trees. Taking a deep breath, he lifts his hand to knock, but it falls to his side when he hears a door slamming, someone calling—sounds coming from behind the house. He goes back down the porch steps, moves gingerly toward the light in back. It is pitch-black night and way later than the time he had said he'd be there. A thick and ancient hedge, as high as his head, encircles the backyard, but at its base, the heavy old stalks leave small triangular openings. He drops to his knees and crawls until he can see into the yard.

A world such as he has never seen before is before him, springing up from the darkness, a world lit by candles and oil lamps and a dazzling string of multicolored electric Christmas lights. The yard is full of hollyhocks, their pale blossoms like small moons scattered about the yard. There is a red cloth on a picnic table and a yellow hammock strung between two magnolia trees. The smells of meat and onions and garlic and chocolate fill the air. And the sounds! Cats meowing, dogs barking and growling and the *gssfs, gssfs,* chatterings of a monkey! The Sandflats have a monkey!

Into the middle of this Maxine strides, wearing a white blouse and a long black skirt. A great jug of wine is on the table, and Maxine comes toward it and then, from the outer perimeter of darkness, there is the crisp click of hooves and across the terrace, the stone terrace, a little white goat trots. Mr. Sandflat, stretched out in a chaise longue by the charcoal grill, playfully grabs one horn as it trots by. And now a bright moon breaks over the trees, throwing a silver sheen over everything. If he had been taken up and set down in another world, Bobby couldn't have been more astonished.

"Princess, Princess, Princess," like a hoarse gull Mr. Sandflat calls, "let me pour you a glass," and with surprising lightness he is up and pouring and handing a glass brimming with red wine to Maxine.

"Papa, he's not coming. I don't care. But he's not coming!"

"Princess, these small pale boys in this small pale town. Either he comes or he doesn't! He is not for you. Sit, sit," and he pulls a chair forward (how many times Bobby has seen this courtesy at the cafeteria), and she eases her great bulk into it. Then he picks up a guitar and strums a few chords.

"Mama," he calls, "come out. I've poured the wine. Come out!"

And Mrs. Sandflat, in a red blouse, wearing a long black skirt, comes down the steps, stepping around a duck that runs along by her side until she sits in the white swing. Then the duck jumps upon the seat beside her and, tucking its feet under, eases itself down as if to nest.

As Bobby gazes at the scene before him, he feels a tremendous yearning, for here, before his eyes, is another life, one he could not have imagined, and yet (he feels this strongly), here is a way of living that is more generous, more extravagant than any he has known. And seeing it satisfies him in some indefinable way.

The string of Christmas tree lights winds around a tree branch over Maxine's head and, for the first time, he looks at her, sees her long straight nose, her mass of thick black hair. And her eyes—large, dark orbs in her pale face. He remembers the sound of her voice saying the strange Latin words with such sureness and ease, and with all the lights and animals and color, she seems to Bobby like some magnificent Roman goddess.

Suddenly a cry of anguish, a long wail shattering the night, rises above the clattering of animals: "Papa, Papa," she cries, "he's not coming!"

Immediately knowing he is the subject of her sorrow, Bobby hugs the ground, afraid to breathe, but feeling as if he must stay there forever. It is as if all his life has been lived in a desert, and he has now come to a green and fertile jungle only to find it filled with sorrow. He has never seen his mother cry, has only seen her dab at her eyes with a handkerchief before rushing to her bedroom, and Maxine's racking sobs release some tightness he has always felt.

Mr. Sandflat kneels by her chair, takes her hand, pats it tenderly. "Princess, what do you want? I'll get it. Tell me what you want."

And Maxine makes a bell-like sound and, leaning forward, throws up her hands: "The moon, Papa, I want the moon!" And looking up at the bright moon, she begins to weep, proudly, without covering her face or lowering her head.

Mr. Sandflat pats her hand once again, rises and walks to the center of the yard. For a long minute he stands there, looking up at the moon.

"Such a little thing for a princess to want," he says. He drinks the last of the wine from the glass and tosses it aside. "Well, I'll give you the moon." And then Mr. Sandflat raises both arms, swings them backward and jumps. With a tremendous effort, he pushes himself off the ground, perhaps as many as six inches off the ground, and Maxine's voice, sounding like the tolling of bells, comes again. "Jump, Papa! Jump for the moon!"

And again he pushes himself away from the earth. "Please, Papa! Jump again!" she cries.

"Papa," Mrs. Sandflat calls. "You've lost your senses. Maxine, stop him! Stop your papa." But neither of them hears.

"Jump, Papa! Oh, I want the moon," comes her anguished cry. And he stands, clenching his fists, looking only at the moon, and then he jumps, his labored breathing clearly heard above the excited barking of the dogs, the quickened *gssfs* of the monkey, the shrill bleating of the goat. With the perspiration pouring from his body, he jumps again and again.

And to Bobby, his unbelievably awkward efforts are the bravest thing he's ever seen, and he finds himself leaning forward and, crazy as it sounds, hoping against hope that Mr. Sandflat can get the moon for his daughter.

Mr. Sandflat sinks to the ground, finally. When he can no longer lift his arms, he falls to the ground. And as Mrs. Sandflat comes to kneel beside her husband and cradle his head in her arms, Bobby slips away.

After school the next day, he climbs the steps to Mr. Sandflat's office and puts the money on Mr. Sandflat's desk. "Sir," he says, "Maxine knows more Latin than I do."

On Sunday, when the Sandflats arrive and heave themselves up on the curb to stand breathlessly before they walk into the cafeteria, Bobby looks into their faces as he passes. "Hello," he says.

Only Mr. Sandflat acknowledges his greeting. "Hello, Bobby," he growls.

Chapter 4

· *1* ·

GRACE Gillian has just come from her Saturday tennis game. Amelia had fallen, trying to return Grace's serve, and Grace had gone home with her and seen her inside to be sure no bones were broken. Grace volleys *very* well, but ordinarily she does not serve well. But this morning she had; the perfectly placed balls had *zing*ed satisfyingly over the net. When Amelia fell, Grace felt a twinge of guilt at her own aggressiveness. Now, sipping a cup of hot tea, she is snuggled in the blue-and-yellow lounge chair on her gallery. From time to time she glances through the windows into the treetops to see bare limbs swimming in a haze of tiny, almost invisible, green leaves. The forsythia has bloomed overnight. And the smallest of the finches, the gray ones with yellow breasts, have returned. Spring is here, the smell of it as enveloping as incense.

Spring. The elixir of emotion. When she had read "The Lady of Shalott" to her class, she had been so emotional she could hardly get through the poem. The class had assumed it was because of Bucy, and afterwards they had all looked so solemn that she wanted to cry out: *This is not about my husband!* But of course, she couldn't. Full of sympathy, Dixie Balderidge offered to return Grace's books to the library. Steve Schuster said he would stop by and mow her lawn. "As long as

I have the mower out, might as well run it over yours, too," he'd said, his eyes on the toes of his shoes. And, most surprising, Maxine Sandflat had glided slowly into her classroom with a bouquet of jonquils and irises. Watching Maxine's slow, sad exit from the room, *Who are they, these Sandflats?* she asked herself.

John is leaving. When the thought comes again, Grace gets up and turns on the burner for another cup of tea. All week she has read poetry in the daytime (indulging in self-pity, she tells herself sternly) and at night she has listened to the voice of her grandmother, dead these twenty-five years: *"Honey, it'll get easier. Just let enough days go by, and you can live with it."* This had been Gran's refrain when Grace's grandfather died. Nothing in the world was truer than her grandmother's voice. Lullaby sounds.

The weekend that stretches before her is as empty as John's house will soon be. If she had the money, she would be on the first train to New York as soon as school was out. She still has some of the money Bucy gave her, but not enough for New York. She spent two thousand dollars when he left, changing things around so she wouldn't miss him. And now she's getting ready to do the same thing—change things around, missing John. And Anna. She misses Anna, too. But who would believe it if they knew?

She could take in roomers. With the defense plant and the soldiers in town, there is a big demand for places to stay. And with the two bedrooms downstairs, she could take in several soldiers. It would help her financially. And it would help the War effort. Toying with the idea, she dunks the tea caddy in the cup of hot water until it is a rich amber color. Cradling the cup in her hand, she surveys her backyard. The flower beds are in good shape. But winter's accumulation of debris—fallen limbs, decaying leaves and the boxwood, hit by a freeze—needs to be removed. A yardman is what she needs. Back to money again. And if she takes in roomers, she'll need a painter, some kid who needs the money.

As if summoned, here is Bobby Moore, cutting across her yard. His pants an inch too short, his shirt hanging out a fraction on the right side, a sweater tied carelessly around his waist, he walks with his shoulders hunched, his slight figure leaning forward as if facing a strong head wind.

A curious thing. She had seen him the day before walking down the hall with Maxine Sandflat, the two separated by her bulk, Bobby listing toward her, a tug piloting a ship.

She raises a window: "Bobby, come up here a minute. You got time?"

"Where? Upstairs?"

She laughs. "Yes. Come on."

She hears the back door opening, his footsteps hurrying up the back stairs, taking two at a time. When he stands in the doorway, she smiles. "I'm not in that big a hurry. Bobby, you know anybody who needs a job?"

"Yes, ma'am. I need one."

"Well," she says. And after a minute, "You do?"

"Yes, ma'am. I had a wreck, and I've got to pay for it."

"Let me fix you a cup of tea. No. A Coke. You'd probably like that better. Sit down and we'll talk."

"Thanks."

Mrs. Gillian is wearing a very short skirt. White. It takes a minute for him to recognize that it's a tennis skirt. She gets a Coke out of one cabinet and a glass from another. She has nice legs for a teacher. Brown. Calf muscles moving when she walks. Her hair is in the same old bun, and with the bun and no lipstick she looks older, but then everybody knows she has been through a lot. Chipping ice, she smiles over her shoulder at him and—before his eyes!—a metamorphosis! A younger Mrs. Gillian!

"Here you are, Bobby," she says, and hands him the Coke.

He sits back and looks around, wondering what his mother would think of Mrs. Gillian's house. Their house is plain. But Mrs. Gillian's walls are yellow where she's got her dining room table and living room, and in the kitchen she's painted her walls blue. And she's got bright blue-and-yellow upholstery, some red, too, on the furniture. Magazines and books are scattered along the pine table. On the floor she's got a tall vase of yellow flowers. It's nice.

Following his glance, "The first forsythia," she says, tongue against white teeth.

When Mrs. Gillian comes into the classroom, she looks tall. Now he sees that she is no taller than he is. Leaning forward, he peers out through her windows into treetops. "This is real nice up here. It's like a tree house."

"Thank you. Now, first of all, there's the yard. And I need some painting done. So, let's get down to business."

Business. He longs to talk to Mrs. Gillian, but not about business. He'd like to tell Mrs. Gillian about seeing Maxine the other night. For a hairsbreadth, like a goddess. And her father, jumping for the moon. Like one of those heroes with impossible tasks. The memory imprinted. He'd like to tell her about everything—the white flowers, how the food smelled (chocolate and garlic, spices all mixed together), about the goat and the monkey. A monkey! He'd like to tell her about all that courage and love and sorrow under the gauzy light of the moon. Maybe Mrs. Gillian, with her poetry and all, could understand why everything looks different now.

Grace, sitting on the sofa, draws a pillow to her and hugs it. "Bobby, I've decided to take in roomers." And having said it, she realizes she has made up her mind. "Are you handy?"

Hugging the pillow has made Mrs. Gillian's breasts move upward.

"Ma'am?"

She laughs again. "Are you handy with tools?"

"Yes, ma'am. I think I am."

She leans toward him, the movement outlining her breasts. In her excitement she sits on the edge of her chair, scooting up her skirt. Seeing the shard of white between brown legs, *Oh, Lord,* he thinks.

"Let me show you what I think we need to do." Jumping to her feet, she leads the way past the table, "Bobby, I have everything I need up here, but," hurrying through the kitchen, flinging open a yellow door, "a bathroom. And see here. There's plenty of room for a bath. Don't you think so?"

"Sure."

Now she is inside the pantry (he can see that it is a pantry), taking out brooms and mops and paper sacks. A Christmas wreath. A paper clown.

"Just let me measure this," she says. "I'll have to talk to a plumber first."

He stands in the middle of the kitchen, wondering where she will put all the stuff she is taking out if she puts a bath there. He looks around at the cabinets, looks up and sees the writing in a circle around a ceiling light. Turning in a circle, he reads: COOKING IS LIKE LOVE. IT SHOULD BE ENTERED INTO WITH ABANDON OR NOT AT ALL.

Her voice, coming from the closet, is muffled so that only a few words—*a shower . . . not so expensive . . . quickly*—emerge.

He reads the message again, leans weakly against the counter, considering. *Abandon.* Making love with *abandon.* The word breaks all the rules, turns the steps—the kiss, the French kiss, rubbing the breasts, kissing the breasts, sucking the breasts, finding the right place, getting it in—turns it all upside down. *Abandon.* Schuster's garage is full of fuck books that they've read a dozen times, but there is nothing in a single one of them about *abandon.* Thinking this, he is astonished at the sudden jolt of hardness between his legs.

Oh, Lord, he thinks again. *She's a teacher!*

"Bobby?" Mrs. Gillian comes from the closet, tape measure in hand. "Oh," she says, following his line of sight toward the ceiling, "Mr. Gillian wrote that up there." She stands under the light for a minute, looking up at the words before she turns away, a slight frown on her forehead. "Now that's settled," she says.

What? What's settled? he wonders.

"Here, I'll show you what I'm thinking." She takes a pencil from a cup of pencils, shoves magazines and books aside, spreads butcher paper across the table and begins to sketch. "Here's the sink. The commode. The shower. I like showers better anyway. Of course, we'll need a plumber." She turns, sees him still in the kitchen. "Bobby, come over here so you can see."

"Grace. Grace, come down!" Listening, she raises her head. "Grace!" The call comes again. Together, they look down into her backyard. Mr. Appleby, in a shirt and tie, is pushing a lawn mower over her yard.

She straightens, folds her arms over her chest. "Bobby, we'll begin with the yard. Come tomorrow. Now, please go down and ask Mr. Appleby to come up."

After delivering the message, Bobby heads for home, puzzling over Mr. Appleby. Why would Mr. Appleby be mowing her yard? Does Mr. Appleby know that lovemaking should be entered into with *abandon*? Coming up the walk to his back door, he kicks a basketball from his path. He wishes he were the only one to have ever read the words on Mrs. Gillian's kitchen ceiling. But at least he has a job now. He picks up the basketball and dribbles it along the winding walk to the back door.

· 2 ·

JOHN Appleby has read the words on Grace's kitchen ceiling many times. And while she makes a cup of coffee for him, he reads them again, wondering, always wondering, about Bucy Gillian. Why would a man put that on his ceiling? And now that Bucy's gone, Grace should paint it out. That would be sensible.

He'd be glad to paint it out for her before he leaves.

"John, I appreciate your offering to mow the yard," Grace is saying. "But Bobby is going to do that. He needs the money. Seems he had a wreck, nothing serious, but he has to pay for it."

Only half listening, John has a sudden urge to take her hair out of that silly bun so that it can tumble down her shoulders the way a woman's hair is supposed to. And what was that kid doing up here anyway? Grace should draw the line. Not get so familiar with everybody in the world.

Grace pours his coffee, hands the cup to him. "Sit down, John."

She chooses the sofa, sits up straight, feet primly aligned at the ankles. He takes the big chair, forces himself to lean back.

"I'm leaving for Washington on Monday. I may get as far as Italy if the War doesn't end before then."

"Italy!"

"General Latham is going to Italy, and he's pretty sure he can finagle a way for me to go. But, who knows? The War on the European front is about over."

"People talk about the War being almost over, but every day more of our boys are dying." Her gray eyes, moist with unshed tears, widen.

"Well, maybe I can help. And there's nothing to keep me here."

"No." She wishes he would leave today. She is ready for him to leave. The next moment, she wishes he would take her in his arms.

She says, "It will be good for you to get away from Cold Springs."

"Grace, I can't leave without saying straight out that I never intended . . . that night . . ."

His eyes, bluer than any sky, are full of pity. She does not want, will not accept pity. She stops him with a gesture, holds up her hand, a traffic cop signal.

"John, we're what we've always been. We're friends. Just good friends."

Good. She sees it exactly the way he does. Relieved, he relaxes into the familiar comfort of her presence. "I guess things will go along about the same for you," he says. "You'll be teaching and playing tennis and working in your yard."

Well, after all, she does have a life. John needs to know that. She stands, tucks one leg under her and sits down again. "Things will go along. But not the same. Bobby Moore is going to paint the downstairs bedrooms and help me empty the closets, get rid of Bucy's things. When it's all finished, I'm going to rent those rooms to soldiers. My contribution to the War."

"Grace, I don't think that's such a good idea."

Like a father. Calm. Benevolent. Speaking to a child. "Well, I think it's a good idea," she says, her voice like cold steel.

Jesus, women are crazy! Now she's mad. He tries again. "Grace, taking soldiers, strangers, into your house. A woman alone. I'd worry."

"I hope you would not," she says cheerfully. She looks at his face—blue eyes, nose, mouth (he does have the most beautiful mouth)—looks away. Vaguely she notes that a mockingbird is on a telephone pole in the backyard, singing every song it ever heard. And John is in her house to say good-bye.

"As soon as school is out, I'm going to New York to see Bucy," she says, wondering as she says it, *When does a lie become truth?* His eyes widen, his jaw drops, a reaction that is immensely satisfying. Before he can respond, she adds, "He wants me to come," embellishing further, "and we can decide about our life." Layering it over, "I may be there all summer," she adds, knowing that somewhere in the maze she's woven there lies, surely, the truth.

"I had thought that . . ."

"The marriage was over?" She shakes her head and smiles.

Does she mean that the marriage is over? Or is she shaking her head at his stupidity in thinking it is over? And then she does what he has longed to do—reaches up behind her head with both hands, draws out long pins, and shakes her hair down.

"John, why are you doing this? Going to Italy? To Washington? What reason?"

"You mean besides the War?" He realizes now there's nothing reasonable about this conversation with Grace. Standing, he walks to the windows, walks back, stands over her. "Grace, I'm going because I miss Anna. And because all I remember is sad."

Grief floods his face, but Grace will not allow herself to comfort him. "Well, good-bye, John," she says, holding out her hand. "And good luck!"

"Damnit, Grace," he says. Ignoring her outstretched hand, he pulls her to him. "Dear Grace," he says. He cups her face in his hands and kisses her forehead.

She steps back, away from him. Hands on her hips, she says, "If somebody asks, how can your friends get in touch with you?"

"I'll let you know, soon as I'm settled."

He turns to leave, turns back. "Grace, if I were you, I'd paint out that damn slogan." Gesturing toward the ceiling he adds, "Or whatever you call it." Then he turns again and leaves. She waits at the windows, sees him emerge from her house and cross her lawn to his. He turns and raises his hand in a kind of salute. Then he is gone.

She will not, cannot, bear to see John again before he leaves. But the War won't last forever. It can't. And she has made her plans. She'll stay very busy. Getting the downstairs ready for soldiers will take time. And when summer comes, she will go to New York and see Bucy—that is, if she can find him.

· *3* ·

Bobby waits until everybody is at the table. Because Willie B. is usually off on Saturdays, they have grilled cheese or bacon, lettuce and tomato sandwiches with potato chips. When his father can persuade his mother to go to the country club for supper, that leaves just him and Celia. But, sometimes, the Little Brontës, knowing his mother doesn't enjoy cooking, invite them all over for supper.

Now, finally, finally, they are all there at the table, Celia, like always, the last. He looks at his father. "I found a job." They lean forward, his mother all smiles, his father getting his questions ready. "I'm going to be working for Mrs. Gillian."

"Bobby, that's wonderful."

"Doing what?"

"Taking care of her yard. This morning I mowed. And there's lots more to be done. I've got to rake up all the leaves and fallen limbs and burn them, and all her boxwood on the north side has to be dug out and replaced. She's going to show me how to get the beds ready for spring."

"That's very good, Bobby. Robert, isn't that wonderful!"

"After I finish with the yard, I'm going to paint her downstairs bedrooms and bath."

"That's quite a lot to take on."

"I'll just work part-time until school is out. Then I'll work all day until it's finished. It won't take more'n a couple of weeks."

"How much money is she going to pay?"

Not even Celia can bother him tonight. "We didn't get to that yet."

"Son, what in the name of God—excuse me Barbara—is Mrs. Gillian having her downstairs painted for? Didn't she have all that painted when Bucy Gillian left her?"

"Robert. Now, Robert," his mother says.

"Bobby knows how I feel about Grace Gillian. She may know her poetry, but there's not a practical bone in her body."

"She's going to take in roomers, soldiers, for her part in the War effort."

"Oh, Lord," his father groans, then, "excuse me, Barbara."

"Robert!"

His father blinks, sighs, is silent.

Sometimes his father can go for weeks, and everything's OK. Then the least thing can set him off. Bobby doesn't answer. His waits for his mother to smooth it over.

She reaches across the table and takes her husband's hand and holds it against her cheek. She kisses it. "Robert, dear, it's not up to us to decide how Mrs. Gillian can best help with the War effort."

"All right. All right." He retreats. Some. "Son, there's just one thing. No, there's two things. Tell Mrs. Gillian you need to work out a financial arrangement before you do any more work. And the second thing . . ." He glances toward Celia. "We'll talk about the second thing later."

Bobby's heart sinks. He hates it when his father tries to talk to him about sex. Sometimes, he doubts his father knows one thing about it. Pushing his chair back from the table, "I'm going over to Dixie's," he says.

"Bobby, wait a minute." His mother has left the table and followed him out into the backyard. Slipping her arms into a blue sweater, she pulls her long braid out from under it. "Bobby, don't be cross. Your father has so much to think about right now. The business. The War. His family."

"He won't have to think about me much longer. As soon as I graduate, I'm out of here."

She reaches forward and straightens his collar. "Son, your shirttail's out." Smiling, she pokes at it with a forefinger. Then, suddenly serious, she says, "Bobby, not everyone can get into the armed services. After the War is over, we'll need those who have not been so wounded by it."

"Mother, I'm joining the navy."

"Bobby, they don't take everybody."

"They're taking me!" She is coming too close to what he doesn't want to think about. "Mother, I've got to go."

"All right, Bobby." She stands a minute, hands on her hips, calls once more. "Why don't you bring Dixie over for ice cream? We can all listen to *Your Hit Parade*."

Suddenly lighthearted, he answers, "Maybe I will."

Later that night, Barbara tissues away her makeup, brushes her hair and braids it. *Why didn't they come for ice cream? Is Bobby afraid of how his father might react to this girl?* she wonders. She removes her robe and slips into bed, but everything—the bed, her pillow, her toes under the linens—is uncomfortable. She turns her pillow over, discards the light blanket. *Bobby cannot face the possibility that he will not be accepted into the service. Nor can I.* When she knows this, her heart contracts into a tight ball.

Just yesterday she had seen a young man standing on the corner of Fourth and Main. His hair slicked back to a point at the nape of his neck and wearing one of those zoot suits, he seemed to be pitifully, defiantly announcing to the world: "I'm 4-F!" And now a new law saying that all young men must either fight or work. *What about my son? They're not all draft dodgers!* she wants to cry.

When Robert comes to bed, she says, "I hope they take him."

"Who?"

"The navy. The army. Anybody. He's crazy to go. All his friends will be going."

Her husband runs his fingers through his hair, which in the night light is suddenly grayer and thinner. The small furrows across his brow deepen. He carefully straightens his pajamas. He turns down the linens on his side of the bed. Sighing, he sits heavily on the bed.

"Oh, God—excuse me Barbara—I hope he can get in."

She leans forward to caress his cheek. "You don't need to apologize, Robert. It was a prayer, not a curse." Comforted, she relaxes against her pillow and closes her eyes. Robert wants their son to be accepted by the navy, by some branch of the service, as ardently as she. At least, they are together in this.

· 4 ·

BY the time Bobby gets to Dixie's, he is already dancing, his movements as smooth as Fred Astaire's. Ignoring the steps, singing, "Seems kinda tough now, to say good-bye this way," he leaps lightly onto the small porch of Dixie's house. "But Papa's gotta be rough now," he hums softly as he whirls around three times on the ball of his right foot and leaps from the porch again. Dancing up the steps, and now a little breathless, he finishes with, "So he can be sweet to you another day," and a flourishing bow.

In English class last week Martha Lou had said, "All we hear is bad news. It gets worse every day." Martha Lou's brother is in the War already. And very brave. Now when Martha Lou says anything in class, everybody nods, even the teachers. *Especially* the teachers.

"That's right," Edwina nodded. "I don't even listen to the radio anymore."

"Bad news and good music," Bobby had said, bringing a laugh from the class. They know he loves the music. And dancing.

Dixie loves music as much as he does. She can play anything—"In the Mood," "String of Pearls," "Sentimental Journey"—by ear. She plays all the time. But now, through the thin door on Dixie's porch, it's the radio he hears. A man's voice. Sounding real mad. It's not *One Man's Family*. Could be *I Love a Mystery*, but not on Saturday. He steps closer to the door.

". . . and I don't know. And I wouldn't tell you if I knew. But you ain't gonna leave this house. I'm not gonna let you! Just look at you, for god's sake! You're not even clean. Why don't you clean yourself up! I can't stand to look at you!"

It sounds like a person. Like somebody. But Dixie had told him her father was hunting. *Must* be the radio. He knocks loudly enough to be heard above it. The silence that immediately follows makes his heart beat fast. Then he hears light thumps, a scuffling sound. And in the new silence, he hears the pounding of his heart.

Another minute and the door is flung open. Dixie's father is there, in the doorway. The light comes from behind him so that his face is in shadow. Bobby has never seen Mr. Balderidge up close, but even in this light he sees his small black eyes and black eyebrows. Bobby shifts a little so he can see Mr. Balderidge's face—the forehead that goes a long way before it meets his hairline, a long nose humped in the middle like it was broken and not fixed up right. His mouth is thin, almost unnoticeable.

Coming to himself, Bobby holds out his hand. "Mr. Balderidge, I'm Bobby Moore. I'm a friend of Dixie's."

The mouth widens into a thin smile. "Yessir. Bobby Moore. I know who you are. Now, what can I do for you?"

Mr. Balderidge leans forward, his eyes sliding past Bobby, taking the pulse of Ninth Street. He knows who this kid is. The Moores are neighbors, the closest they have, but the high and mighty Moores are not neighborly. He'd hardly have the nerve to go up to their front door, and he sure didn't need to go to the back. He has a job.

Bobby's heart has quieted some. He stands as tall as he can. "I'm taking Dixie to the Gypsy Dance, and we thought we might practice our dancing. That is, if . . ." The thought of dancing in front of Mr. Balderidge fills him with dismay.

Half expecting to see the old man coming after his son, Mr.

Balderidge leans forward to take another quick look around. "Come in. Come on in," he says. "Dixie's not here, but we might as well get to know each other."

Before he has time to think of an excuse, Bobby is inside, the door closing behind him and closing inside the soft moans that are coming from the bedroom.

As if he is as surprised as Bobby by the turn of an event that was none of his doing, Mr. Balderidge lifts his black eyebrows and fixes upon him a wide-eyed stare. Once Bobby had seen the same look on his father's face when he gigged a snake instead of a fish and almost got it into the boat before he saw what it was.

Mr. Balderidge exhales, blowing out his cheeks. His face, filling out, looks better, temporarily.

"Son, how about a drink? Well, sure. That's what a man needs."

Moving fast, Mr. Balderidge goes to the kitchen, comes back and hands Bobby a glass of tea. Without ice? His mother says they drink it in New York without ice.

Mr. Balderidge stands there, just looking at him and hitting the palm of his left hand with his fisted right hand. He inhales and exhales again. "Whew," he says and then, "Sit down, son. You just sit right down and we'll visit awhile. Take a load off your feet." Drawing a chair from the corner he says, "Take this rocker. It's my wife's favorite chair." And with a nod toward the moaning coming from the bedroom, "Poor soul," he says. "It's a poor soul that's in that room."

Bobby sits in the chair where Mrs. Balderidge had sat the time he and Dixie brought her home from the movie. Looking away from the stare, Bobby remembers the brown rug and sees it again. Everything in the room is dark—the sofa, the rocking chair, the woodwork.

Bobby sits as straight as he can in the rocking chair. He looks at the glass of tea, briefly considers asking for ice. But they probably serve it without ice in the navy. He takes a big swallow.

Lord! It's not tea. Lord, no! It's whiskey. Straight whiskey. Coughing, gasping, he tries to speak. "I didn't know . . ."

"You thought it was a Cokey Cola." Laughing, slapping his thigh, Mr. Balderidge says, "Well, now. Good whiskey don't hurt a man. And I just bet you're man enough. I wouldn't be surprised if you was to say that you'd be joining the armed services pretty soon."

Here was Mr. Balderidge calling him a man and taking it for granted that he'd soon be joining the armed services. Not everybody notices a lazy eye. Gratefully, Bobby takes another swallow, this one smaller.

Mr. Balderidge puts his glass to his thin lips, tilts it and drinks generously. "Whew!" he says again. His eyes are watering. "I'm allergic to drink, but I can't stay away from it. Too handicapped." He places his hand with the glass in it over his heart. "I wish I could get into the War. I truly do. I'm probably the most patriotic man in Cold Springs, but when you've got a handicapped woman, you've got a handicapped man just as well." Surprised by the truth of his words, his black eyes open wide.

Bobby takes another swallow. This one goes down better, and a warmth of understanding floods his heart. He notices that the moans from the other room have decreased to an occasional whimper. "Is Mrs. Balderidge not feeling too well?"

"No, Robert Moore. And that's the God's truth. She isn't feeling too well. Mrs. Balderidge never feels too well. I just pray to God that one day she'll feel well enough." Smiling at his own wit, he waits for the kid to notice. When he doesn't, an irritable feeling descends to rest lightly on his shoulders. "Well, when she feels well enough, if that day ever comes, I can go do my part for my country just like them others. I am true blue patriotic to the core."

It does seem like Mr. Balderidge isn't asking much, just asking for Mrs. Balderidge to feel well enough.

Sliding down the wall, Mr. Balderidge hunkers down on his

heels, ignoring the chair right next to him. Hunkered down, he can think better. He sure would look good in a uniform. He knows it. He smiles at the thought of all the women chasing after him.

"You planning on graduating?" Mr. Balderidge asks slyly. Right in front of him is a boy full of secrets. He can always tell a boy with secrets.

"You mean from high school? Well, sir, I want to join the navy more than anything. I'm going to join the navy. I think I'll like the navy. My parents want me to wait until I'm drafted, but I'd just as soon go now."

"Robert, I know how you feel. Howsomever, I can see your folks' way of thinking. They think everybody needs an education, has to have one. Well, let's just think about that for a minute, Robert. A man can put off an education until hell freezes over, but the War won't wait."

Bobby takes another drink and another. What Mr. Balderidge says makes sense. The War *won't* wait. The whiskey has gone all the way down to his toes and all the way to the top of his head. He leans back in the rocking chair. Mr. Balderidge, still hunkered down on his heels, lifts his glass and empties it. Bobby hears a little sound, a mouse sound, from the bedroom. Leaning forward, he says, "I wonder, sir, would Mrs. Balderidge like for me to step in and say good evening to her? Would it make her feel better?"

"No, son. That takes a woman. Dixie, now, could make her feel better if she were here." *Dadgummit, it's a hard life,* he tells himself. *Too hard.* Tears begin to run, unchecked, down his face. "Lord God have mercy," he says. "What would happen to her, in there, and to my little girl if they was to call me?" he asks. He pulls a handkerchief from his pockets and, snorting, blots the tears.

What *would* happen if they drafted Mr. Balderidge? Thinking about how terrible that would be, Bobby raises his glass and empties it, drinking it down like a dose of castor oil. Mr.

Balderidge may not be the *most* patriotic man in Cold Springs, but he sure is loyal. Bobby rises from the rocking chair and barely restrains himself from saluting. "Sir, if that happened, I would help Dixie and Mrs. Balderidge. I'd see about them. Well, I'd see about them until I joined the navy."

Mr. Balderidge puts both hands flat on the floor and inches up the wall in the same manner he had slid down it. "Robert, I take a man like you on his word. And I'll say this. The navy would be lucky to have a man like you serving our country." He holds out his hand. "Yessir," he says.

Bobby takes the outstretched hand, shakes it firmly. His father would have been proud of the firmness of it. "Well, sir, I'd better be going. Thank you for the advice. And, sir, would you tell Dixie I came by?" he says, and heading for the front door, misjudges, finds a blank wall in front of him.

"Here, Mr. Bobby Moore the Fifth. Here you are." Taking his arm, chuckling softly, Mr. Balderidge guides him to the porch. "Now, you come back. Anytime. You hear?"

"Yessir."

Bobby carefully makes his way home, where he sits on the back steps until Celia's room is dark and shortly afterwards his parents' room is, too, before climbing the stairs to his room. He falls into bed, closes his eyes, feels the room whirling around him. He holds on to the headboard of the bed until the dizziness fades. He is drunk. He has gotten drunk with Mr. Balderidge. He had gotten drunk twice with Steve, but he has never gotten drunk with anybody's father before.

On Monday, watching the crumpled note from Dixie make its careful way down the aisle toward him, Bobby knows what the note will say. He won't be taking Dixie to the dance or anywhere else. If it was a test or something, he flunked it, and it most probably was a test. Mr. Balderidge won't let Dixie so much as walk around the block with him seeing as how he can't handle his liquor.

When the note reaches him, here is Miss Speed, standing right over his desk, gently taking the note, unfolding it. "Bobby, let's share this with the class. Shall we?"

Oh, Lord. The class watches as she unfolds it. Bobby glances toward Dixie sitting like a statue in the front row.

Miss Speed reads the note. "Bobby, you read it to the class," she says gently, putting the note back in his hand.

There's no way out of it now. He pulls himself to his feet and reads:

> *"Hi Bobby!*
> *My dad joined the army last night. He left Mama and me a note that said he had to go because of his duty to God and his country. He said you helped him come to that decision. Come over on Saturday and we'll dance!*
> > *Your date for the Gypsy Dance,*
> > *Dixie"*

The class is watching him and Dixie. Smiling, Miss Speed slowly begins to clap. Then the whole class is clapping and cheering. *Wait a minute!* Bobby wants to say. *What about Mrs. Balderidge? She's a poor soul. And what about Dixie?* He promised Mr. Balderidge he'd see about them. Filled with dismay by the heavy burden he now carries, he can hardly hold up his head, much less smile at his cheering classmates.

Chapter 5

· 1 ·

GRACE Gillian stops her car in front of her house and gets out to pick up a sodden piece of newspaper, a bit of tinfoil, too small for recycling, and a Pepsi bottle before she pulls into the driveway. Inside the house, she puts a stack of English papers, her jacket and her purse on the stairs and walks down the wide hallway to look out into the backyard. Bobby is out there already, taking a tow sack full of leaves to the compost pile. There is something immensely satisfying to her about her new recipe for the compost pile. Since she has begun to add coffee grounds and eggshells and pecan hulls as well as leaves and grass cuttings to the compost, it looks healthier. Richer. Mr. Rhodes gave her the recipe when she bought her azaleas from him last year. She enjoys stirring the compost around, shifting it, but yesterday she turned this task over to Bobby.

She stands a minute watching him work. He is too thin, but then he is a good inch and a half taller than he was last year. He will soon be as tall as his father. If she and Bucy had had a son, and in the early days of their marriage they had talked of children, she imagines he would have been much like Bobby. She is constantly on guard against revealing the special place he has in her heart. And, she reminds herself, he has a mother and she, Grace, never mothers her students as, for example, Miss Hamilton does by having her favorites over, advising them on their love lives, giving them the best parts in plays, putting them forward as eagerly as the mothers of would-be debutantes.

Turning away from the window, she hurries upstairs and slips into khaki-colored pants and an old blue sweater. Tying her hair up in a silk scarf, she sees John's letter on her bedside table and sits down to read it again. For the tenth time? The hundredth? John writes that he is somehow managing to work, even though he has neither an office nor a desk, and that he hopes to leave for Italy soon. He asks her to consider taking in as boarders wives whose husbands are overseas or even spinster ladies. In fact, he does not understand why she feels she must take in roomers at all. He says she must know he only suggests this out of his deep friendship for her. He adds that a girl from his office would be stopping in now and then to see about his house. And then, at the very end, the sentence that fills her with delight: *The War won't last forever, and I am surprised by how eagerly I look forward to coming home to Cold Springs.* She reads that sentence over and over, believing he longs, or at least has begun to long, to return to her. But of course, he cannot write this to a married woman. Regretfully, she realizes it was her pride, only that, that had led her to tell John she was going to New York to be with Bucy. She has not told John how tenuous her marriage was. She has not told him she doesn't even *know* where Bucy lives.

Everybody is saying the War will soon be over. But every day there are more dead, more wounded. Each day three thousand planes fly over the English Channel on their way to targets in France. Each day some of these planes fail to return. So many men. And all so young. Knowing John might soon be in Italy, she greedily reads everything there is to read about the Italian front. The Allies have bombed an Italian dam in order to flood the Nazi defense works. The Americans are still holding on to their foothold on the Anzio beach, their supplies delivered by Allied craft. She imagines John on the beach, hungry and cold.

Tonight she will write to him. She will be completely open about Bucy. Then, she will tell him how glad she is that they had that one night together. She will say: *"When you took me in your arms, I felt that I had come home."*

Satisfied by the unwritten letter, she hurries downstairs. Taking her gardening gloves from a nail by the back porch, she sees that Bobby is dampening down the compost pile. "Bobby," she calls, "when you're through there, come help me with the beds. I want to finish all these beds this weekend."

She stands, hands on her hips, looking over the flower beds. The hyacinths are in tidy rows, white and purple, marching along like little short soldiers. She has never been able to plant hyacinths except in an orderly fashion. But the daffodils, "the host of golden daffodils," are scattered carelessly about the yard in clumps of more than a dozen, sometimes only two or three, and now and then a solitary one that is so beautiful in the sunshine it makes her catch her breath.

The day is partly cloudy and moist, everything dappled and filtered. She works with her gloves at first but soon shucks them off so she can plunge her hands into the humid, fertile earth, speaking to it through touch and smell and sight and, mysteriously, feeling that it speaks to her. Thus, giving and taking, giving and taking, she finds a rhythm to her gardening and relaxes into the work. When she moves to another bed, Bobby comes and, picking up a trowel, watches her work for a minute before taking up the task of uprooting johnsongrass and weeds from the beds. When the beds are clean, together they loosen and tamp down the black earth around the green shoots.

"Look at these hollyhocks," Grace says. "Already up a foot. They might bloom early this year. I brought the seeds from my grandmother's garden in Tennessee." Waving her hand toward the faintly leafed-out vines that climb the fence, she says, "Amelia Johnson gave me those morning glory seeds and helped me plant them. Amelia is my oldest friend in Cold Springs."

"How long have you and Mrs. Johnson been friends?"

"Over thirty years," Grace says.

"Gosh!"

Laughing at Bobby's surprise, she says, "Amelia and I met when we were three. At Miss Patty's nursery school."

Only half listening to Mrs. Gillian talking about her friends and flowers, he longs to tell somebody that it was his fault that Mr. Balderidge joined the armed services after he had promised to take care of Dixie and her mother, who really is a poor soul.

For a while they work in silence, Grace steadily, Bobby in fits and starts. She glances toward him, sees the frown that has been on his forehead all afternoon.

"Bobby, I know you enjoy English, but what subject do you like best after that?"

He likes English all right, but it's not his favorite subject. Relieved that he doesn't have to get around not choosing English, he considers her question. Algebra is easy, but it's dull. Biology. His biology teacher is a better football coach than a biology teacher. "Well, right now, I like Latin."

"Really?"

"Right now I do." And saying this the memory is before him—the smells of garlic and onion and chocolate, the white flowers like small moons scattered about the yard, the strange animals. All of it vivid and Maxine like a goddess, crying, "I want the moon," and Mr. Sandflat jumping to get it for her.

"Bobby, I don't know a thing about Latin. Tell me why you like it?"

"I guess I like hearing about all those impossible tasks that Aeneas had to do. Seeking the golden bough. Going down into the underworld." Sighing, he trowels up another clump of johnsongrass.

Bobby takes everything too seriously. Noting the deepening

frown on his forehead, she says lightly, "Bobby, do you have an impossible task?"

"Yes, ma'am. I do."

With her arm Grace brushes a lock of hair away from her face. She sits back, pulls her knees up and wraps her arms around them. "Bobby, I know that Dixie's father has joined the army. And I know her mother is not well. The situation does seem impossible. But it is not your problem."

"Mrs. Gillian, it is! I promised him! I promised Mr. Balderidge I'd take care of them." The words burst forth, a torrent of them, and then he is telling Mrs. Gillian about going over there and being surprised to find Mr. Balderidge at home and mad and telling Mrs. Balderidge she couldn't leave and that he didn't like to look at her and about going inside and about taking a drink, leaving out the whiskey part, and about the moans coming from the bedroom that changed to whimpers and about promising to look after Mrs. Balderidge and Dixie until he, Bobby, joins the navy and about Mr. Balderidge being about the most patriotic man in Cold Springs and about his handicapped wife and his being handicapped, too, because of it and about how he knew how Mr. Balderidge felt and all the time he's talking Mrs. Gillian is looking at him with her eyes that go from gray to gray-blue to blue and hearing every word he says and caring about it, too. He takes off his hat and replaces it firmly on his head. "I asked if I could go in and speak to Mrs. Balderidge, and he said I couldn't help her. Only a woman could. Only Dixie."

"Oh, Bobby. I never dreamed." Looking at him with her round, gray eyes, she unwraps her arms from around her knees to sit cross-legged. She puts a hand on each knee and leans forward. "Bobby, you need to talk to your parents about this. Nobody could expect you to take care of Mr. Balderidge's family!"

That kind of an answer isn't an answer. He can't talk to his folks. His father would just say that the whole family was crazy. His mother probably wouldn't say much, but she would worry.

Some deep loyalty to his family keeps him from explaining this to Mrs. Gillian.

Grace stands, rubbing the small of her back. The frown is still there, on Bobby's wide forehead. Her answer had not been a satisfying one.

"Let's quit, Bobby," she says. "We got a lot done today. When you come tomorrow, go right ahead with the flower beds. I'll stop by Dixie's and see if I can help. And think about talking this over with your mother or your father. All right?"

"I'll think about it," he says.

Watching Bobby gather up the tow sacks he has emptied, it occurs to her that he always looks as if he is wearing someone else's clothes, his pants too short by a hairsbreadth, his shirt-sleeves too long by as much, and that old brown hat. Surely his father's.

And only Bobby would be reading Virgil and applying it directly to his own life, to his "impossible task." She smiles at the thought. Her answer had been too easy. But it does seem an impossible situation. Why would a man do such a thing? Just go off and leave his wife and child. *Why that's the kind of thing people must have said about me and Bucy when Bucy left.* That thought had not occurred to her before.

That night, upstairs in her little aerie (she has begun to think of it as that), she begins the letter to John. She looks at the sheer (sheer because this letter will, of course, be sent by air) white paper in front of her. She must be completely honest and factual. Especially factual. She uncaps the blue enameled pen that had belonged to her father and fills it with blue ink. Determined to be completely open about her marriage, she writes: *Bucy left on December 22, 1942. He left because he . . .* She gets up and walks into the kitchen. She reads the inscription that encircles the light on her ceiling: COOKING IS LIKE LOVE. IT SHOULD BE ENTERED INTO WITH ABANDON OR NOT AT ALL. She drinks a glass of water and comes back to the table. Frowning, she begins again:

Two days before he left, December 20, 1942, Bucy painted the words that are on my kitchen ceiling. As you remember, at that time it was the ceiling over our bed because the kitchen used to be the bedroom.

She rises again and takes paper, pen and ink to the small table by her sofa. She sits there looking at the sliver of moon and the bright stars below it. Although she cannot see John's house in the darkness, she feels the desolation of the house and the neglected yard. His yard needs work, but then neither John nor Anna enjoyed gardening. It is the empty house that suffers most. The back screen door ajar, the curtains forever closed, the brick path to her swing that John laid just last summer, dust-filled, leaf-filled, undisturbed. She screws the cap on the pen and then unscrews it. She continues:

He left on December 22. This is all I know about why Bucy left. I am still planning to go to New York to see Bucy. If I can find him, I will ask him why he left. I miss you, and I miss Anna, too, although not many would believe it. When you took me in your arms that night I felt I had come home.

After a minute, in her graceful Spencerian hand, she boldly writes:

Love, Grace

She rereads the letter the next morning. Satisfied, she drives by the post office on her way to school so the letter will fly out with the earliest mail.

John's letter arrives in eight days. He has not sent it by air. He writes:

I have been in a dark place for a long time, but now I feel that I am swimming up toward the light. I'm no psy-

*chologist, but I suppose there are several reasons I feel better.
I think of the night we were together. A second reason is that
my work is useful, and I am grateful to be a part of the War
effort. The whole country has sacrificed so much and being
here assuages my guilt. About a lot of things.*

*What do you mean when you say you are going to see
Bucy if you can find him? Does this mean you have not been
in touch with him? All I know is that he was a damn fool to
leave a woman like you!*

*General Latham has wrangled a commission for me to
help me get into this War, late as it is. We will leave soon. If
you want to write to me, you can use the same address.*

Respectfully,
John

She sighs. At least John remembers their lovemaking. But,
she sternly reminds herself, he did not send the letter by air,
and he signed it *respectfully*. If only she could go to Italy. The
Nazis have burned a town in Italy called Terracina and are
falling back to the Pontine Marshes. The Polish forces have
taken Piedmont. The War in Europe has to end soon. Everything points in that direction. School will be out the end of
May, and then she will get on a train and go to New York. Bucy
will be glad to see her. She knows he will be glad. All at once
she longs to see him. *"Why did you leave me? Please tell me
why,"* she will say. And she knows that he will tell her.

· 2 ·

BY the time Bucy Gillian came to town, Grace had settled,
more or less happily, into spinsterhood. Amelia, marrying at
eighteen, had been the first of Grace's six old friends from Miss

Patty's nursery school to marry. Just before Amelia had begun the long walk down the aisle, she had whispered to Grace, who was of course her maid of honor, "Grace, you really ought to settle down." And she had said the same thing through Dorothy Jeanne's wedding and through Mary's and Marcie's and Betty's. But when Emma, the last of the best friends, married, Amelia's plea became a solemn warning: "Grace, if you're not careful, you're going to be an old maid," Amelia had said, turning her hand this way and that so that she could admire her ruby wedding ring.

A little frisson had gone down her spine at the words *old maid*, and Grace *had* tried to marry, had tried so seriously that the very next Christmas two men, one on Christmas Eve and the other on New Year's Eve, had offered, much too seriously, small square boxes with small round diamonds in them.

Dutifully, she tried them on her ring finger, admired each ring, thanked each young man, but found she could accept neither, although, she thought later, if she could have had two husbands and accepted them both, she would have said yes. Instead, she left town to spend the rest of the Christmas holidays with Emma, who was expecting her first baby.

It was during those years of her spinsterhood that Grace fell in love with teaching. Standing in front of her class, "How do I love thee? Let me count the ways," she might read, and then the room would sometimes become suffused with wonder. It happened rarely. She did not know how to call it forth, this look of luminous wonder on their faces. When it came, it was unexpected. A spell cast. Unaccountably. But almost every day, she hurried to her classes, knowing that on this day she might be able to start that certain light on their innocent faces.

One cold, rainy morning in November, she had sat with John and Anna in an easy silence in front of their fire, and John had turned to her. "Grace, what do you like about teaching? Is it shaping those young minds? What is so wonderful about it?"

"When I was a little girl," she said slowly, "at Christmas we would put the lights on the tree, and then we would hang the icicles, and this would take hours. My mother and my sister and I would put a long silver piece of tinsel on almost every pine needle. The tree would be shimmering and alive with the silver. And then we would turn out all the lights in the room and plug in the Christmas tree lights, and the room would be full of . . . of perfection! On the best days, teaching is like that."

Smiling, John had said, "I can see it. I can see that happening in your classroom," and, leaning forward, had given her an avuncular kiss on her forehead.

During these years Grace managed to convince herself that being an old maid was right for her. She could now be quite friendly with the handsome, brown-eyed butcher at the meat market and with her stuffy high school principal and with the husbands of her friends. With John. She reasoned that now that she was an old maid, nobody would mind if she danced or played tennis with somebody's husband. Or if she sat in her backyard swing with John and Anna.

Grace was wrong, and although she could not have put it into words, she sensed the change when she entered a room. They watched her—the men's eyes sliding over her breasts and her long legs, responding warmly to her presence; the women, their eyes, antennae, flicking over Grace's shoulder to their husbands, flicking this way and that, constantly alert, ever ready to place a hand on a shoulder, to smilingly lean forward for a wifely kiss, to gently take his arm. Take him home.

So, is it any wonder that when Bucy came to town, he soon became her best friend? Next to Amelia and Emma. She saw him first at the grocery store. A tall, lovely man, a little younger than she, with a wide smile and an Adam's apple that bounced up and down when he spoke. She ran into him at the high school tennis courts. They played a set and she beat him. At the country club, he asked her to dance. He was easy to follow, could waltz as well as he could jitterbug. After each dance, they came back to the table and sank into chairs only to spring up

again at the first strains of "In the Mood" or "String of Pearls."
When the band stopped playing, they fed nickels into the juke-
box and danced into the early morning hours.

She had never had a friend so lightheartedly interested in
her clothes, her teaching, her house and garden. She had never
had a friend like Bucy.

· 3 ·

GRACE and Bucy had been at the Paramount theater watching
the movie *How Green Was My Valley* when the sound stopped,
the screen went dark and the manager of the theater, looking like a Lilliputian after the giant, on-screen faces of Walter
Pidgeon and Maureen O'Hara, came onstage and said, "President Roosevelt has just announced that Japan has attacked Pearl
Harbor. We are now in a state of war with Japan."

Bucy had turned to her and said, "Where is Pearl Harbor?"

"I haven't any idea."

He took her hand and whispered into her ear, "Let's get
married."

"Are you serious?"

"Dead serious."

Six days later they drove to Oklahoma to be married. By the
time they reached Ardmore, snow had begun to fall, just a few
flakes drifting down, but after Ardmore the wind rose, and the
windows of Bucy's old Ford were not sealed. Afterwards she
thought that only the intense cold made her turn and say, "Bucy,
I have loved someone for quite a long time."

"Loved?"

"Love," she said firmly.

While she waited for him to speak, she saw a Burma Shave
sign, read the first line. DOES YOUR HUSBAND MISBEHAVE? She

smiled at Bucy, but he was looking straight ahead, his Adam's apple still for once. They drove past a pasture where three brown-and-white cows grazed. Just over the hill she saw the next line: GRUNT AND GRUMBLE? RANT AND RAVE? She had never heard Bucy rant or rave. And here was the last line, just ahead. She squinted her eyes to read: SHOOT THE BRUTE SOME BURMA SHAVE! Smiling at the word *brute*, she looked at Bucy.

"Bucy?" she said.

He reached for her hand and feeling how cold it was, he took gloves from the pocket of his overcoat and gave them to her.

"Just love me if you can," he said, and the grace of these words went to her heart. She moved close and drew his arm around her.

They were married by a round-faced and beaming justice of the peace in Oklahoma. They spent their honeymoon night at the Tulsa Hotel, where they had a good dinner and went to bed early. As a lover, Bucy was tentative and sweet. Grace felt safe. Vaguely passionate. Afterwards, they slept well and the next morning, ate hungrily. Driving back to Cold Springs, he took her hand and sang "Let Me Call You Sweetheart," and she read all the Burma Shave signs to him.

On Monday, Grace had a tennis date with Amelia. Amelia faulted on her first serve but recovered to win the game. Grace served. Although Amelia had put on some weight over the years, she moved around the court with astonishing speed. The game was forty–love when Grace called across the net: "Bucy and I got married Saturday."

Amelia, juggling the ball on her racquet, walked toward the net. "What? What did you say?"

Grace walked up to the net. "Bucy and I were married Saturday."

Questions stormed Amelia's throat. "Have you lost—?"

"No."

"Weren't you two a little hasty?"

"No."

"It's because of the War, isn't it? That's it. I know it is! But you don't love . . ."

"Amelia," Grace said, "Bucy is not trying to evade the draft. He has a heart murmur." And then, "Amelia. It's my life," she said firmly.

At that, Amelia, stepping back from the invisible barrier between these two old friends, a barrier she had almost crossed, began to cry, and Grace reached across the net and took her in her arms. "Amelia, it's all right. I'll be just fine, Amelia. I promise I will be."

· 4 ·

GRACE has made her plans. On the third of June, she will leave for New York to find Bucy, although she has no idea how she might accomplish this. The trains headed East are crowded with soldiers on their way to the European front (she feels sure of this), and so she has bought her ticket early.

Bobby is sitting in the chair on her gallery when she tells him. "Bobby, the yard looks great! You've done a good job with it. Here," she says, handing him an envelope containing seven dollars and fifty cents, and a glass of water. She plops down on the sofa, stretches her arms over her head and folds them behind her. "I'm tired," she says. Then, "Bobby, I'm going to New York as soon as school is out."

He doesn't even have to wonder. He knows why she is going. It is like that poem. She will get in a boat (only it will be a train) and lie back, and it will take her to her Sir Lancelot. On the long journey her breasts will rise and fall while she sleeps. He wonders if Mrs. Gillian's breasts would feel like Dixie's. Last night Dixie had let him touch hers. Remembering, he feels a pleasant arousal. Mrs. Gillian's are bigger. Probably softer, too. If Mr. Gillian saw her now with her legs brown from the sun and her nice smile and her big gray eyes—well, he never would have left.

"Bobby, this will be a perfect time for you to paint the downstairs bedrooms," she says. "Move the furniture to the middle of the room and cover it up. I have some old sheets for this. The woodwork's fine. Just leave it. When I come home, I want it to be finished. I'll call your father and ask him to charge the paint to me. Or maybe it would be better if I stopped in to the store to tell him. I think so. Yes. That's what I'll do."

There's no telling what his father might say to Mrs. Gillian. When he mentions English or English teachers, his father always bristles: "All that poetry. Makes them frivolous." He can hear him saying it. He wishes she wouldn't stop in to see his father. But he can't think of a way around it.

"Uh, Mrs. Gillian, what color?"

"Bobby, I like yellow. Do you think a soldier would like yellow?" and thinking of a future with John, she adds, "Or a soldier's wife?"

"I like yellow," he says. "I don't know about a soldier." He grins widely. "But you can ask me what a sailor would like pretty soon."

"Bobby, when will you be eighteen?"

"In December."

"Good! The War's bound to be over by December."

"I'm going in early," he says, trying out words he has not said aloud before.

"Bobby, don't be in a hurry to go over there and get yourself killed! I can count twelve boys—and they were just boys!—from high school who have been killed or seriously wounded. Steve Schuster's brother came home in a wheelchair. Sally Bryan's brother will never come home. Never! You go talk to Steve and Sally before you join early."

"Steve's gonna join as soon as he's eighteen. And you don't have to be so . . . to get so . . . All I said was . . ."

"I know what you said. And you know what I said. Don't you join *anything*! You hear?" Grace doesn't think he can get in with his eye problem, but they seem to be taking everybody now.

Bobby stands and picks up his hat. He swats his pants leg with it. His face is flushed.

Relenting, "All right, Bobby," she says. "You do what you have to do." She holds out her hand. "OK?"

He grins at her. Instant forgiveness. "Sure," he says.

He is too young! They're all too young. Boy that he was, Wilfred Owen knew about war. "Lend him to stroke these blind, blunt bullet-heads/Which long to nuzzle in the hearts of lads," he wrote.

"We're squared away, then. I'll see you tomorrow," she says. And the rest of that poem? What was it? Something about, "his teeth seem for laughing round an apple."

One thing Bobby likes about Mrs. Gillian is that she doesn't remind him to read his assignment or ask if he has a paper ready. School is school and yard work is yard work with Mrs. Gillian. He really likes Mrs. Gillian. In some ways, he likes her more than Dixie.

On her way home from school, Grace stops to tell Amelia. They sit in the breakfast room Amelia has papered with purple grapes and green vines and leaves. She named it *the arbor*, sending Ed into a paroxysm of laughter. Amelia names all her rooms. The living room with its blue ceiling and a painting of a sailing ship over the fireplace mantel is the cove. The dining room, for whatever reason, is the island.

An afternoon ray of sunlight comes through the window, turning Amelia's eyes to a hyacinth blue and highlighting small wrinkles around them. Amelia has gotten out her wedding china and silver and linen napkins, making Grace's visit an occasion. Grace adds sugar and lemon to her tea and stirs it. She takes a bite of an oatmeal cookie.

"As soon as school is out, I'm going to New York."

"Oh," Amelia says carefully. Patiently, she stirs her tea, picks up a cookie and looks at it thoughtfully. She looks at Grace. Smiling, she lifts her eyebrows.

Laughing at Amelia's restraint, Grace says, "I'm going to see Bucy."

"Good. That's exactly what you should do." All restraint gone, Amelia is full of enthusiasm. "Ed and I have talked about it. I'm glad you're going. Ed will be glad, too. But not to stay! You're not going to stay!"

"No. Not to stay," Grace said. "Now tell me when to plant morning glories. I lost about half the vines this winter."

That afternoon, Grace burns a pile of leaves a safe distance from the trees where birds have already begun to build nests. Reassured by Amelia's approval, she watches a plume of smoke rise, straight up, into the blue sky. A smoke signal. Suddenly lighthearted, she takes off her sweater and waves it through the smoke: *Bucy, I'm coming to New York. I have my ticket. I'll be there soon.*

If only it were that easy, she tells herself. *I have to get in touch with him. Somehow.*

Suddenly awake in the middle of the night, she sits up in bed. It has come to her as clear as anything. She will put a message in the personal pages of the *New York Times.* Bucy always reads the personal columns.

Before Bucy left her, she once asked him: "Why do you read them?"

"I don't know."

It had been a Sunday morning, the papers lazily on the floor and the two of them still in nightclothes. Bucy had handed her a glass of orange juice.

She picked the paper off the floor and read: "Slightly overweight girl looking for male friend who likes to play bridge."

"Are you interested in a slightly overweight girl who plays bridge?" she teased.

He had grinned. "You know I'm not. But it's interesting. Each one a story without an ending. Most sound . . . Oh, I don't know." Then he had headed for the kitchen, calling over his shoulder, "How about pancakes this morning? And, don't forget, we're on for tennis this afternoon."

Remembering, she lies down again, smiling at the idea of Bucy at a bridge table with a slightly overweight girl. Relaxed by the idea that she can get in touch with Bucy, she turns over and falls into a sound and restful sleep.

· 5 ·

On the last Saturday in May, the old postman (called out of retirement by the government) rings the doorbell. "Mrs. Gillian, there's a letter here. Looks like Mr. Appleby is a captain! I don't think most folks know he's in the army."

Mr. Bartlett's face is wizened, his back bent. In spite of his age, he knows that nobody in town takes care of every letter, every card—not to mention packages!—the way he does. Sometimes his job is so hard he can hardly finish out the day, but he thinks of himself as an old soldier doing his share for the War. This morning, his black eyes, mere slits under drooping lids, are alive with excitement.

"Thank you, Mr. Bartlett. Thank you!" Grace takes it from his hand, turns, rips it open and reads it as she slowly climbs the stairs.

Shaking his head, the postman reaches inside and pulls the door closed until the latch catches. *Something's up with those two,* he tells himself. And Mr. Gillian still in the picture. Thinking of it, he walks a little faster. Mrs. Bartlett will have his dinner ready around two, and while he rests she can chew on this bit of gossip.

By the time Grace has reached the top of the stairs, she has read the letter. She sits on her sofa to read it again.

Dear Grace,

Things move fast. As you see, I'm in the army now and in a place I've always dreamed of visiting. I wish I could tell you more, but I can say that the experience has taught me that every day is precious. When I come home I intend to enjoy every sunset, every rainfall and, most of all, your friendship.

The War will soon be over. I know it.

I hope you have been able to work things out with Bucy. I want you to be happy.

Affectionately,
John

John hopes she can *work things out* with Bucy. Does this mean he hopes she will divorce Bucy? With the letter in hand, she walks outside and into her garden. The brightness of new leaves is everywhere. Gulf clouds move lazily across the sky. She sits in the swing and frowns at the letter. *Working things out* could mean he hopes she and Bucy will reconcile. Sighing, she folds the letter and tucks it away. It has become unfathomable.

But John *is* in Italy. That's clear. Since he left she has read everything she can find about the war in Italy. Ernie Pyle has won the Pulitzer for writing about it. But Wick Fowler's columns are the ones she reads first. This week he wrote about soldiers on the Anzio beachhead who count the Liberators when they return from a bombing mission because when one doesn't come back, they know ten of their buddies are missing. Then the soldiers hurry over to ask the returning crews if they saw any sign of parachutes when the plane went down. He has written about American soldiers taking in dogs and adopting Italian children. And during a lull in the battles he wrote that some of the soldiers were building small houses of stones and

making furniture and planting gardens. But Wick Fowler said
not to be misled by these domestic scenes. Our boys are fighting and dying every day in Italy.

The invasion is bound to come soon. In early May Eisenhower was sending three thousand planes across the Channel
each day. Now he sends six thousand.

When the invasion begins, the fire trucks are going to sound
their sirens all over town, day or night. Thinking of it, a shiver
goes down her spine. The invasion has to come. But at what a
cost! One can only imagine the terrible, tragic losses that will
come when it happens.

Made restless by her thoughts, she moves through the
house, opening windows, opening doors. Bucy's clothes hang
in his closet, waiting, just as she has waited. John hopes she can
get things straight with Bucy. He wants her to be happy.

She stands there, looking at Bucy's clothes—his white shirts,
starched and ironed, his suits, his jackets—hanging there as if
he had left only yesterday. Waiting.

Well. She can't wait forever. She needs this closet. Feverishly, she takes his clothes, all that he has left behind, out of the
closet. She leaves the jackets and shirts on hangers and folds the
sweaters in a neat stack. By the time Josie comes, his closet is
empty.

"Josie, I've got some of Mr. Gillian's clothes for you. Hope
you've got somebody in mind who can use them."

Josie won't work for new people. She says she can't understand a word those folks from up north say. But there are a
number of women in line for her services. Josie—small, wiry,
her hair in a braid around her thin, dark face, the apron she always wears, like snow—is one of Grace's blessings.

Josie sets the laundry basket on the hall table. "Mr. Gillian?
He home?" she says, beaming, her hands on her hips. "Well,
now, ain't that something?"

"No, Josie, he's not home. Truth to tell, I don't know if
Mr. Gillian is coming home. And I don't care whether he does

or not!" She bites her lip to stop the tears, to control her voice, gone suddenly trembly. Her lighthearted mood of yesterday seems years ago.

"Miss Grace, you just let those tears come. You needs to cry. You's had a harder time of most anybody. Mr. Gillian jumping up and leaving like that. Wonder what got it into his head to do that?"

"Oh, Josie. I don't know. Maybe it's something to do with the War. I just feel like everything will be all right when the War ends." She takes a deep breath, the tears gone as suddenly as they came.

"You right about that, Mrs. Gillian. Now, here's your laundry. Let me just put this here laundry up."

"I'll do that, Josie. I'm rearranging the closets down here. Let me get your money, and here's Mr. Gillian's clothes. Gosh, I don't know what got into me."

"Ain't nothing but the War. Gets into us all. Like a dark cloud. Now, you sure about getting rid of Mr. Gillian's clothes? You sure you wants to do that?"

"Absolutely."

When Josie leaves, Grace puts the sheets in the linen closet, runs her hand over their smooth softness. Every Wednesday Josie takes her laundry, bundled in a sheet and balanced on her head, to her house. On Saturday, she brings it back, starched, ironed (even the sheets), all pristinely finished and smelling of wood smoke.

When Josie leaves, Grace gets scissors from the house and cuts a lavish bouquet of daffodils. A consolation. Each one is the soft, butter color she likes. She will tell Robert Moore that this is the color she wants her bedrooms painted. She must remember to take a daffodil in to show him.

She puts the flowers into a green vase and buries her face in their aching fragrance. Then she takes the flowers upstairs and puts them on the gallery table. "I'll be seeing you in all the old familiar places, that this heart of mine embraces all day through," she hums. When the War is over, John will come home and sit in her swing and walk up her stairs and sit on her gallery. *Home.* John will soon be home.

After supper, she composes the message to Bucy: *I will be at the Cosmopolitan Club in New York on June 6th. I must see you. Please tell me how to get in touch with you. Grace.* She provides dates for the advertisement to run, asks the *Times* for a bill and addresses and stamps an envelope.

Satisfied, she opens the back door to feed Cal. Startled by the cries of birds, she stands motionless. The air is filled with sound. The black limbs of the trees are lined with migratory birds, hundreds of little black silhouettes against a sky like old silver. She takes a step into the yard, and the birds spiral up with one accord, swing this way and that. A ballet. She stands quite still. They return, and the trees are again filled with their cries. Excited little gossips. She wishes John were here to see it. Or Bobby. Bobby would enjoy it.

His friend Dixie hasn't been in school the past three days. She needs to finish high school. With a high school diploma she could get a job at the defense plant.

Impulsively, Grace slips into a skirt and blouse, stockings, heels. School clothes. She hurries downstairs and then, remembering the flowers, turns and runs back up to get them.

She walks out through her back gate into the alley that smells of tar and creosote. She feels the gravel beneath her thin-soled shoes, stumbles over a rock. A dog barks, and another, setting off all the dogs in the neighborhood. Coming to the end of the alley, she smells the fetid odor of the uncovered drainage ditch across Ninth Street. Josie lives somewhere over there. Here and there she sees a faint light in one of the small houses. She hopes Josie's house is one of these with a light.

The Balderidge house is here, just to her left, at the end of the alley. There is someone on the porch. A woman, muttering angrily. "Now you better get out of here. Get out. I took the piano. Yes, I did. That and my suitcase. Papa said . . . what? I don't know." Now the rocking is faster, the voice frantic. "I wish. I wish. What do I wish? Don't you come here. Don't. Don't come. Don't."

"Mrs. Balderidge?" Grace calls softly. But before she can say more, can even think what to say, Mrs. Balderidge has gone silently into the darkness of the house. The empty chair rocks faintly even as Grace places the flowers on the porch beside it.

· 6 ·

WHEN Robert sees Grace Gillian coming into his store, he gets up. Sits down. Gets up again. Positioning himself. Raising defenses. Walking lightly, as if her feet were about to leave the ground, she comes toward him with a flower. Now, who else but Grace O'Brian would walk around town with a yellow flower, holding it toward him like some damn prize or something! And in that green dress, looking like a girl, still.

"Hello, Bobby," she says. *Bobby.* He hasn't been called that since—well, since that night. Well, damnit! Nobody but his old aunties and Grace have ever called him that. Grace always said *Bobby* like she was laughing about his name or about him or something. He still has the ring she refused in the back of a desk drawer in his office.

Wearing a dress the color of lilacs, she had put it on her finger that night. "Let me think about it," she said, but after no more than a minute or two, turning it this way and that under the porch light, she took it off and gave it back. She was laughing. "Bobby, we'd drive each other crazy. I drive you crazy now."

And she had. But back then he had thought that with a few years on her she would settle down. But she hadn't. If anything she has gotten worse. More high-spirited. Even reckless. Yes.

He would go that far. *Reckless.* Marrying that man from Mississippi and not knowing a thing about him. Well, what could you do with a woman like that? What could you do?

But Grace had been much favored by the Little Brontës until she turned him down. After that they were in his corner faster than a robin on a worm. "Not the girl for Bobby." "That Irish blood." "A girl like that won't ever settle down." "Liable to turn out just like her great-grandmother." "*Likely* to."

"Bobby?" Smiling (still those white teeth, that generous mouth), she waves her hand in front of his face.

"What?"

"This is the color I want my bedrooms," she says, and hands him the flower.

"What color is it?"

"It's yellow. I want my bedrooms this shade. A soft color. Like butter. Remember butter?"

"What is it called?"

"I don't know. Is there one called daffodil?"

"No."

"Or jonquil?"

Now she's laughing again. He shakes his head. "Leave the flower. We'll see if we can match it."

So serious. Almost stern. She longs to say: *"Forget about that silly ring. Remember the fun we had together. Remember, we were young."* Instead she says, "Oh, Bobby, you have a fine son. He has done a good job with my yard. He works hard."

"Thank you, Grace."

Formal. As if we haven't known each other for years and years. Not yet ready to leave, she says, "How are the Little Brontës? I haven't seen them in some time."

"Aunt Emily's been a little under the weather. Keeps Aunt Anne busy looking after her."

"Bobby, you remember that time we took their car and got stuck in the mud and they came by and . . ." Laughing, she bends over, holding her side.

The same Grace. Getting so tickled she cannot finish her story. "And they insisted on helping us," he finishes for her.

"And Anne was so muddy, Emily had to hose her off before she could come in the back door."

Robert is smiling now. "They told that story all over town. They were rather proud of it," he says, chuckling.

"Bobby, ask the Little Brontës to stop in to see about Mrs. Balderidge. She's not well."

"Who?"

"Your neighbor. Across the alley. That little house on Ninth."

"I know who she is."

"Well, ask them. They go all over town visiting the sick. Will you ask them?"

"I'll mention it."

"Thanks." She leans to kiss his cheek, and with a wave of her hand she is gone.

Standing to watch her walk lightly down the aisle and push open the outside door, *Lord, you'd have to be a stone not to enjoy Grace,* he tells himself. He sits at his desk, and fumbling in the back of the drawer, he takes out the ring. He really should do something about it. If he dropped dead, Barbara would wonder about a diamond ring in his desk. When Celia is a little older he could give it to her. Yes. That's what he will do. Celia would probably like a little diamond. Not wanting to make the same mistake twice, he had proposed to Barbara before he bought another ring. A plain, gold band was what Barbara had wanted. And got.

He looks at the clock, surprised to see that it is almost noon. The morning has been wasted. Grace coming in has turned it all upside down. Since she refused his ring all those years ago, they have seen each other only at big affairs—weddings, funerals, that kind of thing. But they have never talked, just the two of them, until this morning. He will mention Mrs. Balderidge to his aunts. He will do that for Grace.

Chapter 6

· 1 ·

WATCHING for Dixie between classes, Bobby sees nothing else. When she appears, he walks with her down the hall. "Kiss me once and kiss me twice and kiss me once again," he whistles softly, although he's never kissed her. Not on her lips. Not one time. Although she lets him kiss her neck, and she lets him touch her breasts, when he tries to kiss her lips, *abandon* is not in her vocabulary. But if it's dancing, well, Dixie dances with more abandon than any girl he's ever known!

The dance is two weeks away, and every night he hurries through supper so they can practice. Mrs. Balderidge is always at home, but she never comes into the room when he is there.

The first time they practiced after Dixie's father left, Bobby said, "Could I say hello to your mother?"

"Not tonight," Dixie said.

"I promised your father I'd help if I could."

"But not tonight. She's upset. Somebody left some flowers on the porch. It upset her."

"The flowers?"

"No. Well, maybe. They were in a green vase. She's always trying to remember something about a green bottle. She cries when she tries to remember."

Dixie had leaned forward and put her head on his shoulder. "Oh, Bobby," she sighed.

Pulling her to him, feeling thin, sad shoulders, he is filled with longing. *Oh, Dixie! Of the Coke bottle glasses! Of the boogie-woogie and tapping saddle shoes. The brave swing of skirts. If I could only make you happy!*

Tonight the meal will take forever. The Little Brontës have come for dinner. The table glistens with his Grandmother Charlotte's cut glass and heavy silver. Sprays of japonica and wild plum blossoms in cut-glass vases on each end of the sideboard fill the room with balmy scents of spring.

Entering the dining room, Aunt Anne says, "Barbara, it is such a comfort to see our dear sister's things on Robert's table." Her eyes fill. By the time Robert seats her, she has recovered. "Thank you, dear," she says, smiling moistly up at him.

Aunt Anne's eyes are always moist—with happiness, with sadness, seemingly embracing both immediately, bouncing instantly from one to the other. She spends her money, her energy, her emotions carelessly, ceaselessly. She has never married, although she had her chances. Several chances.

Aunt Emily, twice widowed and financially sound, is careful with love, careful with life. After the precipitous, *literally* precipitous, deaths of both husbands (one by falling from a horse, the other by falling down the stairs of a hotel in Paris), she has become exceedingly careful of her money and her name, her family name. The Moore name. The only luxury she allows herself, she tells her banker, is her chauffeur. She and her sister must have a driver. Robert is far too busy to drive them about.

Emily quietly and steadily loves her sister, her nephew and his children. Because her nephew's marriage has lasted almost twenty years, she recently has begun to love Barbara. A little. Now, picking up her sister's mantra, she smiles at Barbara, touches a glass and runs her finger around its rim. "Not a chip. So treasured."

Tonight the aunts are wearing navy dresses, identical at first glance, and single strands of pearls around their necks (Emily's, of course, much larger), and pearl earrings. Their hair, dyed brown, is cut and curled tightly against their heads. Emily wears a pink flower at the neck of her dress, and Anne wears a small wisteria blossom on her shoulder. Both flowers are artificial.

Oh, but who would guess they were sisters? Anne is short and sturdy, round cheeks polished with color, lips bright, eyes innocent as a child's. Emily is tall and thin, her face long, weary, her eyes guarded. They have almost always lived together.

As Robert takes his seat at the head of the table, he lifts his glass to his wife. While they were dressing, Barbara had flirted shamelessly with him, inviting him in to dress while she was in the tub, dropping her dressing gown down around her waist, asking him to fasten her brassiere. With her hair up and in that black dress, his wife is especially beautiful tonight. Already he looks forward to the time—the dinner's end, his aunts safely delivered, his children asleep—when they can make love. At times Barbara is rather wild. Noisy. "The children," he whispers at such times. "The children."

But now they are at the table. His family. Celia looks exceptionally happy tonight. And healthy. Expansively, he leans forward. "Now, Anne, tell Celia and Bobby about the time the three of you brought home a stray dog and told Grandmother it was a fine Dalmatian." And they are off, into the past. The glorious past.

Tonight, Bobby's mother looks like any other mother, only prettier. Her hair is up and braided in a coil on top of her head. She is wearing a soft black dress and Grandmother Charlotte's ruby lavaliere. He wonders if she misses having a family of her own. She never had one. Not really. But she loves the aunts. She loves for them all to be together.

Now Aunt Emily is telling about the time his father got Emily's car stuck in the mud, and they came along in Anne's car and tried to help him and got so muddy they couldn't go in their own front door, a story he's heard a million times.

While the conversation rises and falls along easy and familiar paths, Bobby gives himself over to thoughts of the Gypsy Dance. He and Dixie have not decided about the song they will dance to, but they're leaning toward "It's Been a Long, Long Time." The beat is right. And the ending is good. Not too fast for him to tumble her over his back, dance four beats together, separate, swing out and finish with Dixie across his left arm, her head almost touching the floor.

Dixie is making her dress in home economics. All he has to do is get a bright scarf to wear around his waist, a gold earring, and then paint on a mustache.

He looks at the tall clock in the corner. An hour at the table and the dessert not served. Seeing his edgy attention, his mother says, "Bobby, I'm sure the aunts will excuse you." And to the aunts: "He has so much to do these last weeks of school, and he's got this yard work, too."

"Son, we're having bread pudding for dessert. Now you don't want to miss that. Barbara's new maid is a great cook," his father tells the aunts. "And now that she's here, Barbara will have more time to get into things."

For as long as he can remember, his father has wanted his mother to get into things. The aunts smile at his father and turn to gaze hopefully at his mother.

Turning her iced tea glass round, his mother says, "I have plenty of time. I'm just no good at it."

A great chorus rises from the aunts: "Now, now, Barbara," says Anne.

"Oh, dear, that's not true," says Emily.

"Just because you're not one of us!"

"Anne, you don't mean that!"

Anne, her eyes filling, murmurs, "Of course not."

Suddenly realizing what has been said—*not one of us*—the aunts grow pale at this alarming honesty.

His mother throws back her head and laughs. Relieved, his father chuckles; the aunts smile. It's going to be all right. But oh, Lord, if he doesn't leave right now, Willie B. will be bringing in the dessert. He hurries around the table to hug the aunts. He kisses his mother's cheek. "You look nice," he says, and whispers, "Thanks." Almost through the kitchen door, he turns. "Good night, Dad."

His father, off on another story about Robert Moore III, waves cheerfully and goes on with his tale.

· 2 ·

MRS. Balderidge is rocking slowly on the small porch when Bobby puts his hand on the gray, rickety porch railing. "Good evening, Mrs. Balderidge," he says, but already, Mrs. Balderidge is half out of her chair. "Oh, please. Don't leave," he says, stepping back. "Maybe I could just sit out here on your steps for a minute."

He remembers his grandfather, gentling a high-strung horse, talking to it with his hands and with his voice. "Whoa, now. Whoa, boy," holding the bridle with one hand, stroking the horse's throat and muzzle with the other and talking, talking.

"It's all right, Mrs. Balderidge," he says softly. "It's just me. Bobby Moore. You remember me? Remember when Dixie played 'Deep Purple' for you? She said it was your favorite song."

Mrs. Balderidge has eased back into the chair. Looking straight ahead, she sits as still as a statue. He can barely see her face—her dark eyes, her black hair falling round her shoulders.

"It's a mighty nice night, Mrs. Balderidge. Well, I guess you're sitting out here, waiting for Dixie. Maybe I could keep you company. Would that be all right with you?"

When she doesn't answer, he slowly eases himself down on the steps. Should he ask about Dixie? He looks up at the stars, finds an easy subject. "The sky is clear. The Big Dipper is real bright tonight."

He waits a minute for Mrs. Balderidge to step into the conversation, but Mrs. Balderidge does not seem interested in the stars. Looking straight ahead, she sits still as a stone. The conversation doesn't seem to be going anywhere. Maybe he could ask about Mr. Balderidge. No. Too risky. Well, pretty soon he will have to think of something to say. Talking to Mr. Balderidge was a whole lot easier.

Slowly, Mrs. Balderidge begins to rock again.

"That's a mighty comfortable-looking rocking chair," he says hopefully. Giving her plenty of time, he waits. He has about run out of subjects.

Then, so quick, she jumps in: "Stinging nettles did this." She traces the scar on her face. "It wasn't a fence. It was stinging nettles."

"You got into a bunch of stinging nettles? That must have hurt real bad."

"A Balderidge did it. . . . And the dogs."

"How? Do you mean that—? Did some dogs attack you?"

"My daddy said . . . My daddy told me . . . He said, 'Coming to Texas, Maggie, you'll need . . .' "

"What? What would you need, Mrs. Balderidge?"

"Sixteen. I was sixteen."

"What would you need in Texas, Mrs. Balderidge?"

"Mustn't talk! Mustn't talk!" The rocking becomes frenzied. Then, gripping the arms of the chair, Mrs. Balderidge begins to cry.

Standing up, he leans to touch her shoulder. "It's all right, Mrs. Balderidge. It's all right. You want me to ask my mother to come over here? She can help you. She can help anybody."

Swiftly, silently, Mrs. Balderidge is out of the chair and has vanished into the darkness of the house.

Damn! He's fouled it up. Asking questions. Saying the wrong thing.

He wishes Dixie were here. She'd know what to do. Where is she, anyway! They were supposed to be dancing. She is probably out with Jack Pearce. He hates to think about her out in a car driving around with Pearce. Pearce is always horny. He gets horny when a girl walks by. Any girl. He'd go crazy over *abandon.*

Kicking at a rock, he follows it halfway down the alley. He could go on home, but the aunts will still be there. No point in walking into a hornet's nest of questions.

In just two more weeks, he and Dixie will be dancing in the high school gym. For a single dance, they will be almost like, well, like movie stars. Thinking about the dance, his heart lifts.

About halfway through the dance, Sophie Anne White will stand, lift the trombone to her lips and slide into "Saint Louis Blues." Even before Sophie blows the first round notes, the kids will begin to clap, and then they'll fall silent, swaying quietly to her song. He can see it. Sophie standing, lifting her straight, long hair back over her shoulders and blowing that horn like all she has ever known is loss and suffering. And then, after Sophie plays, the crowd will turn and look at him. And he will take Dixie's hand and walk to the center of the floor, and everybody will move back and circle around, and then, he and Dixie, her long brown hair and bright skirt flying, will begin to dance—moving together, apart, together, keeping the beat, jitterbugging better than anybody, better than Ginger Rogers and Fred Astaire.

And after that, the band will play something slow. Maybe a waltz. His mother has taught him to waltz. Or the band might play "Deep Purple." He can make some pretty good moves to "Deep Purple." The rest of the night is a little hazy in his mind, but he's hoping that Dixie will like him so much that Jack Pearce will join the army and leave town.

Suddenly, car lights flash down the alley, startling him so

that he moves back against a garage wall. The car turns into the alley and stops. When the headlights go off, he sees that it's Pearce's old Studebaker. Two heads move closer and closer. Pearce is kissing Dixie!

Suddenly filled with rage, crazy with it, he finds himself trotting to the car. He sticks his head through the open window on the driver's side.

"Get out, Pearce," he says.

"What?"

"Get out!"

"You're kidding. Come on now, Bobby. Cool off."

"What's the matter! You afraid? Get out, you son of a bitch!"

Now Pearce is slowly untangling himself from Dixie's arms and pulling himself out of the car. "Hey, man. Let's just go have a beer or something."

"Bobby!" Just before he swings, Dixie's voice, somewhere between a scream and a whisper, registers, and then he's flat on his butt in the alley, and Pearce is in his car, shifting gears and backing out of the alley. Sticking his head out the window, "Sorry, man," he says.

"Bobby, what's the matter with you! Are you crazy?" Dixie cries. Sobbing, she stands over him for a minute.

Before he can scramble to his feet, Pearce is out of sight. Dixie, too. He pulls out a handkerchief and, blotting his nose, sees the dark blotch of blood. He stumbles down the alley to the back gate, opens it and walks along the path through the old stables to the grape arbor. Dabbing at his nose, he sits heavily on a bench and watches the lights of his house go out, one by one, watches until the house is completely dark before going up to his room.

· 3 ·

THE moon is full and the stars are out and a soft wind is blowing and there's never been a better night for the Gypsy Dance. But before the Buick is out of the driveway, Bobby feels the sweat from his hands on the steering wheel. Is she still his date for the Gypsy Dance? Or is she going with somebody else? Since the fight, if you could call it that, she has ignored him. He hasn't asked her if she's going with him; he hasn't had the heart.

But in case, just in case, she might still be going with him, he has washed the Buick, cleaned it inside and out. And old Rufus, who has a little farm outside town, has sold him enough T stamps to fill up the gas tank.

Since that night, they haven't danced together. By the next day the news that he, Cinco Moore, had been in a fight with the biggest lineman on the football team was all over school. Slapping him on the back, razzing him, Schuster said, "Why don't you pick on somebody your own size the next time? Make it a fair fight." Everybody seemed to think it was pretty funny, him jumping on Pearce. He knew Pearce was big, but he hadn't known he was fast. When he said this to Schuster, Schuster about killed himself laughing.

His dad was really surprised when he saw Bobby's face that night. Bobby had slipped upstairs and gone into the bathroom to look at himself in the mirror. What a mess! His nose caked with blood and the front of his clothes like he'd been in a wreck. His mother had heard him messing around in there and tapped on the door. "Bobby? Everything OK?" And right behind her, his dad was calling, "Son?" and coming in before he could answer. Seeing Bobby's nose stopped him in his tracks.

"Robert," he said. And then there was this big grin. "You've been in a fight! Sit down. Mother, get some ice for that nose," he had said. Making little clicking noises of sympathy, his mother bustled around, getting towels, wringing out his shirt. His father handed him the ice, wrapped in a towel, and sat down on the edge of the tub, grinning.

"Bobby, what in the world happened? What were you fighting about?"

"Now, Barbara. No use in getting all upset over a bloody nose. He's all right, aren't you, son? Lordy, lordy, the fights I've been in. I was the only kid in the first grade who had to wear those damn—excuse me, Barbara—knickers."

"Bobby, who hit you? Who did this?"

"Barbara, let it be. Let it go tonight. Bobby can tell us about it tomorrow if he wants to. Let's get to bed."

Hearing this, his heart had warmed toward his father. At least he understood about fighting.

Getting up his nerve, he has driven around the block twice, but now he's in front of Dixie's house again. He pulls over to the curb and waits for his heart to slow down before going to the door to get Dixie. But here she is! Running out to the car and hopping in before he can open the door for her.

Her dress is low on the shoulders, and the skirt is all ruffles. She's got a red sash around her hips. He's never seen a girl as pretty. Not in his whole life. And she is his date for the Gypsy Dance. She is going with him! Flushed with happiness, he's speechless.

"Let's go," she says, and leans over to kiss his cheek. "You were pretty funny that night. Picking a fight with a guy twice as big," she giggles. Then, suddenly serious, she says, "Actually, Pearce respects you for it. He told me he did." She holds up a foot. "My mother helped me dye these shoes. Are they too red? What do you think?"

Her mother helped her. The thought registers. He has hardly seen Mrs. Balderidge out of a chair. "They look nice to me." Reaching for her hand, he says, "I've got a tank full of gas."

And saying this, in the warmth of the night a thousand

possibilities stretch before his eyes. After the dance, they will drive out to Cold Springs Park, and she will let him kiss her lips and then . . .

"Bobby, come on. We've already missed the first dance," Dixie says, pulling her hand out of his.

All at once, he's as eager to be there as she is, to be there, *dancing*. He puts both hands on the wheel and drives about sixty miles an hour all the way to the gym.

At the gym, the band is playing "We'll Meet Again." Maidie Clayborne is singing, "We'll meet again, don't know where, don't know when," her low, sexy voice drifting out over the parking lot. He hurries around to open the car door for Dixie, but she is already out of the car and hurrying into the gym. They move out onto the floor. Before they've danced two steps, Pearce cuts in. Then Crow cuts in. And now Porterfield. After that, it's Gloria Spearman's brother, home on leave and in uniform, and nobody cuts in—out of respect for God and country. Then he loses sight of her.

Looking around he sees the gym, all decorated with orange and white crepe paper streamers and balloons. Mrs. Gillian is sitting on a bleacher, smiling and keeping time to the music. Now the band is playing "Don't Get Around Much Anymore." Mrs. Gillian, wearing that yellow dress she wore when she read the poem about the lady in the tower, doesn't look much like a chaperon.

Patting the bench beside her, Mrs. Gillian says, "I know every girl here is hoping you'll dance with her."

"Maybe," he says modestly, knowing that what she said, it's probably true. He looks around. Maybeline is sitting this one out with Sam Shaw, his hand resting on her shoulders like a two-by-four. Shaw is a football player who can't play worth a damn. Or dance, either. Maxine, spreading out over at least two seats, is sitting on the opposite side of the bleachers. She wears the black skirt and white blouse she wore that night in the moonlight. He stares at her, trying to see her like she was

that night—a goddess, and with all those animals and her father, jumping for the moon. But with Maxine sitting there,
right before his eyes, she just looks like the same old Maxine.

Now the band is halfway through, "Don't Get Around
Much Anymore." He wonders if Mrs. Gillian is thinking about
the words and missing Mr. Gillian. She doesn't look sad. He
could ask her to dance. Should he? He takes a deep breath.
"Would you like to dance? With me?"

"Bobby Moore, I was hoping you'd ask me!"

Mrs. Gillian does have the best smile he's ever seen, except
for Willie B.'s. Now the saxophones take over: "Awfully different without you/Don't get around much anymore," they wail.
He puts his hand on Mrs. Gillian's back, holding her a respect-
ful two or three inches out. Even not holding her in an ordinary
way, she is following him like a feather. Maybe he should say
that. Would it sound fresh if he said it? He wouldn't want her to
think he was fresh. But the truth is, Mrs. Gillian is as good a
dancer as Dixie. Maybe he will dance the next one with her.

When the last note fades away, she grins. "Bobby, I enjoyed
that. It's my turn at the punch bowl. Go find your date."

He looks around for Dixie, sees her and starts toward her.
Hollingsworth has his arm around her waist. Now Bane is moving in, but before he can cut in, Schuster's there, his arm
around Dixie, and dancing her his way. Good old Schuster!
The floor is crowded. Everywhere he looks everybody's happy
and dancing. When Dixie sees him, her lips curl up into a smile.
Oh, the Lady of Shallot! As he moves to claim her all else—the
music, the dancers, the dance—is forgotten.

By the time Sophie plays "Saint Louis Blues," the dance is
an hour old, and he hasn't danced more than a step or two with
Dixie. He has danced with Maybeline, but he hasn't had the
heart to ask Maxine. But now Sophie stands and begins to play,
and Dixie comes and squeezes his hand, and his heart about
jumps out of his chest. Dixie is so excited she can hardly keep

her feet on the floor while Sophie plays her sad, sad song. Then the first happy notes of their song, "Kiss me once and kiss me twice and kiss me once again," bounce out over the floor, and the crowd moves back and circles, and he takes Dixie's hand and the crowd is singing along with the band and after the first few steps, he knows it is as good as it is ever going to get with Dixie in his arms, knowing what he is going to do before he knows it, her eyes flashing and her dress swinging out so pretty around her waist and couples moving back and moving back and beginning to clap and his feet hardly touching the ground. And then it's over. It's over before he's had time to know it has begun. But the guys are crowding around and slapping him on the back, saying, "Atta way to go, Cinco!" and "Fred Astaire, wow!" and he is one of them like he's never been before.

He feels her hand pull away. As the guys turn back to their dates, he looks for her, and out of the corner of his eye, he sees the ruffles and red sash going out the gym doors with Pearce right behind her.

Schuster has seen it, too. "Come on out to the car, man. You need a drink," he says.

Bobby tilts the bottle of Jack Daniel's to his lips, lifts it like a trombone and drinks about a gallon, and then he is back on the dance floor and dancing with everybody and anybody. He even hauls Maxine around for the last half of "I'll Get By." And in between dances, he goes out for another drink, and Schuster, good old Schuster, keeps on saying, "Hey, man, slow down." But nothing can slow him down, and then he is dancing with Maybeline and leaving with Maybeline and taking Maybeline out to Cold Springs Park, and she is reaching for him, whispering, "I've always liked you, Bobby," and lifting her skirt, and he is giving it to her about a mile a minute, for about ten seconds, and then it is over and he is sorry. Not sorry it is over, sorry it ever started.

Maybeline is pretty disgusted. "Bobby Moore, before you try that again with me, you better go over to Fourth Street and get some practice," she says, throwing her panties out the window, brushing at her skirt.

Sometime the next morning he hears his mother outside his door. "Let him sleep, Robert. Just this one Sunday morning, let him sleep until he wakes up."

He turns over and puts the pillow over his head. More than anything, he wants to sleep. He wants to sleep until he can forget the whole crummy evening.

Chapter 7

· 1 ·

GRACE and Amelia have decided to spend the day together because Grace will leave for New York the following day. After lunch they go to an early movie. Grace wants to see *Mr. Skeffington* with Bette Davis, but Amelia has seen it. They decide to see *Snow White*, smiling at the idea of grown women choosing a children's movie.

And then, strangely (Grace can't imagine why), as she watches the beguiling little dwarfs and Snow White's mothering of them, she imagines Bucy—tall, very tall, lean, handsome— wearing his periwinkle blue shirt (the one she has most recently given to her washwoman), his eyes squinched up with laughter, his Adam's apple going up and down. She is not sure John would like the movie. But Bucy would love the funny dwarfs, the music, the color, the *artistry* of it. Perhaps they can see a movie in New York after she has said, "Tell me why you left." *Had* he known she couldn't love him enough and been too kind to say it? Was that why he had painted those words over their bed and left?

During the early months of their marriage, their lovemaking, although sporadic, had been . . . pleasant. But afterwards, *always* afterwards, it seemed to her that a faint melancholy filled the house. She had longed to say to Amelia, to say to someone,

Is this how it is for you? But then she had made love to John and had known such passion, had known such, yes, such *abandon*, that in the midst of it, she clearly remembers thinking: *Why, this is why we are here, on this earth, on this blessed earth.* She had realized then that she had never loved Bucy the way a man should be loved. And he must have known it, too.

After the movie, Amelia comes home with her to see the clothes she has bought for the trip. "A trousseau!" Amelia says.

"Not exactly," Grace says wryly. "Come on up. Let me fix some iced tea, and I'll show you what I bought. I went a little crazy, really."

A hard summer rain has begun to fall, and for a few moments they stand on Grace's gallery and watch as torn, dark clouds move across the lighter, but still very dark, sky. Then Grace moves around, turning on all the lights, putting on the teakettle, shifting books and a shawl from the chair where Amelia usually sits.

"I'll make the tea," Amelia says. "You get the clothes. No, go put them on. I want to see how you look in them."

Feeling excited (after all, the trip is only hours away), Grace hurries to change into the blue-and-white-checked skirt and bolero. Coming back into the gallery, she turns in a slow circle before Amelia. "This is to wear on the train," she says. "It won't wrinkle. Do you like it?"

"I saw that dress in Klein's window. I love it. I love checks in the summertime. And with that pink blouse. Wait until Bucy sees you!"

"But, Amelia, you should know—" Grace begins, but stops. If she says she is not even sure she will see Bucy (although she has run the ad three times in the *New York Times* personal column), or if she says she is going to straighten out her life, Amelia will be polite but perplexed. And her unspoken questions will lie there, almost palpable, between them.

"What? What should I know?"

The impulse to confide vanishes. "You should know that I also bought a dress to wear out in the evening."

"Put it on. Here's your tea. You want lemon? Go put it on right now."

She slips it on. Oh, how she loves the feel of its silkiness on her body. The dress is for John. It is black, bare-backed. It is a dress for John's homecoming. With the black patent leather sandals and the purse and gloves, it has all been expensive. However, she will wear it in New York if there is an occasion, but the dress is for John.

When she comes back into the room, Amelia grins. "That's a drop-dead dress," she says. "And you have the figure for it. Oh, Grace, I wish I were going with you. I've never been farther east than the Mississippi River."

"I wish you were, too!" Grace says.

"Grace, you don't mean that!"

Smiling, Grace plumps up the down cushion in Amelia's chair. "Probably not. Let's sit here, and we'll drink tea and watch the storm pass. You can't drive home in this. It's getting ready to pour down!"

Amelia settles into her chair, takes a sip of tea and adds more lemon. "Did you hear the news this morning?"

"No. What happened?"

"The pope asked both Hitler and the Allies to leave Rome intact. Do you think Hitler will listen to the pope?"

"I don't know," Grace says. "You're the Catholic."

"It would take a miracle."

"I don't believe Hitler will pay any attention to the pope, but the Allies will. And maybe a miracle *will* happen. Maybe Rome will be there, intact, waiting for us when the war is over." Frowning, Grace holds her glass of tea against the fading light. "I wonder if . . ."

"If John is in Rome," Amelia finishes.

"Oh, I hope and pray that he is," Grace says fervently, "and not on some beachhead in Italy."

Amelia doesn't look at her. She doesn't need to. She has seen that look, that mixture of hope and anguish, on Grace's face before. *But John's not the man for you,* she wants to say, but doesn't.

The two of them, these old friends, watch silently as the clouds open, spilling an even harder rain. But neither of them is focused on the storm. Each is wondering a little anxiously about Grace's trip that is to begin the following morning.

· 2 ·

"BUT I have a reservation," Grace tells the ticket agent before the train arrives. "Ray, I reserved a Pullman."

"Mrs. Gillian, I don't know what happened. But with the War and all, the sleeping cars are full. Most are sleeping two to a bed. Some a mother and two kids. What you're about to get on, this here Texas Eagle, not many ordinary folks on it these days. You want me to see what I can do about a Pullman reservation tomorrow?"

"No. I have to arrive in New York the day after tomorrow."

"I expect Mr. Gillian would be mighty disappointed if you didn't."

Ray Benton, you don't know everything about me, Grace thinks, forcing a smile.

The conductor hands her up the steps and, pulling out his pocket watch, looks at it, and then, slowly, sorrowfully, calls "All ab-o-o-o-ard." *Why do all conductors sound so mournful?* she wonders. *Is it part of their training?*

Wishing she had allowed Amelia and Ed to come down to see her off, she steps onto the train.

"Here, ma'am. I've got the door."

A young soldier, with cotton-colored hair and eyebrows and

eyelashes, but with fiery red cheeks, pulls open the heavy door and motions her ahead.

"Thank you."

"Private Russell, First Class. Clay Russell."

His light blue eyes contain the innocent expression of the very young. *Just a boy. Why some of my students are older than Private Russell,* she tells herself.

Looking for an empty seat, her eyes move about the coach, up and down each aisle, taking note of the scattering of sailors, the handful of marines among the seats filled with soldiers.

"Is this a troop train?" she asks Private Russell.

There is a burst of deep, hearty laughter from the surrounding seats. Private Russell does not smile.

"No, ma'am," he says. "But the armed services have preference. A couple of troop trains left Texas in the middle of the night, running ahead of us. I reckon we're the stragglers."

"I'll try another car."

"They're all full, ma'am," he says, pulling his duffel bag from the overhead rack. "You can have my seat."

"No. I won't take your seat."

"Please, ma'am. I want you to have it."

"I've been sitting for ten hours," says another soldier. Older. A sprinkling of gray in his hair. "I'd welcome a change." He stands and takes her small bag from her hands. "Let me stow this for you," he says, smiling down at her. "Will you be going far?"

He reminds her of somebody, somebody she has known. "New York City," she says.

"That's a long trip. Folks will be getting off in Texarkana, and there may be extra seats then."

Taking his duffel bag from the overhead rack, he puts it down and shoves it out of the passageway. He is unshaved. His uniform is rumpled. But when he smiles, his teeth are white and straight. He has brown eyes, a dark complexion, a deep cleft in his chin. *Why, Cary Grant! That's who he reminds me of,* she thinks.

"This is ridiculous," she says. "You've left me and this young . . ."

"Lieutenant, ma'am. Lt. Mark Jackson Smith."

The lieutenant is young, too. Only a few years older than Private Russell. "You've left me and Lieutenant Smith with four seats," she says. "We don't need all this room."

"We'll have plenty of time to sleep this trip. And tonight, Private Russell and I can take turns sitting by the lieutenant."

"How far are you going?" Another burst of laughter.

"As far as the train will take us and then some," the older soldier says, grinning.

When he smiles, a dimple appears in each cheek. He, this Cary Grant look-alike, is extraordinarily handsome. "You're shipping out," she says sadly, her heart quickening at the thought of so many men, most of them boys, on their way to Europe to fight and, maybe, die for their country.

Standing over Grace, his feet apart for balance, the man looks down at her. *He has the softest eyes,* she thinks.

The train jerks forward, he grabs the back of her seat, the train stops, steam hisses, the train jerks again and begins to move, move so slowly that she looks out the window to be sure it is moving. Swaying with the movement of the train, the sergeant smiles down at her. Grace feels a surge of warmth and gratitude toward him and Private Russell and Lieutenant Smith—toward all these men in uniform.

When the train, moving smoothly, has gathered speed, the older man slides his duffel bag close and sits on it. "You remind me of a woman I have known," he says quietly. And at her smile, the shake of her head, "No, it's true. I feel as if I have known you. Somewhere."

"You remind me of a girl I met in Memphis," the lieutenant says. "She had eyes like yours. Dreamy. But she could storm up. Then her eyes would turn black as coal."

Grace smiles. "What brought on these storms?"

"I'm not sure," he grins. "I may have had something to do with it."

Private Russell sits on his duffel bag, elbows on his knees. Leaning toward her, he says, "I can tell when my mother is mad. It's real easy."

"How?"

"She'll be cooking supper. Or cleaning house. When she gets mad, it gets real noisy. If she's in the kitchen, she bangs the pots and pans around. If she's cleaning, it sounds like she's a furniture mover. And she's real little, weighs not more'n a hundred. She doesn't fuss or nothing. She just gets real noisy."

"Evidently, I'm sitting here, on my way to New York, with a bunch of troublemakers," Grace says. They smile, shift positions, shake their heads. "I'm Grace Gillian. I'm joining a friend in New York," she says, wondering as soon as she's said it why she hasn't said *husband*.

The older soldier holds out his hand. "Sergeant Manning. Dan."

"I've never been overseas," the lieutenant says. "But I guess I'll be jumping into places I've only read about."

"Jumping! Then you're a paratrooper."

"Yes, ma'am. Eighty-second Airborne," he says.

"And a lieutenant!"

"Yes, ma'am. I'll be twenty-one the day after tomorrow, June sixth. I'll be old enough to lead a platoon into battle."

"Your first command, and you'll be jumping into battle," Sergeant Manning says. "That's tough luck."

"Sergeant, have you been overseas?"

"No, I've been training men to go. I decided it was time to get over there and find out if I knew what I was talking about."

"I'll tell you one thing, Sergeant. I'll be a hell of a lot better lieutenant than some of those I trained under at Fort Benning. We had one, Lieutenant Dryer—why, he couldn't find his way out of a tent. I swear, he'd get lost in his own tent, and we'd have to go pull him out. One night, after we had blown an old bridge over a river in Georgia, Lieutenant Dryer said good night and started down the road to his tent, at least that's where he *thought* he was headed. But his tent was east and the river was west, and he was going due west. I hollered, 'Lieutenant, remember, we blew that bridge today! Lieutenant, you're headed toward the river. And then, godalmighty, we heard him crashing down the riverbank, falling through the brush and cursing. Man, you never heard such a commotion! We had to run down there and fish him out. The water was ice cold, and I'm telling you, we all got wet. Just about froze to death. We should have let him drown. Think of a man like that commanding a troop in battle. Why, every morning of the world, Lieutenant Dryer has a hard time finding his own feet when he gets ready to put on his socks."

Listening to the young lieutenant's story, the sergeant smiles at Grace, sees her live, gray eyes, the perfection of planes and inclinations of cheeks and nose, her berry-colored mouth. Listening to Smith, she leans toward him, her face alight, her entire body revealing her delight in his humor. She wears a gold ring on the ring finger of her right hand.

A widow? No, he tells himself. *She doesn't have that look about her. That deep sadness in her eyes.*

"Hell, Lieutenant Dryer's on this train," the lieutenant is saying. "Two cars back. At least I hope he managed to get back on board the train when we made that last stop."

The lieutenant has black, curly hair and the merriest blue eyes. His face, his nose, both narrow, give him the look of a feisty terrier.

Sitting on his duffel bag, Private Russell crosses his leg, jiggles a foot. His face is flushed with admiration. "Lieutenant, how many times have you jumped?"

"I don't know, Russell. But I tell you this, every damn time I jumped, I was scared as hell. And it never got any better. After we blew that Georgia bridge, Lieutenant Dryer and I were sent to Maryland for a month to train in munitions. By the time we got back to Fort Benning, the whole damn camp had shipped out."

"The invasion," Sergeant Manning says.

The men are suddenly quiet. After a few minutes, "It has to come soon," Sergeant Manning says. "Eisenhower is flying six thousand missions a day now, bombing the hell out of the coast. We're going to be part of the assault forces."

"I hope it comes before I get over there," Private Russell says. "My mother doesn't want me to be in the invasion."

"Private Russell, the invasion will be over before any of us get there," Lieutenant Smith says.

"Just the first waves, Lieutenant," Sergeant Manning says, forcing himself to tear his gaze from Grace's face. After all, he's seen beautiful women before, women with gray eyes and berry-colored mouths.

"I've got this lucky charm," Private Russell says, pulling out a worn billfold, taking out a small, gold four-leaf clover. "My girlfriend took it off her charm bracelet and gave it to me. Just as the train was pulling out, she passed it to me through the train window. Here's her picture," he says, handing a frayed snapshot to Grace.

In the picture a cloud of dark hair frames a young girl's face. A smile shows slightly crooked teeth. Her eyes are in dark shadow. The white lace collar of her dress is the clearest part of the picture.

"She's very pretty," Grace says.

"Thank you, ma'am. We're not engaged or nothing, but she's going to wait. She said she would. We went down to Woolworth's and both of us got our pictures made. She's got mine in a gold frame by her bed."

The sergeant and the lieutenant look at the snapshot, nod gravely.

"She is pretty," Sergeant Manning says.

"How old is she?"

"Sixteen," he says proudly.

"Private Russell, how old are you?" Asking the question, Grace feels a kinship with him. He could just as well be one of her students.

"Eighteen." Looking anxiously up and down the aisle, he adds, "Almost."

"You'll do all right," the sergeant says kindly. "You'll be fine."

Another boy who can't wait to be a hero, Grace tells herself.

"Let me show you *my* lucky charm," Lieutenant Smith says. Reaching up, he pulls boots from his duffel bag. "Snow pacs," he says proudly. "Got 'em in Maryland. And I guarantee that with these boots and three pairs of socks, I'm coming back with all my toes."

"But it's June over there," Private Russell says, frowning. "You see, Lieutenant, if it's June here, then it's June over there, too. Isn't it? You don't need snow boots in June. If it's hot here, it's hot over there, too. Isn't it?" he says, looking toward Sergeant Manning for confirmation.

"Hell, I know it's June," Lieutenant Smith says. "But I don't know where I'll jump or when. If I have to haul these damn boots all over Europe without putting them on, I'll do it. Why, man, I've hunted in snow and freezing rain over every hill in Tennessee. Forget about keeping your powder dry. When it's freezing, what you got to do is keep your feet dry."

The sergeant chuckles. "Lieutenant, you're right about your feet. The first winter, we had more injuries from frostbite than bullets."

"Why, hell, man. I'd leave my gun behind before I'd march without these boots."

Private Russell's mouth falls open in astonishment at the thought of abandoning one's weapon in the middle of a war. Grace smiles. The sergeant, as if responding to an outrageous child, winks at Grace.

The train slows; the whistle blows. They peer out a window, struck by the cavernous size of the train station in Texarkana.

Then, "Here they come," says the lieutenant.

"Yep," Private Russell says. "I been on this train eight hours, and I haven't spent a dime on food."

"If you like doughnuts and sandwiches, you won't ever have to spend a dime on food," Lieutenant Smith says, pushing a car window up.

Leaning forward to peer out the window, Grace sees women and young girls hurrying to the train, some pushing carts, others carrying trays, all of them hurrying, hurrying, spreading out alongside the train. Soldiers push windows up to lean out, calling, "I'd like some coffee," and "Thank you, ma'am," and "You're real pretty. Wanna be my pen pal?"

Below Grace's window, a pink-faced, gray-headed woman hands doughnuts and coffee through the window. A half a dozen girls (even younger than Private Russell's girlfriend), all with trays of sandwiches and coffee, cluster around the woman. The girls look up at the soldiers, smile, look down.

"If you want to stretch your legs, you got about fifteen minutes," the conductor says, gold watch in hand, hurrying through the coach. "We're taking on water and coal here."

Grace watches the men get off the train, their faces alight with pleasure. The young girls smile while the soldiers drink coffee and eat sandwiches. They pull billfolds from hip pockets to show snapshots of sweethearts and wives and babies. When Private Russell takes out his gold four-leaf clover, it catches the sun's reflection, scattering its brightness alongside the train. *Blessing us all with good luck,* Grace thinks.

"He's proud of that charm, isn't he?"

Sergeant Manning, who has not left the train, moves from his duffel bag to a seat across from Grace. "He'll need it," he says.

Sitting across from her, he catches a faint scent of flowers.

"Sergeant Manning, do you have a lucky charm?"

"No."

She waits, expecting more, but he does not go on. He watches the soldiers and the girls for a few minutes; then he takes a book from his duffel bag and begins to read. The book he is reading is *The Red Badge of Courage*. Oh, how well she knows this book. Since the War began, she's had her students read it. "This is what war is like," she tells them. "Wait to be drafted. Wait until you're older. Wait until you're out of high school."

The sergeant looks up from the book. "Well, Crane got it right. He got everything about war right," he says.

"My students read that book and go right out and lie about their ages to get into the armed services," she says sadly.

Tiny wrinkles have appeared at the corners of her round, gray eyes. *And I love her.* The realization sweeps over him. It is total and complete. He loves her. But how could he? He doesn't know her. It's the War. It's the gut-wrenching knowledge that he might die next month. Or sooner. Maybe next week in convoy, crossing the Atlantic. It is because he is afraid that he loves her. He's never been in love. Long ago, he decided it wasn't for him. He's had his share of women, but he's never been head-over-heels in love. And now he loves a stranger. It's crazy. He closes the book, puts it away and gazes out the window.

Now the conductor is on the steps, calling, "All abo-a-a-a-rd," and the soldiers are swinging back onto the train. The girls, casting off their shy demeanor, are blowing passionate kisses to the soldiers and calling, "Come back safe," "Be careful," "Thank you, oh, thank you." Some of them are crying.

Abandoning her food cart, the gray-headed woman is walking alongside the slowly moving train. "My two boys, Billy and Lawrence Junior, are over there," she calls through the open window. As the train begins to move faster, she begins to trot. "Tell my boys—" she cries, trotting still faster, "Tell them I love them." Now she is running, trying valiantly to keep up with the train. "Tell them to be careful over there," she calls. Tears stream down her face. "And tell them their daddy . . ." The rest is lost in the sound of the train's whistle. As they continue to watch, she suddenly stops, falls to her knees and buries her face in her hands.

Private Russell waves until he can no longer see her. "Gosh," he says, turning away from the window.

Lieutenant Smith says cheerfully, "I had a dog like that. He'd chase every train that came through."

Grace's eyes fill. She smiles, lowers her head, smoothes her skirt over her knees. The lieutenant's remark makes her feel like laughing and crying, both at the same time. Private Russell stares uncertainly at the lieutenant.

Sergeant Manning smiles. "It's hard to know what to do with a comment like that, Lieutenant."

Acknowledging the sergeant's remark, Lieutenant Smith nods. Then, "Get ready, Russell," he says. "They'll be waiting for us in Little Rock. I hope to God they have fixed something besides pimiento cheese sandwiches."

"Doesn't it make you feel like . . . well, like we're their protectors?" Private Russell says.

"We *are* their protectors," Lieutenant Smith says cheerfully.

The word drums its way to Dan Manning's heart. *Protectors. Her protector.*

"This is powerful stuff," he says soberly.

Grace gazes at him, trying to decide whether he is referring to the emotional stop in Texarkana or to the book he was reading.

"Both," he says, answering the question in her eyes.

He knew what I was thinking. And then, astonishingly, she begins to imagine his nude body, his smooth, well-muscled shoulders and arms, broad chest, not too hairy, and below, a generous brush, darker than the hair on his head. Looking carefully over his head, she imagines her head on his chest, the smell of his male body. *Grace, for goodness' sakes!* she tells herself, and for composure folds her hands in her lap.

Between Texarkana and Little Rock, Lieutenant Smith keeps up a lively monologue about Lieutenant Dryer's lack of any sense of direction. About the mystery of Lieutenant Dryer's brain. About other soldiers he has trained with, trained under and, lately, trained. About the common sense he, Lieutenant Smith, has. About how uncommon common sense is. About how in the Georgia swamps, the men under him saw a snake, thought they saw a snake, thought they saw a *nest* of snakes and started shooting. "Did you shoot?" he asked each one. Then, "Well, what were you shooting at?" he asked. When they couldn't answer, he took their guns away. "They almost shot me. Almost shot each other."

After a while Grace stops listening, but the soft Tennessee voice goes on and on, merging with the rhythmic sway of the train, the brisk sound of the wheels of the train, all of it, somehow, reassuring. She watches Private Russell's face, the myriad expressions—amusement, bafflement, admiration—on it mirroring his every thought as he listens to Lieutenant Smith. Feeling the sergeant's eyes on her face, she gazes out the window, sees the small knolls just outside Texarkana transform themselves into small hills and, as they near Little Rock, she sees tall stands of lush, thick trees.

It is after three when the train pulls into the Little Rock station. And, again, the Red Cross women are there, leading scout troops of girls even younger than those in Texarkana, and Junior League women (older, but still quite young), and still older Civic League women alongside the train. They hurriedly (the train is running behind schedule, and passengers may not disembark) hand sandwiches (pimiento) and coffee through the windows to soldiers, already heroes in their eyes.

"Gee whiz," Private Russell says again, again overwhelmed.

After Little Rock, the lieutenant hurries off to see if Lieutenant Dryer is still on the train. "Hell, Lieutenant Dryer probably got off by mistake in Texarkana or Little Rock. But I guar-an-tee that wherever he is, he's lost. Probably thought he was getting on the train, went out the wrong door and got off," Lieutenant Smith says, straightening his hat before leaving.

"If he's still on the train, bring him back here," says Private Russell. "I'd like to see him."

The afternoon passes slowly. The train stops, young girls come with food, the train jerks into movement. The sergeant reads again, looks up, meets her eyes and smiles. Before they cross the Mississippi into Memphis, Lieutenant Smith returns with Lieutenant Dryer in tow.

"What has this crazy man been telling you?" Dryer says.

"The truth, man. The reason I brought him back here, Miss Gillian, is we're getting ready to cross the Mississippi, and I thought that if anybody could keep him out of the river, you could."

Lieutenant Dryer grins. "Hell, I thought I was walking away from that bridge we'd blown, and I fell right into that damn Georgia river."

Lieutenant Dryer is small, dark, with a long nose, a sharp chin, eyes as black as a beetle. He slaps Lieutenant Smith on the back. "I'll tell you one thing, Miss Gillian. This is a man will come through the war without a scratch on him. If a man is left standing, Lieutenant Smith will be that man."

"That's right," Lieutenant Smith says seriously. "As long as nothing disturbs my concentration. And I don't intend to let anything disturb my concentration."

"Lieutenant, could you explain the concentration part? I'm planning on coming back, too," Private Russell says.

"The one thing that can disturb a man's concentration is a woman. When I get over there the thing I'm gonna do is sleep. Sleep and eat every chance I get. And keep my feet dry. That's the best thing for concentration. There'll be plenty of time for women after the war."

"That's a, a *damn* good thing to know, Lieutenant," Private Russell says.

Hearing the awkward cursing of the boy, Sergeant Manning looks at Grace. Her eyes are dancing, and she smiles so broadly that a small dimple appears in her left cheek. He wonders how it would be to see her hair down, soft around her face. He forces himself to return to his book and reads the same page over and over.

By the time they reach St. Louis (where they will change trains and where they have a one-hour layover), Grace feels she has known them all her life. *Why, I know them better than I knew Bucy when I married him,* she thinks, surprised by the thought.

Private Russell pushes his duffel bag close and whispers, "Miss Gillian, when you laughed back there in Little Rock, you sounded just like my mom."

Touched by the boy's longing for his mother, she says, "I consider that a compliment, Private Russell."

A few minutes later, when Lieutenant Smith, leaning to get a flask from his duffel bag, touches her breast as if by accident, she holds the straying hand, yet feels no resentment toward it.

He leans close, his shoulder touching hers. "If you want to know the truth, Miss Gillian," he says softly, "I'm scared as hell. But I'm coming home. I guar-an-tee it."

"Of course you are, Lieutenant. I know you will."

After midnight Lieutenant Smith leaves again to find Lieutenant Dryer. Private Russell follows to stretch his legs. Sergeant Manning, seated opposite her, closes his book. "Miss Gillian."

"Please," she says, "it's Grace."

He nods and says, "In the olden days, knights carried a favor—a lady's colors, a scarf, something—into battle. It sounds a little crazy, but I was wondering if . . ."

Already fumbling in her handbag, "I'd be honored," she says. "What about this?"

Holding the lacy handkerchief to his face, he says, "It smells like a meadow, fresh-cut."

He folds it carefully, puts it inside his book and tucks the book inside his shirt.

"Oh, I hope it brings you luck."

"I'll take care of it."

"Will it be the Italian front?"

"I don't know. Probably France. Maybe Holland."

"When?"

"My guess is as soon as we get to England."

"Oh, dear."

"It's all right. I've been in the army most of my life. I like it, but it's no life for a woman. I guess that's why I never married." He sits back, arms folded, a smile playing around his mouth. "No, that's not true. I never met a woman I wanted to marry." *Until now.* The urge to say this is strong. Instead, he says, "You might want to get a little rest. You'll be meeting your friend in New York."

She puts her head back. Beneath closed eyes, she believes that if she opened her eyes and looked at him, his gaze would be on her face.

In St. Louis, they board the Pennsylvania Railroad train, and as if by common consent, flasks are broken out, the dining car becomes a bar and sleepy, drunken soldiers stumble up and down the aisle. When Grace moves through the car to freshen up, to stretch her legs, the aisle is immediately cleared as men spring from their card games and shove duffel bags aside to speak to her. Pulling pictures from billfolds, they tell her about their sweethearts, their children, their homes. And almost always, they show Grace some keepsake—a pink ribbon from a little girl's hair, a toy truck from a little boy, a child's first tooth, a pressed flower from a bridal bouquet. She looks out the dark window, sees a reflection of a redheaded, slender-faced soldier who stares at her image in the train's window. She smiles at the reflection and sees him give a mock salute. She puts her head back, closes her eyes. And is dazed into sleep . . .

  . . . *and then, dreaming and somehow knowing it is a dream, she is moving down the aisle of a train. She sits by a soldier and welcomes his head on her shoulder as he falls asleep. She rises. Moves on. A soldier beseeches her, the wound on his leg open, seeping blood. Tenderly, wordlessly, she bandages the wound. Now, a sailor*

*looks at her, his face flushed with desire. She unbuttons her blouse,
drops it to her feet, unfastens her brassiere and feels his lips on her
lips, and on her throat, her breasts. Farther down the aisle, the
endless aisle, a young boy holds out his arms. Her embrace is tender and loving. No words are spoken. All are strangers, yet fully
known to her. Sensing what each man needs, she offers that and is
comforted.*

Hearing a deep, contented sigh, she realizes the sound is
coming from her own throat. She opens her eyes. All movement up and down the aisle has stopped. The darkened coach is
filled with sleeping men.

"Lady Grace. You were dreaming. Go back to sleep,"
Sergeant Manning says.

"I *was* dreaming," she says.

"A good dream?"

"Yes. I was taking care of . . . of everybody."

She reaches for his hand and falls asleep.

The next day everyone is subdued. At noon the conductor
comes through to announce that the train is behind schedule.
"There's no telling when we'll get to New York," he says. The
soldiers cheer, whistle, clap. Dan Manning grins, and opening
his book, settles into his reading.

As night falls a soldier in the front of the coach plays "I'll Be
Seeing You" on his harmonica. Another soldier sings the words.
His voice is true. The words are clear. He sings softly but with
such yearning that Grace turns her head to hide the tears. *If only
I were stepping into John's arms when we reach New York,* she tells
herself. Looking out the window into the darkness, she watches
the car lights on a road that runs parallel to the railroad tracks,
watches until dawn breaks.

In the middle of the morning, the train slows, jerks to a
stop. "Baltimore, Baltimore," the conductor calls. In the distance, she hears a murmur of voices. The sound grows. Men
are clapping. Cheering.

A soldier bursts into their car, shouting, "We've invaded Europe! We're on the beaches!" Unable to contain his excitement, the soldier jumps and twists up and down the aisle in a frenzied dance.

"Wa-hoo!" Private Russell hollers.

Lieutenant Smith springs from his seat. He hugs Grace and slaps the soldiers on their backs.

"The War will be over by the time we get there. Sergeant, how about that!"

"God help those on the beaches," Sergeant Manning says. "God help us all. The next time you jump, Lieutenant, you'll be jumping smack-dab into the middle of the biggest battle the world has ever seen."

· *3* ·

WHEN the train pulls into Pennsylvania Station, soldiers push open the train windows, but there are no women hurrying toward them offering coffee and sandwiches. There are too many men in uniform. Too many trains.

The easy mood of the trip has vanished as Grace and the three soldiers stand near the train in a knot of formal leave-taking. They exchange addresses, promise to write, promise to come see Grace after the war ends. Disregarding Private Russell's outstretched hand, Grace hugs him warmly.

Lieutenant Smith laughs and kisses her cheek. "Miss Gillian," he says, "you'll open your paper when the War ends and read about me, Lt. Mark Jackson Smith, coming home and bringing every one of his men back with him."

It's easy to believe him, she thinks, watching the two shoulder their duffel bags and turn to make their way through the crowd.

"In this mob you'll never find a taxi," Sergeant Manning says. "I'll stick around. I'm in no hurry to report."

He grabs his bag and picks up her suitcase. Following the sergeant's broad back, she realizes the very air is filled with talk of the invasion. Snatches of conversation—"over by Christmas," "figured they'd take Italy first," "Eisenhower damn well knows"—follow them through the crowded station. Grace has never seen so many people in one place.

Outside, they find a long line of people who are waiting for taxis. "Let the sergeant and his lady through," a man calls. Another asks, "Sergeant, are you on your way to Europe?" A woman with hair the platinum blond of Jean Harlow's and bright red lips says, "Honey, I'd love to be your pen pal."

Effortlessly, Dan Manning shoulders his way through the crowd to the cluster of uniforms at the front of the line. Turning to her, he says, "I'll write you. You don't need to answer my letters. Just read what I have to say. Will you do that?"

"Of course I will."

"One thing more. And this is a promise. One day you'll look up and there I'll be and there you'll be. One day we'll meet again." He taps the book where her handkerchief rests inside his shirt. "And I'll take good care of this." He cups her chin in his hand. "Let me look at you. If we had a little time. Just a little. I'd show you . . . Well, hell."

She puts her hand on the back of his neck and pulls his face down to hers. The kiss she gives him is warm.

"When you see that friend of yours, remember what I've said to you. Now go," he says. "You have to go."

As the taxi pulls away from the station, she looks back. He stands, hands on his hips, watching her leave.

Leaning forward, she says, "The Cosmopolitan Club on East Sixty-sixth. Between Park and Lexington." She sits back and, feeling a tear on her cheek, brushes it away.

"It's tough, miss," the cab driver says, "seeing them off like that."

"Yes. It's the hardest thing I've ever done."

Their route is through a canyon of buildings, some so tall she cannot see their rooftops from the cab. Outside the Cosmopolitan Club, a boy cries, "Extra! Extra! Invasion Spearheaded by Paratroopers!" She stops to buy a newspaper before checking in.

In the lobby, a woman sits behind a curved wall of mahogany paneling. She is small. Her blond hair is in a roll. She wears rimless glasses with rhinestones at the corners. She is sorting papers. She does not look up.

"I'm Miriam Chamberlain's guest." Before the woman can check her register or reach for a key, Grace asks, "Are there any messages for me?"

"Let's see. It's Miss Gillian, isn't it? No. No messages. Annie here will show you to your room."

"This way, miss."

The young girl, Annie, black-headed with a smattering of freckles, picks up the bag and leads the way toward the elevator.

In the elevator she says, "You'll like it here, miss. There's a restaurant on the second floor, and there's great stores near. I love to see the pretty things, but they're dear." Her blue eyes shine with enthusiasm.

"You're Irish," Grace says. "How long have you been in this country?"

"Only just. I stepped onto the shore the very day they bombed Pearl Harbor. And, oh, the poor lads! Going down in the ships."

Grace follows Annie down a small hallway and into a small, airy room. The curtains are lace; the wallpaper is white with pink sprigs of rosebuds. Annie opens the drapes and raises a window.

"Miss, before you turn on a light this evening, be sure the drapes are closed tight. There's going to be a blackout tonight."

"Yes, Annie, I'll be sure to do that."

When Annie leaves, she curtsies, almost imperceptibly, but still it is a curtsy.

Grace kicks off her shoes, props pillows behind her on the single bed and opens the paper. She reads every word about the invasion, her heart lifting at Roosevelt's magnificent speech, telling the nation that the invasion is "a mighty endeavor" and that it is to "set free a suffering humanity." As she reads, a part of her mind turns to Private Russell, so young that he misses his mother more than his girl, and to Lieutenant Smith, so feisty, so *scared*. And the sergeant. In any war, he's the one she would take her chances with.

Suddenly, she sits up straight. Wondering why she hasn't thought of it sooner, she flips through the paper until she finds the personal columns. This is where Bucy's message will be. He knows where she will be staying. She has put that into her ads. But a message might be here. There are hundreds of them, but none is from Bucy. Sighing, she turns on the small radio by her bed. Frank Sinatra is singing "Perfidia" when she falls into a deep sleep.

When she wakes the room is dark. Feeling her way to the window, she looks out into total darkness. Then, across the way (it is impossible to tell how far), a single light shines from a window, but as she watches, it, too, is swallowed up by darkness.

After she draws the drapes, she turns on the ceiling light, the bedside table lamp, the closet light, the bathroom light. She floods the room with light. Then she calls the desk.

"Is there a message from a Mr. Gillian? For Grace Gillian?"

"No message." The voice is triumphant.

"Wait! Don't go! Is the restaurant open?"

"The restaurant closes at nine."

"Is there a place nearby, another restaurant—?"

Rudely, the line has gone dead.

She splashes her face with tepid water, combs her hair, picks up her purse.

At the desk she asks, "Is there a message for me now? Perhaps a message came while I was on my way downstairs."

"No." The woman is too busy sorting mail to look up, to smile.

She steps outside into a darkness that goes on and on, enveloping the hotel, the sidewalk, the street. She hears footsteps. The shadowy form of a woman taps briskly by. The sound of her footsteps fades. Grace stands still, longing for the inner compass that might direct her toward a restaurant. More footsteps. Two shadowy forms, entwined, stroll past. She walks along behind them.

From a doorway, a man lurches toward her. "Hey, doll. Wanna come with me? Show you a good time."

"No!"

"Well, whatever you say, doll."

She hurries on. More footsteps, a man's, just behind her. The footsteps draw closer. She hurries to the corner, certain she is being followed. She will circle the block, get back to the hotel. Has she turned the wrong way? She stumbles, slows. The footsteps fade. Harmless, she tells herself. But now the doorways, the sidewalks, the streets—all are empty. Footsteps draw close again. She breaks into a fast sprint. *Dear God, where is the hotel?*

"Stop! Is that you, Grace? Grace, wait! Wait!"

Although she cannot see him, she knows it is Bucy—tall, very tall, lean—and, now that she has stopped running, walking casually toward her.

He chuckles. "Goodness, girl. Have you been training for a cross-country race?"

His voice, his walk, his laugh, all casual, as if he were just coming home from a game of tennis or golf.

By the time he reaches her, astonishingly, Grace has burst into sobs. Deep, harsh, guttural sobs. Bending over, clutching her stomach, she sobs.

"Bucy, how could you? How could you leave me?" Sobbing out the words, gasping for breath. "How could you do that, Bucy?"

His arms are around her. "It's all right, Grace. Dear, dear Grace."

"No, it's *not* all right!" She catches her breath, gasps, sobs. "I've given all your clothes away. And Amelia thinks my new clothes are for a second honeymoon. You were mean to leave!" Bending over, still clutching her stomach, "O-o-o-o-oh," she wails, "I thought I didn't care. But I did care. I cared. You were so—so mean!"

"Grace, I'm surprised. I never thought you . . . Grace, you're exhausted. Have you eaten?"

"Why did you leave? That silly postcard! Tell me why! No, I haven't eaten!"

"You're coming home with me. I'll fix scrambled eggs and hot tea."

"And a cold cloth. I need a cold cloth for my forehead."

"Yes. A cold cloth," he says gently.

Still gasping for breath, she cries, "And I hate it that everybody in town feels sorry for me. And on the train I said I was coming to meet a friend. *A friend!*"

"My apartment is a couple of blocks from here. Come on, Grace. You'll feel better when you've eaten."

"I'm not coming. I'm going to sit on these steps and cry."

"Don't sit down, Grace. Grace! Please get up. Don't cry, Grace! Get up. Please don't cry."

"Don't say that to me! I'm going to cry. I *need* to cry!"

Arms around her knees, she sits on the steps, a small ball of gasping, keening misery that is heartrending to Bucy, now speechless, who stands over her. *What to do with this woman, this once sweet, reasonable woman?* he wonders. *Now gone mad. Completely mad. About everything. It's not like Grace. It's the trip. It's the War.*

Finally, the sobs become long shuddering sighs, change into

hiccups. "I gave my handkerchief to a sergeant on the train," she says. "He looks like Cary Grant."

Pulling his handkerchief from his pocket, "Here," Bucy says.

"He called me Lady. Lady Grace. And there was this boy, just a boy, missing his mother. And a young lieutenant. Young. And scared. He was scared. Oh, Bucy, there were so many on the train, all on their way to the front. And I loved them. And you know some of them will die. And there was this woman whose sons were over there and she was desperate, trying so hard to keep up with the train and . . ."

Softly, Grace is crying again.

"Now, Grace. Now, now," he says tenderly. Then, "Can you get up?"

"Of course I can get up."

He puts his arm around her shoulders. "Can we go?"

"Yes."

At his apartment, they climb three flights of stairs. He unlocks a door, and they walk into a very small living room. He leads her to a sofa, puts a pillow under her head, brings a dampened face cloth and lays it across her forehead. Then he brings a small glass of whiskey. "Drink this," he says, and she does. Next he is standing over her with a cup of hot tea and lemon. "Drink this," he says. She drinks it.

He looks anxiously down at her. He chews his lip, wheels and goes into the kitchen. After a minute he calls, "I'm poaching your egg. Is that OK?"

"Yes."

She smells the bacon frying, and suddenly, she feels very, very hungry.

"I've got a surprise for you. Real butter for your hard rolls."

Hard rolls. Why hard? she wonders.

She looks around the room, sees walls almost white but softer than white. A big armchair, deeply carved, is upholstered with burnt red and flame. And green. Only a little green. The sofa she is sitting on is not orange. But it is not quite red either.

It is soft and long and warm. Paintings hang on the walls. She counts them. Eight. The wooden floors shine with wax.

Bucy appears with a tray of toast, bacon, orange juice, jelly (almost as good as Amelia's strawberry preserves) and a poached egg. He pours more tea for her. A cup for himself.

He sits in the carved chair, sips his tea. He chews on his lip and watches her eat. She eats hungrily, too ravenous for speech.

When she finishes, she folds her napkin and lays it on the tray. "Thank you," she says, her tone now that of a supplicant.

"Grace, I am so sorry that . . ."

She holds up her hand. *Silence!* the hand commands.

"Bucy, when I saw you I was furious. But I didn't know I was mad until I saw you. I was mad because you left me. And mad because of the War. Those soldiers on the train. They were sad. So very, very sad. And scared. And trying not to be. I was tired. Oh, I don't know," she finishes lamely.

He leans forward to speak, but the hand is again aloft. "Bucy, I knew you weren't over there. I wasn't worried. I knew they wouldn't take somebody with a heart murmur." She leans back; her eyelids fall shut; she opens her eyes, blinking. "Bucy, I am going to sleep now."

Immediately, he is on his feet. He hurries out, returns with a pajama top, a robe, a toothbrush.

She stumbles to the bathroom, undresses, slips on the pajama top and the robe. She brushes her teeth.

In a small bedroom, the bed is turned down. She falls into the softness of it.

"You can sleep here. With me," she says, her voice fading. "It's all right."

He stands in the doorway. "We have two bedrooms. We'll talk tomorrow."

She nods, closes her eyes and turns on her side.

"Grace, I have to go to work tomorrow," he says. But already she is sound asleep.

The next morning, she finds freshly squeezed orange juice, cinnamon rolls and coffee. A note is propped on the coffeepot:

> *Pick you up at the Cos Club at 7:00. Wear your fanciest duds. We have a reservation at the Algonquin.*

By half past six, Grace is ready. She has dressed carefully, spending more time than usual on her hair. It is done up on the sides and then allowed to fall, a tassel of silk, below her shoulders. Looking into the mirror, she adds a touch of powder, a little lipstick. And Chanel No. 5. Another extravagance.

When she steps out of the elevator, here he is, Bucy, gracefully climbing the few steps to meet her. Bucy, clean cut, looking wonderful in a blue suit. Bucy, smiling widely, and always with that happy, expectant look on his face. When he leans to kiss her cheek, the fresh smell of his face is so familiar that she raises her hand to his cheek.

"We're having dinner early," he tells her, hailing a cab. "I want you to see a little of New York before it gets dark. The Algonquin," he tells the driver, and turning to her, he says, "I like that perfume you're wearing. And you're prettier than ever. Did you know that?"

"Thank you, Bucy."

At the hotel, they stand in line. Again, as at the train station, men in uniform are motioned forward and permitted to enter. When, finally, they reach the head of the line, the maître d' says, "Sorry. The tables are filled. We might have something at the late seating."

"Look again, please. I have a reservation. Gillian. Bucy Gillian."

"We're overbooked. Sorry, sir. It's all the soldiers who'll soon be shipping out."

"Bucy?" she says.

"It's all right." He squeezes her hand. "Let's walk a little. We'll find some place to eat."

They walk a block. Two blocks. The restaurants they pass are filled with people in lines spilling from the doors to the streets. A gray-headed man rudely shoulders past them, snaps, "Buddy, why aren't you in the army?"

"He's got a heart murmur!" Grace calls indignantly.

"Yeaw, yeaw, that's what they all say."

"Grace, forget it. Come on! Everybody's tense because of the invasion."

They stroll down another block, walk past shuttered stores. They turn a corner.

"Bucy, do you wish you were over there? Fighting?"

"Sometimes." He smiles at her. "Here's a deli, Grace. Let's try it."

They sit at a small table, eat corned beef sandwiches and drink wine, quite a lot of wine.

Bucy fingers the stem of his glass, turns it round and round. His brown eyes glisten, grow black in the candlelight.

She puts her fork on her plate, places her knife beside it. "Bucy, tell me now. Tell me why you left."

"Grace, there were so many reasons. I felt closed in, and I knew I had to get out. But a postcard is no way to say good-bye."

"Closed in? You felt closed in?"

"By small-minded attitudes, by my job, by the routine of my life. I had to live my own life. Maybe I had to leave town to find a life. But I loved you then. I love you still." He touches her cheek.

"But it wasn't enough."

"No. And when I painted those words about love on the ceiling, I knew it wasn't," Bucy says, carefully rolling small bits of bread into pill-like shapes. "I knew you'd be all right. I wasn't worried about you because . . ." Taking her hand, he looks at her, his gaze unblinking and direct. "You have always loved John."

"Oh, Bucy. How did you know?"

"By the sound of your voice when you spoke his name. By the look in your eyes whenever he came into a room."

"Oh, Bucy, I do love him. But I love you, too. I love you both!"

He throws his head back and laughs, a great laugh that causes heads to turn as people walk past the deli.

"But not the way you love John. No," he says as she leans forward to protest, to offer regret. "It's all right. I'm glad. You told me you loved him before we married. But I wanted to marry you anyway. Grace Gillian, who wouldn't want to marry you!"

"Anna died."

"I am sorry."

"Marrying you was a careless thing."

"We just made a mistake. It's all right."

"I think we should get a divorce."

He reaches for her hand. "Of course. We will just as soon as we can."

That night Grace sits at the small desk in her hotel room. The hotel stationery is elegantly heavy, a light gray color embossed with an orange crest. She is pleased with it, for what she is to write is important. She takes up her pen and writes:

> *Dear, dear John,*
>   *I came to New York to straighten out my life and I did.*
> *Bucy and I are getting a divorce. We will always be friends.*
>   *John, I am so much wiser now.*
>   *Love,*
>   *Grace*

The next morning Bucy takes her to the train station. He kisses her cheek. "My best girl, always," he says.

She steps up onto the platform, turns and comes back down. Throwing her arms around his neck, she whispers, "Oh, Bucy! So many kinds of love."

*P*art

TWO

Chapter 8

· *1* ·

HUSBANDS. Sons. Fathers. Lovers. Dead on the beaches of Normandy. All through summer the telegrams have come to Cold Springs. The first, Captain Newton, forty-five years old, married, a father of two children. A month later, young Frank Conroy, dead a month short of his eighteenth birthday. And now, the first day of high school, September 4—only it isn't the first day because at eleven this morning a memorial service at the First Christian Church was held for Lt. David Taylor, shot by a German sniper in Marseilles a day before the Germans retreated.

Flags are flying at half-mast at the post office where David's father is postmaster and at the high school where he marched in the band. Those who did not know David know his mother at the Red Cross or his father at the post office or his sister just two years younger and off at the University of Arkansas so that she had to hear it from a stranger. All his relatives over in Arkansas, more than a dozen, were there, and so the church was filled to overflowing with those who came to grieve with the Taylors.

Later that afternoon the First Monday Bridge Club is to meet as usual (today at the Carringtons' house), but only for lunch. The cards will not even be shuffled. Arnie Carrington's mother did not attend the service, couldn't bring herself to go, because Arnie, her only son (and she a widow), had enlisted in the army the middle of July, and although he is still in basic training and the War is bound to end before he can finish and be sent *anywhere*, the thought of what might happen to Arnie is more than his mother can bear. Still she wants to hear about the service for David. Who was there. Who had managed to hold up. Who hadn't.

Before the other members of the bridge club arrive, Amanda Carrington has the cucumber and chicken salad sandwiches all made and covered with a damp cloth in the icebox and the iced tea in a pitcher. However, as she places the tray of tea sandwiches on a table in the living room, she decides to forgo the tea. This afternoon, something stronger is needed, so she gets out her cut-glass sherry glasses and opens a bottle of sherry left over from the Christmas before.

After two glasses all around (two because after only a sip or two the first is empty), the four women have scarcely touched the sandwiches. Relaxed by the sherry, they find themselves returning again and again to the death of David Taylor, despite their determination for Amanda's sake not to dwell on it.

Martha says, "Why David? Why him?" She pushes her glasses up over her forehead, takes a sip of the sherry. "He was too fine, too young to die on a foreign beach," she says, red-faced with anger.

"And the saddest thing—the Red Cross notified them two months ago he was missing, but his family kept telling themselves he was alive, either escaped or a prisoner. They just *knew* he was. Now, to find out he was dead all that time. It makes it harder," says Sarah, of the soft eyes, the soft heart.

"His father has already aged ten years," Miriam says, matter-of-factly.

"If it's any consolation to his family, David never took a step in the wrong direction," says Sarah, her voice going trembly.

"Everybody loved him. All that energy. That smiling face. Gone."

"He threw my paper for two years, and it was never anywhere but on the porch."

"Halfway through the service, his fiancée fainted. Just keeled over. Did you see that? The poor thing."

"But fainting. That seems a little . . ."

"Excessive?" Martha finishes boldly.

Coming to the girl's defense, "Well, it was too hot in that church, even with all the windows open and the ceiling fans going," Sarah says. "All the crowd."

"Girls, I know it's too warm in here, but I've got the attic fan going," says the hostess. "Now, would anyone like more sherry? Might as well finish it. A bit more in each glass?"

"If you ask me, it's his mother I grieve for," says Miriam, holding out her glass. "The girl's young. She'll get over it. But his mother. This will just about kill his mother."

"She was pitiful, sitting all through the service, pale as a ghost. Not shedding a tear," says Martha, her anger dissolving into grief.

"All those years, taking care of David, loving him. Who would ever have thought it could end like this?" Mrs. Carrington says. And with this, she puts her face in her hands and sobs so violently the women have to call her doctor to come to the house.

By the end of this first week of high school, the students have found their lockers, found their classes, changed their schedules, but they have not settled in. Too much has happened; too much *is* happening.

Late Friday, Bobby, just about worn out with it all, flops down on his bed, puts his hands under his head and stares at the ceiling. When he was a little kid, his mother had painted it blue and glued silver stars up there. If they were still up there, he could count them and not think about the worst summer he's ever had.

The worst was David Taylor. He had known David, at least he had known who he was. Mobley's older brother, Richard, had been David's best friend, and since Richard was overseas, Mrs. Taylor asked Mobley to sit with the family at the service. Mobley had looked so pale and sick all through the service that Bobby thought he might faint any minute, right along with David's girl.

But the whole summer was terrible. The night after the Gypsy Dance, he had woken up in a cold sweat thinking about Maybeline, worrying that she might be pregnant and he'd have to marry her. That had kept him awake night after night, but then, thank God, she married a soldier she met at a USO dance and left town.

And Dixie! He still can't believe Dixie! Nobody saw her for four days after the Gypsy Dance, but then she came home without Pearce. Married. When he heard it, he felt like somebody had hit him in the stomach with a sledgehammer. All summer it was all anybody talked about, even the parents. *His* parents.

One night he had come back to get his billfold when he heard them. They were sitting on the screened-in porch after supper, and when he heard the word *Dixie*, he stood still and listened.

"Dixie may not be the girl they would have chosen, but they are interfering with their son's marriage! With his life!"

"No use in ruining his life because of one mistake."

"But forcing them to live separately! And now they're trying to get the marriage annulled. It seems cruel."

"Well, they're Catholic. What else can they do?"

"What about Dixie! What about her feelings? I don't know her, but Bobby does. And they've been friends a long time."

"Barbara, Barbara. Let's not quarrel. It's not our problem, let's just . . ."

At this Bobby had quietly retrieved his billfold and left. But all summer it had been like *Gone with the Wind*. Only instead of

Rhett Butler and Scarlett, everybody was talking about Pearce and Dixie. First, they said Pearce had joined the navy, and Dixie would soon be going to wherever Pearce was sent after basic training. Then, when he and Schuster were fooling around, shooting goals, Schuster said, "Hell, Cinco. Pearce isn't in the navy, never has been; he's been visiting relatives in Memphis all summer." And just before school started, Bobby heard Pearce was back in town, and Dixie was looking for a room for them to rent. But that hadn't happened either. Dixie is still living with her mother, and Pearce is living with his folks. Pearce is in Bobby's English class, looking as stupid as ever.

The only good thing about the summer was Willie B. and Mrs. Gillian. All summer the kitchen has been filled with the smell of bread baking and, sometimes, sugar cookies, and filled, too, with Willie B.'s whistling and her gold-tooth smile.

When Mrs. Gillian had come home from New York, she and Bobby had painted her downstairs rooms. It had taken all summer with him doing most of the painting and Mrs. Gillian putting new tile in the new upstairs shower. Not at all sure she wanted to turn part of her house—the soft yellow bedrooms—over to strangers, "There's no hurry about any of this," she told Bobby.

When Bobby wasn't painting, he was working in her yard. There was plenty of yard work to do. When he finished the brick path, he and Mrs. Gillian sat on the back steps drinking lemonade and admiring it. It was pretty, curving in and out around the trees, all the way to the swing.

"Bobby," she said, "you have a wonderful sense of design. In November, we'll plant bulbs, jonquils or daffodils, and maybe some wood violets, on each side."

Mrs. Gillian's mouth had looked so soft and full, smiling at flowers that weren't even in the ground yet, that he had to make himself think about Maybeline until he didn't have a hard-on.

Mrs. Gillian had started him on poetry during the summer. Memorizing it. One hot afternoon, she took off her gardening hat and fanned herself with it. "You enjoy poems," she said. "Why don't you pick out one and learn it? If you're ever in jail, it will be a great comfort."

He had laughed at the idea, but that very night he flipped through his English book, looking at the poems. Short ones. A lot of them, even those written a hundred years ago, seemed like they were written about Dixie. Take the one he's just memorized:

> *Tell me not here, it needs not saying,*
> *What tune the enchantress plays*
> *In aftermaths of soft September*
> *Or under blanching Mays,*
> *For she and I were long acquainted*
> *And I knew all her ways.*

Boy, is that Dixie! Especially that second line. He can see her, not exactly an enchantress, but *still*, playing tunes on her piano in her yellow sweater and plaid skirt, her penny loafers bouncing at the foot pedals. And that last line. He knows *all* her ways. Maybe that's why he still loves her.

This morning he had walked down the hall with Zelle Hodges. Zelle spent the summer on Lake Michigan and came home good-looking. Her locker is next to his, and after English she asked him to teach her how to jitterbug. Thinking about Zelle and Mrs. Gillian and joining the navy pretty soon, for the first time in a long while, he feels like happiness is about to hop on his shoulder.

But when he wakes up the next morning, the first thing he's thinking about is Dixie. She hasn't been in school all week, and he had promised Mr. Balderidge he'd see about her until he joined the navy. He makes himself get out of bed and get dressed. Nobody else is up yet, so he makes three pieces of toast, piles on the apricot preserves and drinks a cup of coffee. By then, it's nine o'clock and not too early to go over there. He dreads it, hates to see Dixie all sad and, maybe, crying.

Taking his time, he walks over, steps up on her porch and knocks. But when she opens the door, she's got this big smile on her face!

"Guess what, Bobby Moore!"

Wearing white shorts and a blue shirt, she looks so cute, standing there and smiling at him, that he laughs. "What, Dixie Balderidge?"

"Dixie Pearce," she laughs. "I'll be in school Monday. Judge Baker went to the school board and said if they weren't going to let me attend school, they couldn't let Jack attend either. So they are. Letting me come back."

"You mean they weren't going to let you finish high school? Why?"

"They said if they started letting married girls come, it would be bad for morals."

"What!"

"Oh, I don't know, Bobby. That's just what they said. But Mrs. Gillian talked to Judge Baker, and he said they had obviously made a mistake. I'll be there on Monday, and I'll get to see Jack. I can see him every day."

Bobby wants to tell her what a louse Pearce is. But instead, "That's swell, Dixie," he says. "I'm glad."

· 2 ·

By September Cold Springs had lost thirteen men to the War. Of these, Grace had known eight. David Taylor's death, coming so soon after the others, had struck at the very heart of the town. A pall of mourning hung over the high school students. That first week Grace had heard it in their subdued voices and seen it in their solemn faces. In the stiffness of their movements, it was as if premature old age had struck the very young.

Now, the despair, the lassitude, has gradually been replaced by a kind of reckless energy. The school is filled with recklessness—students cutting classes, playing hooky, not turning in assignments, not *listening*.

This morning Grace is reading *Romeo and Juliet* as the students come into the classroom. She does not look up as the room fills with the autumn colors they are wearing, colors heralding a season not yet come to Texas. Hearing the hurrying footsteps of the stragglers, she lifts her eyes from the book, sees them almost running to get to their desks before the tardy bell rings.

In this class, her nine o'clock senior English, the majority are girls—urgent, self-absorbed, yet yearning. The boys, and there are only ten of them, are reckless, bold. And they are afraid.

Steve Schuster strolls in, carelessly. He takes his seat a minute after the tardy bell has rung, looks at her and grins.

She returns his smile. "Steve, stop by the office after class and get a tardy slip," she says. "Today let's begin with Act Four. Friar Laurence and Paris are speaking. Read through that first scene and jot down anything that catches your attention. It's an important scene."

But is it? To them? So greedy for life, so desperate to live. Reluctantly books are opened, pages turned.

Stay the course, she longs to say to them, knowing their answer would be, *Why?* She is not sure she, herself, could answer.

Bobby, looking strained, sits on the last row, as far from Dixie and Jack as he can get. He looks up, smiles quickly, looks down. Dixie sits in the front row, her young husband right behind her.

Dixie, wearing a new navy plaid skirt and navy sweater, is aglow with happiness. Thank goodness for Judge Baker! He may be bumbling and old (some say senile), but he is fair. An honorable man.

Grace leans against her desk, crosses her ankles. "Let's not go on with this play," she says firmly. "Families feuding. Young lovers. What has that to do with us when we know that at this very minute some young man from Cold Springs might be fighting for his life in Europe or the South Pacific?"

They look at her. Surprised. Interested. "Shakespeare wrote about love and lovers, and we may, perhaps, come back to *Romeo and Juliet*. But Shakespeare also wrote about war. One of his plays, *Henry V,* is about a war in Europe. I just wonder if, in some ways, all wars are not alike. This week, let's read *Henry V.*" Now her students seem mildly interested, but not yet engaged. Elizabeth has pulled a strand of hair over her shoulder and is idly twisting it around her finger. Mobley is rubbing his lower lip with a forefinger, a sign that he is, at least, thinking. Grace plunges ahead. "But before we begin Shakespeare's play, let's think about the war that is being waged right now by our country. First, who commands our forces in France and Holland—all the Allied Forces? Who commands them?"

The boys straighten in their seats. A few hands are raised.

"Mobley?"

"General Eisenhower."

"Right. General Eisenhower. Now, what has just happened over there? The papers have been filled with it. Remember? As we were trying to secure the Arnhem Bridge in Holland, what happened?"

Morris holds up a finger. "Morris?"

"We were outnumbered, and Poland lost thousands of soldiers. Nobody knows how many. We lost hundreds. Maybe more. But we couldn't get across the Rhine."

"That's right, Morris."

He leans forward to speak again. "And the soldiers we lost. I think they were paratroopers."

Paratroopers. The young lieutenant on the train. Was he there? So cocky. So sure he would come home. She takes a deep breath. "It failed, tragically. In *Henry V,* Shakespeare wrote about a battle that, in many ways, is like that battle. And I wonder if there is something we can learn from him? First, let's remember that in *Henry V* the commander is not a general. He is a king. King Henry. In the play, sometimes Harry or Hal, and . . ."

And as Grace carefully introduces the play, outlines the history of the battle and the reasons for it, describes the armor worn and the arms used, she is excited, made almost breathless, by what she is trying to do. By the time the class ends, the room is full of questions and opinions and arguments about battles and generals and strategy. All that week, they compare and contrast the War with the ancient battles in France, following the course of each on the wall map. When Grace talks about the power of words, Bobby brings Churchill's speech, which rallied the citizens of England in their darkest hour, the speech that contains "We shall fight them on the beaches . . ." and reads it to the class.

By the middle of the second week, the class is filled with wonder as Mobley reads King Henry's speech in which he exhorts his soldiers to almost certain death:

> *"And Crispin Crispian shall ne'er go by,*
> *From this day to the ending of the world,*
> *But we in it shall be rememberèd—*
> *We few, we happy few, we band of brothers;*
> *For he to-day that sheds his blood with me*
> *Shall be my brother."*

Driving home that afternoon, she finds herself singing. It has been a good week. The students are coming to class, listening, turning in their assignments. They will stay in school for a little while longer. Maybe long enough to graduate.

· 3 ·

AT home, Grace takes the mail from her box, looks through it and finds a letter from John. Running up the stairs, she kicks off her heels and looks at it again. Only the letter is not John's. She tears it open, finds the signature. It's from Dan Manning, the sergeant on the train. He had said he would write. From time to time she's thought about him, hoped he was all right. Smiling, she reads it:

Dear Grace Gillian:

I write this letter under a bridge where I sit with three peaceful companions. A cow and two sheep.

Casualties in my company have been light, but I don't let down my guard for a minute. I mean to come home.

For weeks now I have not known where we are, but each day is a challenge. Sometimes, we can move fast and some days it's one foot at a time.

Since I can't say much about the War, I'll tell you a little about my life. I grew up on a ranch in New Mexico. When I joined the army, I began to buy land out there, a few acres at a time. It was dirt cheap. My dad died in '39, and with what he left me I've got about 3,000 acres now. I'm not sure what the land is good for, but I'd like for you to see it. It is a part of the country like no other. It is downright beautiful.

Grace, I think of you. You are always on my mind, like a meadowlark, unseen, but whose song is never far away. You were not wearing a ring on your left hand when we met. I hope it means you are free.

Dan

She reads it again. She looks at her watch. *Good Lord!* She's already late. Amelia's probably on her way to the club right now. Slipping on shorts, tying her tennis shoes, she decides to show Amelia the letter. She can hear her now. "Grace!" she'll say. "What do you think he means by that last sentence? Why, it's practically a proposal."

She won't show it to her after all. The sergeant is not serious. He couldn't be. She certainly doesn't want him to be serious.

Amelia is waiting impatiently when she arrives. "Where have you been, Grace Gillian? We've just got about thirty minutes to play. I promised Ed fresh vegetables for supper tonight."

"Sorry, Amelia. I got a letter from a soldier I met on the train and stopped to read it."

"Really. What did he say?"

"Just a note. He wrote it under a bridge with a cow and two sheep for company."

"What about John? Have you heard from John lately?"

"No," she says. "But in his last letter he wrote that he was up to his knees in paperwork. I think he's pretty safe, probably in an office in Rome. I'll get a letter soon."

"Of course you will. Now, after the game, I want you to come have supper with us. Ed said to tell you he's been missing you."

Chapter 9

· 1 ·

"I can't keep good help anymore," his father says at the dinner table that night. "Barbara, you're lucky. Willie B. has been with us, let's see, about eight months now, and I've had five cleaning girls at the store during those eight months."

He says it like Willie B.'s not there, right at his elbow, with a plate of hot cornbread.

"Folks finding all kinds of jobs at the defense plant," Willie B. says cheerfully. "Piece of cornbread, Mr. Moore? Just out of the oven." She retreats to the kitchen, and they hear her whistling "Coming In on a Wing and a Prayer" through the dining room door.

"Why work for white folks, when they can make three times as much at the Lone Star Defense Plant?" his mother says, sounding every bit as cheerful as Willie B. does.

His mother is a puzzle to Bobby's father. He doesn't understand her. "I don't understand you, Barbara," he'll say. He says it pretty regularly. Now he looks at her like he's trying to figure out a crossword puzzle. He frowns. "Barbara, I declare, you sound like you're . . . one of them."

His mother throws her head back and laughs. "Well, I am pretty dark," she replies, her eyes glistening with humor.

Bobby looks at his father, hoping to see the slight smile that will signal his capitulation to his mother's good spirits, but at such times his father effortlessly resists what he calls "Barbara's notions."

Shaking his head, "Barbara, Barbara," he says, like he really hates to correct her. And then, in mitigation, "Barbara, I've never known a girl to catch on so fast."

"Robert, she's very bright. There was hardly any need for me to show her anything."

"Yes. Well, the Little Brontës and I were just saying that now with summer gone, you will have more time to get into things." His father says *this* all the time, too.

"Get into things?" Distastefully she stirs her coffee, adds cream.

His father retreats. A little. "You know, help Celia. With the house running smoothly and the children in school, you might plan a little party for Celia's friends. A Christmas party. Just yesterday the Little Brontës remarked that the Christmas season would soon begin. It's already October. Not too soon to plan."

His mother sighs, a long, shuddering sigh. She removes the gold ring on her finger, gazes at it and replaces it. "Robert, Celia's too young to be pushed into all this debutante business. It seems quite unnecessary."

"Unnecessary?" He is genuinely puzzled.

"With the War going on. You know the minute Bobby's eighteen, they'll take him. Even with his eyesight. They're taking everybody now."

"Dad, I'm ready now. I want to get in there and get it over with. Leroy Elkins joined the army last week. His father signed the papers."

His mother's eyes fill. "Oh, Bobby."

"How in the hell did we get on this subject!" His father's face is slightly flushed, his voice is raised. Nothing upsets his father more than seeing his wife unhappy. "We're talking about a

little Christmas party for Celia and her friends. We're not talking about the War, for God's sake—excuse me, Barbara."

He clamps his lips together. A muscle on the right side of his
face tightens. "Celia has to live here after all, and somebody has
to help her."

His mother is very good-hearted. The aunts say that all the
time. She loves things like sunsets and crippled people and
china bowls that have been mended. Willie B. is always saying,
"Miss Barbara is a good spirit." When his father is sorrowful or
worried, his mother jumps right into his corner. To Bobby it
seems like she is always trying to make up for some terrible
wrong that has happened to his father. Maybe it's because his
father is a motherless child. Whenever he gets crossways with
his father, "Remember, Bobby," she always reminds him, "your
father never had a mother."

Whatever the reasons are, tonight she goes back to feeling
sorry for his father. She reaches across the table and takes his
hand and holds it against her cheek. She kisses it.

And then his father plays his trump card. "You know, the
Little Brontës love the children, and they love you, too," he
says. "They'll help. It hasn't been that long since they went
through this."

"I'll call them," she promises.

Oh, this mother of his. Unlike any other. At once the source
of his greatest pride, his deepest despair. Bobby is painfully
aware that his friends, jabbing elbows into each other's ribs,
falling onto the living room rug in exaggerated excitement
whenever she leaves the room, notice her loosely bound bosoms and see the sway of her hips, although in his presence,
they dare remark only on her long hair, as unconfined as her
bosoms. But she is as indifferent to their crazy teenage admiration as she is to his embarrassment over it, as indifferent as she
is to the ladies' Friday afternoon bridge parties and to the Sunday tea dances at the club. While the other mothers carefully
count their tricks and politely tally their scores at bridge, his

mother is teeing off, usually by herself, or worse yet, suited out
and swimming laps in the pool.

In the early years of marriage, his father gently urging,
would say, "Don't you enjoy their company? Wouldn't you enjoy sitting with them and watching our children swim?"

And she, a newcomer (*"Your mother's a Yankee,"* Butch
Henderson had called out when he was in first grade, the other
children taking it up, crying, *"Yankee, Yankee, Yankee!"*), would
answer, "Oh, Robert. It's tiresome. All that talk about lazy
maids and bridge hands when the whole country is in the middle of a depression."

But, now, she invites the aunts to tea, an Irish tea. Hot
scones with cream and apricot preserves that Willie B. has
made. The aunts make suggestions, at first tentatively. "Do you
think Celia would enjoy ballroom dancing lessons? This is the
time to learn," Aunt Anne says. "Then at Christmas a little
party for her friends. A tea dance. At the club."

Aunt Emily loves the idea of a party, especially one that will
please his father. "Or what about a Mardi Gras ball later in the
season?" she says, straightening the skirt of her rose-colored
dress. "Celia will be sixteen then. It could be a masquerade
party. Young people love costumes." She chooses a hot scone,
splits it and spoons apricot preserves into it.

Anne nods. "That will give us more time. We'll have to go
to Dallas for her dress." She bends to brush a dust mote from
her navy blue pump.

His mother leans back in her chair and splays her legs out
before her, deliberately evoking raised eyebrows. "What about
a hunt breakfast? We could ship the horses in from Virginia."

After a minute, the Little Brontës smile and pull their chairs
close. "Now, Barbara, be serious."

She pulls her mane of black hair forward over her shoulder,
sits straight in her chair, feet together, the very picture of com-
pliance. "Let's make a list," she says.

After dinner that night, she reads the list. The aunts beam. Her husband is confounded. "My God, excuse me, Barbara, that would cost a fortune!"

She smiles, reaches for his hand. "We'll have Celia's party here. At the house. With lots of flowers and good food and somebody in to help Willie B. And a piano player."

Celia bursts into tears. "I'd be so embarrassed! Nobody has parties at their house. Nobody will come. Nobody! If I can't have a party at the club, I just won't have a party at all!" Celia cries, storming out of the room.

"Barbara, Celia's still not strong," his father reminds her. Since Celia's rheumatic fever, the family tries not to upset her.

The Little Brontës agree. The party must be at the club. And for her first grown-up party, it will be a tea dance, closer to Christmas and not so demanding as a Mardi Gras ball.

After this, a kind of serenity descends upon the household. Homey smells of corn bread in the oven and pot roast on the stove waft through the house. In the kitchen Willie B. snaps beans and shells pecans for pies. And whistles. Often, Willie B.'s whistling is the sound that wakes the Moores. "Though there's one engine gone, we will still carry on," she whistles cheerfully. "Coming in on a wing and a prayer."

Although his father never praises Willie B. to her face, he sometimes compliments her to his mother. "Barbara, ask your maid to make some more bread pudding," he might say. "Until she served it last week, I thought the making of bread pudding was a lost art."

The middle of October, Celia, accompanied by the aunts, drives to Neiman's to choose a dress. "Barbara, don't you want to go? The child might need your advice," his father says.

"No, dear. The aunts have insisted the dress will be a gift. If I know Celia, she will show no mercy when it comes to cost. Of time or money. Robert, it does seem so foolish to spend all this money. Things haven't been going well at the store. You're not sleeping well. And with the War, this is not the time . . ."

He cups her chin in his hand. "Sweetheart, you mustn't worry about money. That's my job."

She brushes his hand away. "Oh, Robert," she says despairingly.

That same afternoon, Schuster, who by working all summer and carrying a paper route has managed to buy a '37 Chevy, gives Bobby a ride home. Turning into the driveway, Bobby sees the two women sitting on the back steps, barefoot, their skirts hiked above their knees to catch any breeze that might come their way. His mother is almost as dark as Willie B., and from this distance, coming upon them, they might easily have been mistaken for sisters. As they watch, his mother, overtaken with mirth, throws her head back and slaps her thigh, and Willie B., with a hand on each knee, laughs along with his mother, a rollicking laugh that bounces through the open windows of the Chevy.

"Why, that's your mother!" Schuster says.

"So? Want to make something of it?" Suddenly, his fist is in Schuster's face, and Schuster draws back, astonished.

"Bobby, are you crazy! My God, man!"

But Bobby is stalking across the lawn to his back door, and Schuster takes off, squealing his tires around the corner.

His mother says, "Oh, Bobby, Willie B. just told me the funniest joke about Hitler. A colored man went up to . . ."

She stops when she sees his face, and he storms into the house without a word to her or Willie B. Throwing himself on his bed, he hears his mother's voice, sounding not at all disturbed, blending with her maid's.

He lies there, furiously willing his father to come. He *wants* him to see her. He wants him to *do* something. But when Bobby hears his father's car in the drive, his stomach tightens. He gets up and goes to the window. His father closes the car door and walks quickly across the lawn. "Mrs. Moore, come inside, please," he says.

The family is usually divided, when there is a division, into two camps. He identifies with his mother. As Bobby sees it, they are both outcasts—he, because of his lazy eye and his acne and also (he feels this acutely at times) because of his mother. She is from the north—a Yankee, a newcomer, not caring what anybody in town thinks of her. Or of the family.

Now, hearing his father's voice, iced by controlled fury, he understands his father's humiliation. The Moore family has, as they say, come down in the world. But only financially, and not so far as to keep Celia from being a debutante. In that single moment in Steve Schuster's car, he realized that his mother was hastening their downfall. And he knew that she didn't care. Listening to his father's angry voice, for the first time he feels that he, Bobby, has a right to be angry at his mother.

"Barbara, sitting out there, barefoot, for all the world to see! And with your skirt hiked up over your head! Damnit, Barbara!"

For the first time his father's use of a curse word in his mother's presence is not followed by an apology.

That night his mother knocks on his door, a soft, tentative knock. Steeling himself, he remains silent, his eyes on an open book. She comes in and sits on the edge of his bed, but he keeps his eyes on the book. She gently takes it from him, places a book marker in it and closes it.

"Bobby?"

"Mother, he's right. You did look like a maid this afternoon. Steve was shocked. I was embarrassed."

She sighs. Then, "Oh, Bobby," she says. "You and Steve Schuster! Don't you know there's a world out there, and there's a War being fought in that world! Just this week thousands of brave Polish men lost their lives in an uprising that failed." Her blue eyes narrow. "Well, you'll soon find out there's more to be shocked about than your mother sitting on the back steps on a hot day with the best damn—excuse me, Bobby, as your father would say—maid we've ever had!" The ice that had been in his father's voice when he spoke to his wife has traversed into hers.

"Bobby, you've been mad since Dixie eloped with Jack Pearce," she says more gently. "Mad at the whole family. Sometimes rude to Willie B. And now, mad at your best friend. Whatever happened that night at the Gypsy Dance hurt you. And I'm sorry for it. But you just be careful you don't hurt somebody else because of it. You hear, Bobby?"

Stung into silence, he does not answer. After a minute she leaves the room.

After that day, although his father does not dare fire Willie B. (after all, she is his wife's maid), he finds a dozen reasons for her dismissal, and his mother finds a hundred reasons to keep her. Under his father's polite, remorseless siege, he finds himself again allied with his mother.

Once again, his father has his breakfast served in the dining room, where he rarely speaks to Willie B. And, sighing often, she goes heavily about her tasks. Now she refuses to make his father's favorites—bread pudding (takes too much sugar), fried okra (too much bacon grease). In the war that is being waged, she is heart and soul on his mother's side.

Bobby is changing the tire the day he hears Willie B. ask his mother for money. "I hates to ask. I surely does. You got so much on you right now, but Dr. Bruce, he say I need to have this knot out, and he has to have some money down before the procedure."

His mother puts her arm around her maid's shoulders. "Oh, I am sorry. Does it hurt?"

"No'm. But he say it will."

"Of course you can have the money. I'll speak to Mr. Moore tonight. How much does Dr. Bruce need?"

"He say fifty now and fifty when I comes in."

"I'll speak to my husband tonight."

Lately, with her husband somewhere in Europe, Willie B. has got in the habit of leaving supper on the stove so she can be home in time to listen to the news. "Of course she needs to leave, Robert," his mother had said firmly when his father protested.

In fact, maids from households all over town are slipping out into the falling darkness, allowing back screen doors to whisper to a close behind them, hurrying, hurrying to be home in time for the news. As the town prepares to listen, all activity ceases and chairs are drawn close to the radio.

Tonight, Bobby's father settles into his leather chair, his mother takes the rocker, and Bobby sits on the floor to be as close to the news as possible.

"Where's Celia?" his father asks.

"Probably polishing her nails."

"That's good. She doesn't need to be worried with all this bad news."

Tonight, Walter Winchell begins as usual. "Good evening, Mr. and Mrs. North America and all the ships at sea. It's good news tonight. General Douglas MacArthur has fulfilled his promise. He has returned to the Philippines, this time in the company of the greatest armada ever to sail the Pacific."

His mother walks over and turns the radio off.

"Barbara!"

"Robert, our maid needs money for surgery. It's quite serious."

"Where does she plan to get this money?"

"Why, Robert, from us, of course."

Rising from his chair, his father slaps a folded newspaper against his leg. "It's out of the question."

His mother's hands are outstretched. "You can't refuse."

"Our expenses are heavy. I don't have it. Barbara, you know what the War has done to my business. You've been in the store. You've seen the empty shelves."

"I know how much we're spending on Celia's Christmas party."

"That is totally irrelevant."

"Not to me."

With a final *whack* against his leg, and, "No, Barbara. And that's final," he leaves the room.

The next morning, his mother, still in her pink gown and robe, is down before his father. "Willie B., I'm going to work something out today. You tell Dr. Bruce to schedule the surgery."

Willie B. turns from the sink, her shoulder blades wings beneath her yellow dress. "I thank you, Miss Barbara. And I wrote my sweetie. He'll send the money for it. He surely will."

Frowning, Willie B. leans against the icebox, clasping her arms beneath her breasts. "Trouble is, I ain't heard lately. Nothing. And last night I had this dream." Her voice is mournful, keening. "He wore dead in my dream, by the side of a wide, wide river. Now his spirit got to haunt the river. It can't ever leave it." She shakes her head, denying the dream.

"Willie B., there's no such thing as ghosts. It was just a dream. You'll hear from him soon. Try not to worry." Mother turns to leave, turns back. "And, Bobby, I want you to drive me on an errand after school. I'll tell your father we need the car," she says before hurrying back upstairs.

After school, his mother comes out before he has a chance to get out of the car. She is wearing her black dress, black hat, high heels and stockings. Seeing his mother, he feels a surge of pride, knowing she has asked him and not his father to drive her.

"Bobby, drive me to Morris's Jewelers," she says. When he parks in front of the store, she says, "You can wait out here."

"I'll come in. Mother, it's too hot to wait in the car."

She hesitates. Then she says, "You might as well."

She walks into the store with her head high, removes the ring from her finger and places it carelessly on the square of black velvet that Mr. Morris has placed in front of her. She takes another ring from her purse, the diamond that had belonged to her mother, and places it beside the gold ring.

"Dick, I want to sell one of my rings. Which one will bring a hundred dollars?"

Now, Dick Morris is one of his father's oldest friends. Their friendship had begun in Miss Elam's School for Boys when they were five years old. Although they seldom see each other now, on social occasions such as a christening or a funeral or a wedding, Dick Morris is always in attendance. "I can count on old Dick to be there when he's needed," his father frequently says.

Mr. Morris, his hands behind his back, looks at the rings, looks at his mother, looks at Bobby. He strokes his tidy beard.

"Which one, Dick?" she says calmly.

Dick picks up the gold ring, puts it down. With his forefinger, he moves the diamond ring a fraction of an inch to the right.

"Dick?"

"Barbara, I'll have to do a little investigating. Excuse me a minute."

They wait silently. His mother sits in a chair in front of the black velvet square, her hands folded on the table in front of the rings. Staring at the rings, she crosses her legs and rotates an ankle. She picks up the diamond ring and puts it on her finger. She replaces it, stands and walks around the store, touching a porcelain unicorn, a porcelain rose.

Dick Morris returns, a deep frown on his face. "Barbara, I'm sorry."

"You called Robert."

Hands still clasped behind his back, he does not answer. He looks down, solemnly shaking his head.

She picks up the rings and drops them carelessly into her purse. As they leave the store, Bobby turns to glare at Mr. Morris. But he, watching Barbara Moore's swinging hips as she leaves, is unaware of Bobby or of Bobby's glowering expression.

They drive home in silence. Bobby parks and hurries to open the car door for his mother, who goes immediately upstairs, and there she moves his father's things from her room to the guest room at the end of the hall.

That night at the table, only words such as *please* and *thank you* and *pass the butter* are spoken. Bobby and Celia warily circle their parents all evening and go quietly to their rooms after supper.

The next afternoon, his mother and Willie B. are again on the back steps. Today their dresses, his mother's blue one that matches her eyes and Willie B.'s familiar yellow one, are tucked below their knees. His mother's face is pale, her eyes sad. He speaks and they answer, but then they fall silent, waiting to resume their conversation when he leaves.

As he enters the house, he hears his mother: "Oh, Willie B., with this terrible, heartbreaking war, the hardware business is difficult. But you tell Dr. Bruce that we . . ." He is sure she said *we*, but that is all he hears.

Willie B. does not come to work on Monday. On Tuesday, a glimmer of gold on the dining table causes him to veer from his path to the kitchen. His mother's gold ring lies beside his father's folded newspaper. Gazing down at the ring and at his father's carefully folded paper, he senses the storm that is about to engulf the entire family.

Willie B. is gone a week, a week of cold cereal for breakfast, an empty cheerless kitchen, and only polite greetings and leave-takings between his mother and his father. If his mother knows the reason for her maid's absence, she doesn't say. His father doesn't ask. Every morning, they come down to a cold kitchen and cold cereal, and they leave as soon as they can. His father continues to use the guest room at the end of the hall, and only one time does he knock on her door. It is in the early morning hours. "Barbara" he calls softly. "Barbara, please." But if she answers, Bobby doesn't hear her.

A week later, Willie B. returns to work. When he comes down and sees her at the kitchen sink, his heart lifts. "Willie B.!" he says. "Here you are. You're back."

She nods and smiles (such a small smile), her lips curling around her teeth. "What you want for breakfast?"

"Willie B., I don't care. But where have you been? I've missed you! Mother's missed you, too!"

"I be all right, right soon," she says. "Done had my procedure."

It is when she stoops to get the iron skillet from a stove drawer that she grimaces, and he sees the gaping hole where her gold star tooth had been. "Oh, Willie B.!" he says, shocked by the change in her appearance.

She covers her mouth with her hand. "Ain't nothing to be done about it," she says. Placing his breakfast before him, she touches his shoulder. "It all right, Bobby. Just a tooth."

"No. It's not all right," his mother says softly. Neither had heard her come down. Wearing the velvet robe his father had given her on her birthday, she stands, with her hands in her pockets, her chin thrust forward. "Willie B., I'm glad you're back. We've missed you. We'll have a little visit after breakfast."

At Celia's wail, "Mother, I can't find my blue angora sweater!" she turns to go back upstairs just as his father comes down. "Robert, Willie B.'s back. She had her surgery. She sold her gold star tooth to pay for it," she says, speaking as if to a stranger.

"I knew she would work it out," his father says reasonably.

"Robert, I never intend to be placed in that position again."

The next day she is dressed before Bobby leaves for school. She dresses early the next day and the next. The following Monday, Judge Baker, his father's first cousin once removed, stops by the hardware store for "a little visit."

Robert Moore cannot contain his anger when he comes home that evening. "Goddamnit, Barbara, do you know what you're doing to me?" he shouts, not caring that his children are listening to every word. "Going all over town, looking for a job. As if a man can't take care of his family. I don't understand you, Barbara. What in God's name do you want?"

"Robert, you really don't know, do you? You haven't any idea," she says, a sad wonder in her voice.

That afternoon Willie B. helps his mother pack. Bobby watches, disbelieving. "Mother, I can't believe you're doing this! Just going off to Washington."

"Miss Barbara, all this here ain't necessary. It wore just a tooth," Willie B. says.

"It's more than a tooth, Barbara. It's much more than a tooth."

Later that afternoon, he hears them laughing, giggling like schoolgirls. *Maybe she's changed her mind,* he thinks. *Maybe she's not going to leave.* He knocks on the door.

"Come in, Bobby," his mother calls cheerfully. "We're talking about ghosts. This girl believes in ghosts. Tell him, Willie B."

"They is ghosts. I knows it. And I knows I has to haunt the house where I passes. All us coloreds knows it." So caught up is she in the telling that she forgets to cover her mouth. "All I wants is for yore mama to say that if I passes here, here in this house, she be here, too. With me."

"Oh, Willie B., you're not going to die."

"I has to haunt the house where I dies, and I don't want no strangers round. I wants them I knows. If I passes in this house, you got to promise to come back home."

"But you're not going to die," his mother says. "Your sweetie will come home from the War, and you'll live happily ever after." His mother, excited by what she is about to do, is taking her clothes from hangers and tossing them on the bed for her maid to pack.

"I got to know."

"All right, I promise."

When she is packed, Bobby takes her bags downstairs, and she calls a taxi. When she comes down, she makes her hand into a fist and touches his chin. "Bobby, you're a man now," she says. "But I want you to promise you'll wait to be drafted. Don't join the army. Promise? You can find another way to help. Will you promise?"

In the Moore family, promises are not given lightly. Dismayed by what his mother has asked, he shakes his head. "Oh, Mother!" But then she looks so stricken that he says, "All right. I promise."

Talking to herself, Willie B. comes slowly down the stairs. "A tooth don't matter," she mutters. "You'd think Hitler had come in here on us. Or that that gorilla had caught Ma Perkins. A tooth ain't nothing." She starts into the kitchen.

"Wait a minute, Willie B. I want a promise from you, too."

She turns and comes back. Her face is alive with eagerness to promise anything, everything.

"I want you to promise to find enough sugar to make bread pudding for Mr. Moore."

Willie B. frowns. His mother smiles.

"I want your promise. Promise."

"I will," her maid says solemnly. "And now I got to see what I can find for supper. I don't hold with good-byes."

All that afternoon Celia has refused to come out of her room, but now she storms out, sobbing, throwing herself into her mother's arms, begging her to stay. And when she refuses, she makes a frantic telephone call to their father. But he cannot stop her. Somehow, perhaps from one of the aunts, she has the money for the ticket.

During the next weeks, Willie B. continues to work, becoming thin and stooped as the weeks pass, growing old before their eyes. But the kitchen is still the first place Bobby comes to when he is at home. After school, there is the smell of bread baking or cookies just out of the oven, and Willie B.'s whistling fills the air.

With his mother gone, Willie B. seems like the only good thing about home. Like today when Miss Dolby returned their Latin tests, his with a big, fat F. The night before the test, he and Schuster had been out drinking Jack Daniel's until three in the morning. He could hardly get out of bed the day of the test. After school he came into the kitchen, sat down and closed his eyes. Rubbing his temples with his fingertips, he says, "Willie B., what's that smells so good?"

"Bread pudding."

"You're making bread pudding? He doesn't deserve it."

"I promised. And don't be criticizing your daddy. Can't you see he's about on his last leg? Here, you take one of my pills. Take care of that headache."

After the pill and a glass of iced tea, his headache is gone, but the F on his Latin test remains. "I wish she'd come home," he says.

"Bobby, don't fret now. 'Bout your mother. You got this chance to grow up, all of you. And she got to try her wings. One of these days, she be coming home. When you gets low, just write her a letter. That's what I does."

And it helps. He writes his mother that night, not telling her about things like the F in Latin, but instead, telling her about the bread pudding and Mrs. Gillian's yard.

Winter 1944

Chapter 10

· *1* ·

WINTER has come early. Unbelievably, a light snow on Thanksgiving Day. The sound of Robert's car has brought the Little Brontës out to the front steps, where they stand shivering with the cold and their anxiety over this first Thanksgiving without Robert's wife.

Three days getting ready. First, Emily had set Ruth (who has been with them longer than anyone cares to say) to making the cakes, chocolate for the children, and the orange layer—that takes all day—for the grown-ups. Yesterday, Anne had insisted on accompanying Henry to the greengrocer's for cranberries and lettuce and red pears and to the grocery store with the main order and, finally, to the butcher's, where the twenty-one-pound turkey Emily had ordered was dressed and waiting.

It was while Anne was setting the table that the two had a discussion, one that bordered on argument. "Won't it be strange not to even mention her name?" Anne had said. She waited a minute, and as there was no response, she continued. "After all, she is the children's mother. I just think a casual remark, such as, 'Robert, I hope Barbara's work in Washington is going well,' would be appropriate."

Emily never explains her views; she saw no need to explain

them now. After all, Anne had been there and, doubtless, remembered as well as she how Robert's face had fallen when
Barbara's name had been mentioned last Tuesday. After that
encounter, there had been a tacit understanding between the
two that Barbara's name would not be mentioned again.

"Absolutely not," Emily said. And saying it, she fixed her
mouth.

Anne retreated momentarily. Then, not quite ready to sur-
render the field, she added, "Well, it seems abnormal to me not
to mention her name."

Seeing Emily's mouth—obdurate, imperious—Anne waited
a few minutes before trying another approach, one even more
daring. Straightening the candles in silver holders, "We could
ask Grace O'Brian Gillian to stop by for dessert," she said.
"Grace would be the one to cheer up Robert, if anyone could."

This idea, even with its hint of scandal, had been surprisingly appealing to Emily, so that she lingered over the bronze
chrysanthemums she was arranging while she considered it. To
see their Robert happy again. What wouldn't she dare to see
that! Then, "No, sister," she said. "It wouldn't do. It just
wouldn't do."

And Anne, of course, had known it wouldn't.

Now, hearing the sound of Robert's car being leisurely
driven through the cloudy shadows of pin oaks and pine trees,
the aunts, dressed in familiar holiday silks, their cheeks flushed
with excitement and the cold, stand on the steps, exclaiming
with pleasure at the arrival of Robert and his children. Celia,
ethereal in gray velvet that sets off her blue eyes (like her
mother's) and her blond curls (from her Grandmother Charlotte), runs up the steps, gives each aunt a fragile hug and vanishes into the house. Robert, looking especially handsome in a
gray pinstriped suit with a black overcoat over his shoulders,
steps forward and gently hugs his aunts.

"Bobby's moving the car along the drive in case anyone else

is coming along," Robert says. "Come. Let's go in. It's too cold to be out here. It's downright wintry."

In the entrance hall, Anne stands on tiptoe to take Robert's coat from his shoulders. Giving it over to Henry, she says, "Bobby will be along in a minute, Henry. After you take his coat, you can see if Ruth needs anything in the kitchen."

And then Anne, leading the way across the hall and throwing open the great mahogany doors, says, "We've got a wonderful fire going in here. Sit close until you're warm."

Coming into the room, seeing his aunts happy and excited, it almost seems to Robert that Barbara, her eyes glistening with excitement over the first snow, might come hurrying in to stand beside him in front of the fire. And for a fleeting minute, he is able to believe that this day might be a little better than just another day to get through.

Twenty-three days. Letters flying into the mailbox. Letters to Celia, to Bobby, even to Willie B. And last week, the Little Brontës had come into the store, specifically (he was sure of it) to tell him they, too, had heard from her and that Congressman Patman had arranged a position for her in the State Department. The letter was halfway out of Anne's purse before he told her he didn't have time to read it, and confused, bewildered, she had slipped it back.

"Robert, dear, more eggnog? No?"

At the sound of her voice, Robert turns from the window to see Aunt Anne pouring eggnog from a silver pitcher. Whipped cream and lots of eggs and generous dollops of whiskey. Barbara has always loved Ruth's eggnog.

Barbara. Despairing, he says, "Not just yet, Aunt Anne."

Taking another swallow, he sees his aunt refilling Bobby's empty cup. Leaning forward to remonstrate, he notices that Bobby is wearing an old blue sweater.

"Bobby," he begins, "couldn't you find a jacket for Thanksgiving dinner?"

Bobby shrugs his shoulder, indifferently turns away.

Son, what in Sam Hill is wrong with you! I'm not the one who walked out! He fights the urge to say it.

Aunt Anne catches his eye, signals something. He has no idea what. He vaguely nods a response. Defiantly, Bobby gets up and pours himself another cup of eggnog.

Robert turns to Celia, who is reclining on the sofa, her arm thrown over her eyes. "Celia, baby, I know you're hungry. You didn't eat a bite of breakfast this morning."

"I wasn't hungry," she says. "I'm *never* hungry."

Exchanging worried glances, the aunts leap to the rescue, although he is not sure who is being rescued. "Celia, I need your help," Emily says. "Would you come pour the water for us?"

"The glasses are on the table," Anne says.

But when they come into the dining room and Robert sees the sideboard laden with the turkey and cornbread dressing, the oyster dressing, the mashed potatoes, the cranberry salad, the relish plate, the English peas, the cakes and boiled custard—evidence of bountiful love—his anger cools.

As they take their places, Ruth comes in, bearing a plate of hot rolls. "Aunt Emily," Bobby says, pulling her chair out for her.

"We'll have the blessing," Emily says, closing her eyes, bowing her head. Opting for brevity and a dearth of emotion, she prays quickly, "Bless this food to the nourishment of our bodies."

"Well, this is a grand day," Robert says, preparing to carve. "Where else in the whole world could you find a meal like this?"

"Celia, we made the salad just for you. And Bobby, wait until you see the cake!" Anne says.

Hearing the conversation, Robert wonders if Bobby and Celia will always be children in the eyes of the aunts. *But they're not children,* Robert tells himself. *Bobby's grown and Celia soon will be.*

"Bobby, I'm sure you're going to the game this afternoon," Emily says. "Do you think we can beat Arkansas?"

"Schuster says we can. I sure hope so."

"Celia, are you going?"

"Maybe. I'm not sure. Elizabeth and I may go to a movie."

"*Going My Way* with Bing Crosby is on at the Paramount. Is that what you're going to see?"

"I'm not sure. Maybe."

Taking another helping of oyster dressing and a sliver of white meat, Robert finds himself enjoying the day, the meal. And his children, if not as high-spirited as usual, seem to be enjoying it, too, although Bobby, turning down the dessert, has obviously ruined his appetite with the eggnog.

It is when they are leaving the table that Emily destroys the fragile weave of the day. "Celia," she says innocently, "we have a surprise for you. Your dress for the party came. After dinner you can try it on."

Celia lowers her head, murmurs something her father cannot hear.

"What, Celia?" he says.

When she lifts her head, her eyes brim with tears. "I'm sorry, Aunt Anne, Aunt Emily. I'm not going to the party!" she cries, and breaking into sobs, she buries her head in her napkin.

"Why, child, do you know what you're saying? It's *your* party. The invitations will be mailed next week. We've reserved the club," Emily says.

"Emily, all that doesn't matter," Anne says rather sharply. Then, her hand on Celia's shoulder, she says, "Celia dear, can you tell us why you don't want to go on with it?"

"I don't know why! And I'm sorry! But I'm *not* going to have a party!" Running from the room, she cries, "I just want my mother to come home!"

Three days later Celia has been invited to stay with the aunts "until she gets over this little spell," and their father has consented, as Bobby knew he would. The following Monday,

Bobby stands by the kitchen sink, looking out the window in the direction of the Little Brontës' house.

"Old Celie's over there," he tells Willie B., "being waited on hand and foot. Ruth will be cooking whatever she wants, and Henry will be driving her all over town. And all that's right down old Celie's alley."

Hands on her hips, eyes narrowed, "Bobby," Willie B. says, "Celia's the only sister you got, and you needs to stay close. Both of you. And you don't need to be getting so high and mighty 'bout Celia. She got her concerns just like you."

· 2 ·

ROBERT Moore refuses to think about Thanksgiving Day. No point in dwelling on disaster. Picking up the newspaper from the front walk, he swats his leg with it. *We have to look ahead,* he tells himself firmly. *By Christmas, things will be better,* he tells himself. He looks at his watch, sees that it's time for the news, but when he enters the living room, he does not turn on the radio. *By Christmas,* he decides. By Christmas he and the children will be organized.

Christmas. Lord, that seems like a long time ago. Barbara had insisted on buying all those Christmas lights to string along the roof of the house. And the poinsettias and candles and ribbons.

Protesting mildly, "When the War ends, we can do all that," he had said. But the truth is he has never been able to resist Barbara's high spirits, her gaiety. Her body. He knows every curve and inclination of her lithe, slender frame, her silken skin, the way she *felt,* curving around him at night.

And coming home from work, it *had* been nice—the poin-settias massed in the entrance hall; on the table, the Meissen bowl of red apples spiced with cloves; the house filled with the smell of smoke and pine and spices. "Isn't this the *best* time!" she'd say. "The house filled with Christmas, and us in it, all together. And *safe*."

Suddenly feeling the bitterness of tears, Robert goes into the bathroom and splashes water over his face. Then he pours himself a good stiff drink. *Well, this time Barbara went too far,* he tells himself. This time she had pushed him into a corner so that he had had to come raging out, so full of anger he had thought he might have a stroke or at least a mild heart attack. Well, he hasn't been a perfect husband. He knows that. But he had always, by God, been able to support his family.

"Mr. Moore? Mr. Moore, you 'bout to miss the news."

"Oh, Willie B. Thank you."

"Your supper's in there waiting."

"Thank you, Willie B."

Willie B.'s been losing weight. He's noticed it. But, then, who hasn't? It's this terrible War. The War in Europe was supposed to be over by Christmas, but it keeps dragging on. And the War in the Pacific. That War is not near over, not by a long shot.

"Mr. Moore, I got this letter from Miss Barbara today. She's liking her job. Sho' is now. I can read it to you."

"No thank you, Willie B."

"Well, I be here in the morning," Willie B. says. Then, talking so that Mr. Robert Moore can hear if he's a mind to listen, she mutters, "Some folks got so much pride, ain't hardly room for nothin' else." And slipping out the back door, she hurries home to catch the news.

Not so long ago, Willie B.'s little lectures, delivered just loudly enough so that he could hear them, would amuse Robert, though he took no notice. But now he often finds himself dwelling on them, turning them over in his mind. He supposes it is the empty house. Wondering where Bobby has got off to, he pours himself another drink.

· 3 ·

THE first of December, another snow. Then the sun comes out before the last snowflake falls, and Cold Springs has a week of summertime weather. On Saturday Grace uncoils the hose and gets out her gardening tools—a trowel, the small rake, fertilizer. Taking the basket of bulbs on her arm, she drops bulbs on both sides of Bobby's brick path. Then she digs a hole for each one, softening the soil, adding chicken manure ("Nothing's better than chicken shit," Amelia raucously says) and rich loam from her compost bed, mixing it all together. Then she fills each hole with water. For seasoning.

Satisfied when each small bed is ready, she looks up at the sun. It must be at least one o'clock. Today, although she has lost track of time, she has not been able to lose herself in the gardening. Again and again she has found herself thinking of school. And her students, still polite. Still attending class. But an air of recklessness hangs over the school. One can feel it, almost smell it. Mr. Lawson has stopped trying to enforce the no smoking rules on the school grounds. But, the drinking. Students are coming to school drunk! This past week he called the fathers of four intoxicated seniors (thank goodness, not her students) to his office. When he calls the fathers in, everybody knows it's serious. Grace admires that. But the recklessness is increasing, and she feels powerless to stop it.

Shucking off her sweater, she decides to stop for a glass of tea and a bite of lunch. Coming into the back hall, she hears the raspy squeak of her mailbox. Mr. Bartlett is a little early today.

"Good afternoon, Mr. Bartlett," she says, taking the mail, turning quickly away. Taking the stairs two at a time, she hurries into the gallery and falls breathlessly into a chair. Flipping through the mail, she drops bills, a yellow folder advertising a sale at Klein's, and a plea from the Salvation Army to the floor.

The last, a letter from Bucy. *Bucy.* Funny. She has been thinking about Bucy. And isn't it always that way! You think about a person and here they are! She makes herself a glass of tea and sits down to read Bucy's letter.

Grace, dear,

We'll always be friends. Best friends. I'm glad you came to remind me of it.

Girl, you can't imagine how often I think of you, coming into a room, lighting it up. Hold on to your foolish, whimsical, openhearted self. God knows the world is full of sensible souls. Too full. It needs frivolity and kindness, Grace.

When the right man comes along, you will know. Listen to your heart. Don't hurry. Listen.

Bucy

Bucy. It's the strangest thing about Bucy. He has gradually become what he always was—her best friend. She loves him. How could she not! And as the days, weeks, months have gone by, it has begun to seem that they were never married, that he was never more than a friend. A dear, dear friend.

But the right man *has* come along. She knows it, and Bucy would know it, too, if he knew John better.

That afternoon, she looks at the bulbs alongside Bobby's walk. Taking the first of them, no more than a husk, really, dry, crumbling, she puts it into the small bed she has made for it and covers it with rich black loam. Tapping the soil down, she imagines the tender, green shoots it will put forth next spring. When she finishes the planting, she waters the beds again, and then she walks out to the swing. Giving herself a push, she imagines the flowering of her yard. The soldiers coming home. Surely by spring. All of them. And a world at peace. *Peace.* The most beautiful word in the English language.

Chapter 11

· 1 ·

WHEN Bobby gets back from Schuster's, he drinks a cup of hot chocolate to get warm, but it makes him feel like throwing up. To get away from Willie B.'s sharp eyes, he decides to walk over to the aunts' house and deliver Celia's letter. With the sun going down, it's getting colder, so Bobby puts on his heaviest jacket over his sweaters and pulls his old hat down over his ears.

Earlier, he had walked over to Schuster's. Unless he has the car, he walks everywhere now. He doesn't know when it came over him that he was too old to be getting around on a bicycle, but one day he was riding his bicycle all over town, and the next day he wouldn't be caught dead on it. It's parked in the garage now, gathering dust.

By the time he got to Schuster's the wind had picked up, and it was almost freezing. Schuster came out the back door just as Bobby was coming up the drive. "Come on, Cinco," he said. "Let's hit the garage."

Schuster's garage is more like a barn than anything else. In fact, they don't ever use it for a garage. Schuster's father likes woodworking, so it's full of tools for sanding and cutting and polishing, and he's got a lathe out there and a power saw and a drill. Stuff like that.

Inside, Schuster turned on the gas stove, and it began to

throw out just enough heat to take the edge off the cold. The whiskey had done the rest.

Schuster's folks were in Kermit, visiting a new grandbaby, so he and Bobby put their gloves in their pockets and settled down on some old tires with a bottle of Jim Beam and some fuck books, kind of laughing at themselves for reading them. But pretty soon, Pearce drove into Schuster's driveway, hollering, "Hey, Schuster. Hey, man, where are you?"

"Oh, shit," Schuster said.

They just looked at each other for a second. With Pearce married, it seemed like kid stuff to be reading about sex in funny books, so they jumped up and threw the fuck books behind an old trunk before Schuster opened the door.

When Pearce came in, he had this phony grin on his red face, and his eyes kept shifting from Bobby to Schuster and back to Bobby again like he thought Bobby might hit him and Schuster might help. Bobby didn't want to fight him, so the three of them finished the bottle. But when Pearce offered him a ride home, he turned it down.

Now, he's about a half a mile from the Brontës' house and so cold his toes feel numb, his hands, too. The cloud-covered sky is pitch-black without the stars. Looking up at it, he stumbles, almost falls. His face feels like it's frozen. He decides to run, but running tears up his stomach so that he has to step behind a tree and throw up. After that, he just walks fast.

When he gets there, the house is dark, except for a couple of lights downstairs. Looking through the windows into the parlor, he sees that it's empty. He walks around to the back. If the aunts are in the kitchen, he'll leave the letter in the mailbox. But Celia's at the sink. Washing dishes. He's hardly ever seen Celia in a kitchen.

"Celie," he calls softly, and opening the back door, steps inside.

She turns around and smiles so widely it shows her braces. "Oh, Bobby," she says. "I'm glad to see you. I'm glad you came." She puts her arms around his waist and squeezes like she used to when she was a little kid. "I've missed you."

"Celie, I've missed you, too," he says, surprised by the truth of these words. "Hey, what are you doing in the kitchen? I didn't think you knew where the kitchen was. Where's Ruth? And the aunts? Where are they?"

"They go to bed with the chickens. That's what they say." And now Celia is giggling and sounding more like the old Celia. "But they don't have any chickens." Stepping back, she turns to the sink. She picks up a cup towel and dries a stove vessel. Then she turns around and looks at him. "I'm lonesome," she says simply.

"Celia, come home. You can come home."

"No, I can't. Ruth has the flu, and Aunt Anne has a terrible cold. Coughing every minute, she can't sleep. And Aunt Emily can't sleep for worrying. I've got to stay here."

"You mean you're not going to school tomorrow? Celia, you've got to go to school."

"Bobby, I *am* going to school. Henry comes in the daytime, but at night he has to stay with Ruth."

"Does Dad know about this?"

"No, and I don't want you to tell him."

"Why not?"

"The aunts don't want him to worry. Please, Bobby. In a day or two Ruth will be back, and Aunt Anne will be better. I'll come home then."

"OK. That's OK."

Looking at Celie, he notices how her hipbones stick out. She needs to eat more.

"Celie, I almost forgot. You got a letter from Mother. That's why I came," he says, and taking off his jacket, he pulls the letter from his sweater pocket and hands it to her.

Celie looks at it for a minute and lays it on the table.

"Aren't you going to read it?"

"Maybe later."

"Celia!"

"She had no business leaving. Now she's got that fancy job in Washington, and pretty soon you'll be leaving, too, and what about me? I can't leave! I'll be stuck here forever in this crummy town."

Now she's sounding more like the old Celia, and he's glad. One thing about Celia, she's got plenty of spunk.

"Mother wants us to come to Washington this summer. Celia, you can go up there."

"And what about you?"

"I've got to get into this War."

"You promised Mother you wouldn't volunteer."

"Maybe they'll draft me. I'm almost eighteen."

"Oh, Bobby, stay a little while. We could talk. We could play a game."

Looking at Celia, he considers this. He could stay all night. His father probably wouldn't notice. Celie looks thin. Like when she had rheumatic fever, and he thought she might die. "Celie, are you OK?" He puts his hand on her forehead.

"Bobby, yes! You sound like Mother! I'm fine. Do you think I'd be anywhere but in bed, being waited on, if I didn't feel good? Want to jitterbug?" she says grinning. "You promised you'd teach me."

"Celie, we'd wake up the chickens and the aunts."

She giggles. "I'll make you some cheese toast."

Now she looks OK. She's always been skinny. "No, thanks, Celie. I'm not hungry. I'm going on home."

"Bobby, it's cold. It's freezing out there."

Putting on his jacket, his hat, "I'll run all the way. Now you get to bed, and I'll see you tomorrow. I'll come by your locker first thing."

"Wait! Bobby, remember? Tomorrow's the last day of school before the Christmas holidays begin. We're having assembly."

"Gosh, Celie. Christmas. What a crazy Christmas!"

He looks at her a minute longer. Then he grins and steps
out into the cold.

Running, he begins to feel a little better. He *hadn't* thought
about Christmas. He would just as soon skip it. But Celie had
been glad to see him. It reminded him of when she was a little
kid, following behind him every step he took. He would check
on her tomorrow, check on the aunts, too. But Christmas. It
would be a hell of a Christmas.

· 2 ·

*I*T *is a hell of a Christmas,* Robert tells himself. Celia, Emily
and Anne not up to par. And Willie B. dragging around. But
Robert can't see that it would be much better if Barbara were
at home where she belongs. What could she do?

Then, just two days before Christmas it dawns on him. They
don't have a tree. He calls the janitor up to his office. "Moses,
get that tree out of the window, put it in the back of your
pickup and take it out to the house."

"You *un*-decorating the store?"

"No. I'm decorating my house," Robert says, trying for a
little humor, but Moses' expression doesn't change.

"I reckon you the boss," Moses says.

The tree hasn't helped. That afternoon when Celia wanders
over from the aunts and Bobby comes downstairs, they look at
the tree. Then they look at him.

"What's the matter?" he says.

"That's the store's tree," Bobby says.

"Those aren't our decorations. Dad, you know we have *our*
decorations. My first year, the kitten in the basket and Bobby's
little elves."

"Celia, if you know where the kitten is, get it! And get the dern elves! And put them on the tree!"

Their father never crosses Celia. Her blue eyes open wide. "Never mind," she says. "Just never mind."

Twenty minutes later she is downstairs with her little overnight suitcase, about worn out from traveling back and forth between the two houses. "I'm going over to the aunts," she says. "Will someone please drive me?"

"Go ahead, Bobby," their father says. "I want to hear the news."

When Bobby comes back, the radio is silent. His father steps outside, picks up the newspaper and brings it in. Then he turns on the radio, but it's *The Adventures of Ellery Queen*. Too late for the news.

By Christmas day, the Moore family knows it is going to be different. Their dinner, picked up from Bryce's cafeteria and delivered to the aunts' house, is good—delicious, really—but it doesn't taste quite like Ruth's cooking. For one thing, there's no oyster dressing.

"I'm fine," Anne says, when Robert asks. "But I just don't have my strength back."

"Aunt Emily, how about you?"

"I think I had a touch of the flu, Robert. But Celia's helped us so much."

"And the little thing can cook. She makes the best Cream of Wheat, doesn't she, Emily?"

"Yes, she does. And just having her running in and out has made a world of difference."

"At least Celie knows where the kitchen is over here," Bobby says, grinning at her.

Basking in the aunts' praise and Bobby's teasing, Celia smiles. When she does so, it occurs to Emily that she looks a lot like her father when she smiles. And seeing the deepening lines on his forehead, the hair a little grayer, she wonders when she last saw a smile on Robert's face, and realizing this, she wishes with all her heart they had invited Grace for Christmas dinner.

To Robert, the Christmas dinner seems much the same—the delicious food, Ruth's serving of it, the aunts hovering over him. And he is proud of the children. Bobby, obviously making an effort, has worn a jacket, and Celia is smiling at the aunts and giggling at Bobby's jokes.

Then, out of the clear blue sky, "I'm going to spend the summer in Washington with Mother," Celia says.

The aunts look sharply at each other.

"She wants me to come as soon as school is out," Celia continues, blithely unaware of the rising tension.

Aunt Anne coughs and takes a sip of water.

"What about you, Bobby?" Emily says.

"I'm not sure what I'll be doing."

Robert sits perfectly still as the conversation swirls around him. He feels outside it, an eavesdropper listening to a strange language. Thoughts, unrelated, mere fragments, drift into his mind. Vanish. A cranberry stain on the white cloth of the table. Bobby, fiddling with his fork. Celia, laughing at something he has said. The empty window at the store. The children. Gone. One way or another. And Barbara. Gone, too. The house forever empty of her teasing. The throaty laugh. The sway of her hips.

He groans aloud, realizes they are staring at him, straightens in his chair.

"Robert! What is it? What's the matter?" cries Emily, half-risen from her chair.

"Nothing," he says firmly. "It's just that the dinner was too good. A touch of indigestion."

That night, the aunts, having assured themselves that Celia is in bed, hold a whispered conference in the parlor.

"She was never the right one for him."

"He should have married Grace."

"Those people from up north. They're different. They just *are*."

"Well, everything's different now. Grace is divorced."

Divorced. The word, unpalatable, causes Anne to raise her handkerchief to her lips.

"Or soon will be," Emily says gamely.

"Robert could plead desertion."

"I'd go to court and swear."

"Oh, Emily, would you?" Anne leans over and pats her hand. "We'll invite Grace to dinner soon."

"Yes. A little party. Small. For Valentine's Day."

Thus satisfied and somewhat consoled, the two old aunties, brave conspirators, go through the house, turning out lights, and then they retire for the night.

· 3 ·

GRACE always spends Christmas with Emma. She loves to go there. Of all her friends, Emma is the most certain, *impudently* certain, Grace believes. In junior high, when Emma had announced she planned to marry and live in the country with a husband and animals and children, Grace had looked at her turned-up nose, *impudently* turned up, and laughed into the freckled face. But Emma, never doubting she would have the life she imagined, has it. Every detail. Down to buggy rides in snow-filled woods.

Always, when Grace turns her car toward Emma's at Christmas, her heart lifts. Days before, she has Christmas shopped for her godchild and namesake, now thirteen years old, and for the little boys. Driving to Paris, she enjoys the trees, bare-limbed against the sky, the fields yellowed by frost, migratory birds in flight, her enjoyment in the journey heightened by knowing what her welcome will be like. No matter when she arrives, the entire family will run out to greet her—the children, their parents, the dogs. Even Spot, the cat, usually shows his excitement by climbing a tree and meowing loudly. Every Christmas but one, the year she was married to Bucy, she has spent the holidays with Emma and her family.

And, now, here they are! Emma Grace, the first to reach the car, is opening the car door, taking her hand. "We couldn't wait for you to get here. Mother's so excited she forgot to put the roast in the oven."

Emma Grace. Tall. Gawky in oversize pants and sweater. And with braces and glasses. But the beauty is there, in the flawless complexion, the red hair thick and heavy as a mane, the vivid green eyes. Then the little boys ("Afterthoughts," Emma says. "Accidents," whispers Lacy) come running, William on short, stubby legs and Ben, toddling, falling, chortling, holding up arms to be picked up.

Grace picks him up and turns to receive Emma's hug.

"Let me look at you," Emma says. "Why, you've cut your hair!"

Grace lifts her hand, feels the curls. "What do you think?"

"I love it. It's so new."

"It's all right," Lacy says. "But, Emma, now don't you be getting ideas."

"We'll cut Emma's tonight," Grace teases.

"Right after supper," Emma says.

"Women!" And taking her bag from the car, Lacy strides ahead of them into the house.

Grace has always liked looking at Lacy. Why, she doesn't know. He's not handsome. In fact, his ears are too big and his chin recedes, but his expression is beneficent. She smiles when she looks at Lacy.

While Grace puts her presents under the tree, Emma Grace takes her bags up to Grace's room.

"We've got a buggy," William says, tugging at her skirt.

"And we're going to take you for a ride," Ben says.

Sweeping the small, warm baby up into her arms again, she asks, "Will Molly pull a buggy?"

Nodding solemnly, he touches her mouth, traces it with his hand.

"Molly's a natural," Lacy says, coming into the room, setting a drink of gin and grapefruit juice on a table by her side. "You'd think she's pulled a buggy all her life."

Coming in just behind her husband, Emma says, "This year, we've gone all out. An old-fashioned Christmas. Midnight Mass in town. Caroling earlier. And buggy rides through the woods."

"If the weather cooperates, it may be the *snow*-filled woods," Lacy says.

"It's perfect," Grace says, "whether it snows or not." She gives Ben a hug before putting him down.

While Emma and Lacy are getting supper on the table—late because of the roast—William and Ben arrange and rearrange the presents.

"I've got four," William says.

"I know I've got . . . William, how many do I got?" Ben says.

"Come on, you two," Emma Grace says. "We've got to feed the dogs."

Savoring surroundings as familiar as her own, Grace sinks into an easy chair. Emma's house seems much like Emma's marriage. Lots of rooms. Light pouring in. Spacious hallways. Books and magazines scattered about. Toys that have to be stepped over or gone around. A disorderly house, but humming with life.

Walking over to a table by the front windows, Grace looks down at the half-finished puzzle. Hundreds of pieces. A landscape. A burning sunset. Canyons. In the foreground, a flowering cactus.

"It's New Mexico," Emma says, coming to stand by her. "We've been working on this puzzle for weeks."

New Mexico. Of course. It looks just as she has imagined it.

"Grace, I'll round up the boys. Supper's ready," she says, adding with a wry grin, "if you like rare roast beef."

Once, Grace had planned to have a marriage like Emma's. Not perfect. But alive. Well, it could happen. She tries to imagine John here—feeding the horses, mending fences, bathing children.

Now, as Lacy comes to the table, he walks by Emma, gives her behind a comfortable smack and kisses her neck.

Be sensible, Grace tells herself. *Every marriage is different.* Hers and John's will have its own shape, its own house.

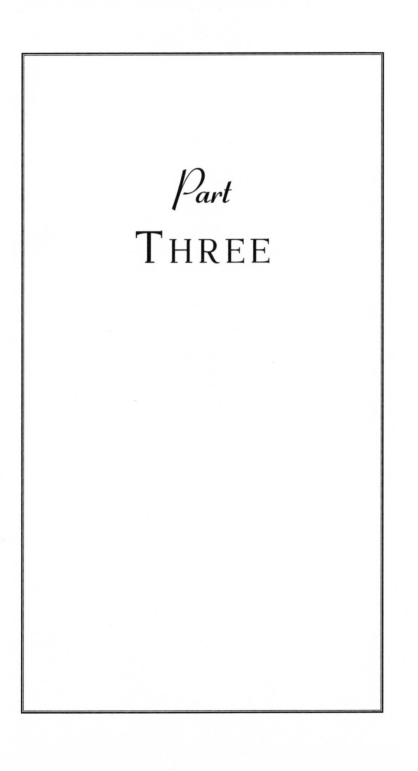

Part

THREE

Chapter 12

· *1* ·

ON a cold March day, but bright with sunshine, Grace Gillian, hurrying down to get the mail, is there before Mr. Bartlett can drop it into the mailbox. Mr. Bartlett thinks Mrs. Gillian is getting to be downright pretty, you might even say beautiful. When Mr. Bartlett first saw her hair, cut short and curly, well, by gosh, he barely recognized her. But now he likes it. Makes her look like a kid. And with those round, gray eyes! Mrs. Bartlett's cat is exactly the color of Mrs. Gillian's eyes.

"Morning, Mrs. Gillian," he says. "Got two letters here. Notice one's from Captain Appleby. This other's from overseas, too. Reckon it could be a local boy."

"Thank you, Mr. Bartlett," she says. Tearing one open, she plops down on her front porch steps to read it.

Noticing which letter she opens first, he ventures a comment: "Hope Captain Appleby will be coming home soon."

"What? Oh, he will be. It can't be long now," she says, waving the letter through the air, waving the postman away.

Dismissed, Mr. Bartlett plods down the narrow sidewalk, watching his step so as not to stumble on the places where old sycamore trees have pushed up the sidewalk. As he walks past the Appleby house (no mail here, of course), "Fancy that!" he says to himself. "Corresponding with her husband *and* Captain

Appleby. And now she's got another soldier on the string, so to speak." Well, two more hours and he'd be home. Thinking about the dinner that Mrs. Bartlett would have on the table and the talk they'd have along with it, he steps right along.

Grace unfolds John's letter, savoring all it will mean—gardening together, reading together, laughing. Sleeping together. How foolish to have thought she was past desire. She reads slowly:

> *Dear Grace,*
>
> *I will be home soon or, at least, back in the States. I am glad you have straightened out your life in New York.*
>
> *I have adopted a mutt—white with a black nose and black paws—whose spirits never flag, hence her name. I think I got the first part wrong. Flag has adopted me.*
>
> *I think of that night we were together. I don't know what it meant to you or to me. But when we see each other again, we can sort it out.*
>
> *As ever,*
> *John*

John will be coming home soon! And he remembers the night they made love! She imagines the homecoming—his embrace, his kisses, his passion. She feels light-headed. She reads the last: *We can sort it out.* Well, now. Here's a sentence to bring her to her senses. A business sentence. John's letters are always . . . ambiguous. *Like Bucy's lovemaking!* The thought pops into her mind. She examines it. Lovemaking and letter writing. She smiles at the idea of similarity. But what does John mean by *sort it out*? And closing his letter with *as ever*? What does that mean? John's letters are nice, but she wants . . . Oh, well. She's not sure what she wants. *Be sensible,* she tell herself. She expects too much from a man recently widowed and fighting a war.

Restlessly, she stands up. The street is empty. If Amelia were home, she would get up a tennis game. A good, fast game might help *her* sort a few things out! But Amelia and Ed have gone to Mount Pleasant to see about Ed's aunt, who fell off a ladder cleaning out her gutters.

Hurrying into the house, she bathes, slips on slacks, a faded blue blouse and tennis shoes, brushes her hair—*she does love it short*—and adds a touch of lipstick. Finding herself on the front porch again, she looks at her Buick, a nice little car, but with tires thin as tissue paper. But the day is too nice—clear sky and faint scent of green—to stay home.

Walking briskly past the Moore house, she notes the sparkling windows and clean-swept walkways. Since Barbara Moore went off to Washington, Robert's house looks lost. The *house* looks lost! And Grace cannot imagine why. Robert certainly keeps it as well as when his wife lived there. Maybe it's Bobby. For most of the semester, Bobby has looked as lost as anything could.

Turning the corner and crossing the alley, she smells the febrile, brackish odor of the open drainage ditches across Ninth Street.

"Morning." A voice floating out of the clear, blue sky. And there she is, Mrs. Balderidge—there!—on her little porch.

"Why, good morning, Mrs. Balderidge!" she says.

Mrs. Balderidge wears a shapeless gray dress and a black shawl with roses on it. Her hair is twisted into a knot on top of her head. Although she looks quite orderly, she still seems *unusual*. It's in her eyes—an amazed expression, as if she's just stepped from another world into this one.

"Mrs. Balderidge, isn't this a beautiful day!" Grace says.

Mrs. Balderidge stands and, leaning over the porch railing, looks up at the sky. "It is!" she says, as if surprised at the beauty of the sky, surprised that there even is a sky. And then Mrs. Balderidge smiles!

Oh, the wonder of it! Grace thinks. *Mrs. Balderidge smiling and saying good morning.*

Lifting her hand in a wave, Grace continues her walk. And now Grace, thinking of Mrs. Balderidge, smiles so widely that folks driving past look back at her, commenting to each other: "Miz Gillian's mighty happy about something. Maybe Mr. Gillian's coming home."

After lunch, Grace turns away from English themes that need marking and goes out into the garden. Buoyed by Mrs. Balderidge's smile, she digs, hauls compost, mulches, snips, plucks. In late afternoon she drags the hose around and waters until the newly fertilized beds are black puddles. How she loves this work—the solitude, the rewards, the *introversion* of gardening.

Upstairs she gets out of her gardening clothes, slips on a robe and pads barefoot into the kitchen. She pours whiskey and water into a glass, adds ice and flips on the radio. "I'll be seeing you in all the old familiar places," Jo Stafford sings. Grace has come to think of this as *their* song, hers and John's. Twirling the ice in her glass, moving to the music, Grace sways into the gallery. Gazing out over her backyard, instead of puddled beds, she sees bowers of roses and hollyhock blossoms on tall, slender stems along the fence and clumps of daisies under the oaks and wood violets scattered about under fallen leaves. She thinks: *John will soon be here, in this place. He'll be sitting in the middle of the swing with his arms outstretched across the back, and he'll smile as I come down the path to sit beside him.*

Not until she steps into the kitchen does she notice the other letter, still unopened, on the dining table. She opens a can of tomato soup, butters a slice of bread. Waiting for the toast to brown, she reads:

Dear Grace,

I do not think I can talk about the War. Ever. But I want to tell you this. I sat by a young man yesterday as he lay dying. I was walking through the field hospital when I saw him. Thinking it was Private Russell, the young boy we met on the train, I stopped. He had the same coloring— white hair and eyebrows—and I sat down by him. It was not Russell, but he squeezed my hand as if he knew me.

While I watched his fingernails take on a bluish cast, I told him he was going to make it. I said I'd write his mother. Morphine eased his going, but when he breathed his last I cried like a baby.

It's cold here now. I keep dreaming that one day you'll look up and there I'll be and there you'll be and the warm fire between us.

I know this sounds crazy, but I write it because I must, because I love you.

Dan Manning

By the time she reads the letter again, she has begun to cry. A boy. Like Private Russell. Away from home for the first time. Away from his mother. And (she feels sure of it), with a young girl's picture in his billfold.

Sniffing the air, she remembers the toast. The toast is burning! Grabbing a hot pad, she opens the oven door and sees that the toast is on fire! She takes it out of the oven, dumps it into the sink, douses it with cold water.

She takes up the letter and reads it again, reads the last paragraph again. *But he can't love me or even think he loves me,* she tells herself. At ten o'clock, she listens to the late news. Led by a young lieutenant (*Was it the young lieutenant on the train?* she wonders. *Could it have been?*), the army has crossed the Rhine River, using a railroad bridge that had not been blown. The tide has turned. The Allies are winning. But at what a terrible cost! At least she knows Sergeant Manning is not dead. But what about Private Russell and Lieutenant Smith? And, of course, John.

She needs to write Sergeant Manning a letter, honest but friendly, warm but restrained. A soldier doesn't need a Dear John letter. But after twenty minutes she tosses her crumpled attempts into the wastebasket. Leaving the unmarked papers for another time, she makes herself another piece of toast and heats the soup. After she eats, she falls into bed.

Awakened by her doorbell in the middle of the night, she is out of bed and reaching for her robe before she realizes it has been a dream. About the Sergeant. A nightmare. *But if something happened to Dan Manning, they wouldn't come here. They wouldn't come to my door,* she tells herself. *But where would they go to say Sergeant Manning has been wounded or is missing in action? Or dead?*

Be sensible. Dan Manning is just fine, she tells herself. She gets out of bed, goes into the bathroom and splashes cold water on her face. Patting it dry, she wonders: *Why Dan?* Getting back in bed, she thinks, *How crazy!* Dreaming about a man she hardly knows.

She thinks about the train filled with soldiers and about Dan Manning and Lieutenant Smith and Private Russell so long that dawn is breaking before she falls asleep again.

· 2 ·

ROBERT Moore had not considered attending the funeral. But when Bobby said he was going and Celia said she was going, he thought it would be better if he went along with them. Now he's glad he came, although he knows it's going to be a long service. Colored services are always long. With the singing and the sermons and the praying, they will be here at least another hour. Old Hardey's speaking now. Seems to have thought a lot of her. Sitting here, listening now and then, his mind drifts off in a thousand directions.

He wishes to God Bobby had not found her! If only Bobby had not been the one. Funny. That very day he had thought about coming home at noon to see if he had received a letter from Barbara. He does that occasionally. After all, she writes the children. She even writes Willie B., but she has never answered *his* letter. He wrote it soon after she left and told her he was sorry she had not understood their financial situation. He even asked her to reconsider her actions and come home. But she had not replied.

But Bobby *had* found her. And called Mrs. Gillian, called his English teacher, and *then* he called his father.

"Dad, she's dead," he said.

He had rushed home to find Mrs. Gillian and Bobby (Bobby crying like a little kid) huddled together on the kitchen steps. He ran inside and saw her. She was at the kitchen table, looking like she had just put her head down and gone to sleep. Even though he knew she was dead, he felt for a pulse before he called the River Jordan Funeral Home.

It was a bad scene all the way around, Bobby crying and Grace looking at him like he was somehow to blame.

"Son, get hold of yourself," he said.

Grace frowned at him. *Hush!* the frown said.

So they sat and waited for the colored hearse in silence, except for Bobby's hurt whimpering like a dog that's been shut out in the cold. And his hiccups. When the hearse came, he had walked out with Old Hardey to offer to pay the funeral expenses. "Hardey, I know you'll be reasonable," he said.

"Yes, sir! Reasonable. Sure will be reasonable," he had answered.

And, as far as Robert can tell, he has been. He wonders if anyone has written Barbara that he, Robert Moore, is paying every cent of Willie B.'s funeral expenses.

To look at Bobby and Celia now, you'd think Willie B. had been a member of the family. When the choir sings "Roll, Jordan, Roll," tears stream down his son's face. He pulls a handkerchief from his pocket and hands it to Bobby. After the hymn, there's the Lord's Prayer, and Robert finds himself praying, *devoutly* praying, that Bobby would get over this spell of his and Celia's heart would be strong and, most fervently, that Barbara would come to her senses!

Then the sermon, he supposes it is called a sermon, begins, and Reverend Pleasant is talking about Willie B.'s devoted husband, a brave soldier fighting somewhere in Europe, and about her fine nephews and nieces, reminding him of how proud he, Robert Moore, used to be of *his* family! Just a few months ago (what seems like years now), his family was a whole lot like *One Man's Family*. When things weren't too busy at the hardware store, he would sometimes turn on the little radio in his office and listen to *One Man's Family*. The children and the mother always came to the father for advice, wisdom, that sort of thing. Listening to his wise, calm voice, Robert would tell himself that he might use those very words, that same wisdom, should Celia or Bobby or even Barbara come to him with a problem.

But, since Celia has practically moved over to the Little Brontës', and with Bobby coming home at all hours of the day or night, what kind of family does he have now? Just this week Jim Baker, his first cousin once removed, had stopped by the store to tell him that on the way home from a poker game, he had seen Bobby, *in his cups* was the expression the old man used, spouting poetry on the corner of Broad Street and Main. Poetry! Makes him wonder about Grace Gillian. He has heard she is getting a divorce. Well, who could blame her! Bucy Gillian was never the right man for her! No, sir! The thought crosses his mind that Grace might not be the best influence on Bobby. But then, *Nonsense!* he tells himself. Grace is flighty, but she's not a bad influence. Grace knows how to make people happy. And what can be better than that?

After the prayers the choir sings "In That Great Gettin' Up Good Mornin'," and it seems to him that with their joyful singing and clapping and swaying, the choir is singing to his own sad heart. And that the colored people, smiling at him and nodding to him and crying and singing, know the burden he carries and know the mistakes he's made and love him, yes, *love* him, anyway. His eyes fill with tears. Fumbling for his own handkerchief before realizing that Bobby still has it, he bows his head and prays: *God, help me! Oh, Lord, hear my prayer. Dear God, hear my prayer.*

· 3 ·

BOBBY reads the newspaper every morning. He props it up behind his cereal bowl and reads so he won't have to talk to his father. This morning, he picks the newspaper up from the driveway, and going up the steps, he looks at the front page. MacArthur has announced that Manila has fallen and five thousand prisoners have been freed. And right beside that: *Matt Robinson is dead!* Matt Robinson! Everybody likes Matt. Always smiling. Leading cheers at football games, seeing everybody in the stands when he led the cheers. *Come on, Jeff. Hey, Bobby! Help me out here! Let's hear it for our team! Come on, Betty Lou.* One time somebody nominated Matt's kid brother to be president of the senior class, nominated this sophomore kid for a joke. Everybody laughed. But Matt stood up and voted for his little brother. The class cheered. The War almost over and Matt dead.

With the War almost over, Matt shouldn't be dead.

He cannot believe it. A kid just a couple of years older than him, dead! Forgetting they hardly ever talk, he calls up the stairs, "Dad, Matt Robinson has been killed. In Germany, I guess. Did you know that?"

His father, frowning, comes slowly down the stairs. "I know it, son. Dick Morris told me about it yesterday." Standing at the foot of the stairs, he carefully hangs his coat over the newel post. "I know your mother will be upset over this. Why don't you write her a note today? Or tell you what," his father pauses, crosses his arms, taps his lip with a forefinger, "why don't you call her tonight? She doesn't know about Willie B. either. She would want to know about her maid."

His father's voice cracks, like he's about to cry. Their family never calls long distance. Not unless it's an emergency. Bobby's eyes fill with tears. Fine navy man he'll be. *Get hold of yourself, son.* He can hear his father saying it.

"Why didn't you tell me? You could have told me."

"I went to bed before you got in. I guess I thought you knew. Bobby, I want to talk to you tonight."

He sounds tired. And Bobby knows what he wants to talk to him about. Bobby had seen Judge Baker drive by the corner of Main and Broad Street the other night. Well, he hadn't seen him, but Schuster had been sober enough to see him and had pulled Bobby back inside the car, both of them laughing like crazy.

Suddenly, he is mad at his father, mad at Willie B. for dying, mad at his mother for leaving and most of all mad about the War. "Well, what about it?" he says now. "How many more kids have to die before it's over?"

His father slowly pulls a chair away from the breakfast table. "Bobby, I just don't know," he says. Sitting in the chair, he leans forward and clasps his hands together. "I guess it's hard to work out an orderly peace."

"Well, nothing's orderly around here," Bobby says, pouring cold milk on cold cereal.

"Everything would be more orderly if we had a maid. We need to find someone to take Willie B.'s place."

"Who in the hell do you think could take her place?" Jumping up from the table, Bobby knocks over his chair and, without stopping to straighten it, storms outside.

"Son, I'm sorry about Willie B!" his father says, standing in the open doorway. "I know you thought a lot of her." Now he's standing in the open doorway and shouting: "Son, I'm sorry!"

Bobby can't believe his father, causing all this and standing

there saying he's sorry. What's *sorry?* What good does it do to
be sorry? Without turning his head, Bobby walks to the end of
the driveway and sits on the curb to wait for Schuster.

In first period history that morning, Miss Speed talks about
the Civil War, and he thinks about Matt. Then, toward the end
of the period he starts to think about Dixie and her dancing
and the way she walks, like a song, and her big brown eyes behind her glasses, and her firm, little breasts. And now he's hard,
so hard he hopes to hell the bell doesn't ring. He is still in love
with her. He must be. To cool off, he thinks about algebra.
Then about Zelle. He's been thinking about her a lot lately. He
likes Zelle, but he doesn't *know her ways.* If he did, would he
fall in love with her? *Love.* He thinks about that a lot, too. During algebra, he decides to go over to Dixie's to see if he still
loves her.

When he steps up onto Dixie's porch, the sky is a soft gray
color with streaks of purple just over the treetops, and Dixie is
playing "Deep Purple." He feels this has some deep significance for him—the purple sky and Dixie playing that particular
song—but he isn't sure what the significance is. He listens for a
minute before he knocks. But it is Mrs. Balderidge who comes
to the door.

"Mrs. Balderidge, I didn't know you played. I thought it
was Dixie."

"Dixie's not here," she says. Then she looks right at him
and smiles. He has never seen Mrs. Balderidge smile, but even
with a broken tooth her face looks nice, smiling.

He says, "It sounded nice. Could I sit out here and wait for
Dixie? I'd like to see her for a few minutes."

"Yes," she says. Then she pushes the screen door open and
comes all the way out on the porch. "I have a job. Mr. Moore
helped me get it."

"You mean my father? My father helped you?"

"Yes." Mrs. Balderidge turns to go back inside. Then she
hesitates. "You can wait for Dixie."

Before he sits down, Mrs. Balderidge is playing again. She plays "Danny Boy," and "Roamin' in the Gloamin'," and "The Isle of Capri," old songs that people went around singing before the War. He thinks about his father, helping Mrs. Moore. That's hard to believe. He looks up at the bright moon and thinks about the music and Mrs. Balderidge and his father. After a while it gets to be chilly, and he wishes he had a sweater.

When Pearce and Dixie turn into the alley, Bobby cannot believe how calm Pearce acts. "Hey, Pearce," he says. And then, getting it in before Pearce decides to hit him or something, he says, "I'm just sitting here listening to Mrs. Balderidge play the piano."

But Pearce doesn't seem worried. Or even interested in why Bobby's sitting on the steps waiting for his wife. He says, "Hey, Cinco. Come on, man. Let's go get a beer."

"I've got to go on home."

"Well, next time, maybe," he says, and gets in the car and leaves without kissing Dixie or even saying good-bye.

Dixie, her hands in her sweater pockets, watches Pearce back out of the alley and drive away. Then she comes on up the steps.

"Hi, Bobby."

"I thought I'd stop by. See how you were."

She shakes her head. "Not too good. Jack's folks are about to die. You know they promised him a Ford convertible when the War ends if he'd get a divorce."

"Is he going to?"

"He hasn't decided."

"Oh, Dixie." He puts his arms around her and pulls her close.

"He loves me. He does! I know he does!"

And now she is in his arms and crying so quietly that he only knows she is crying because he feels her shaking. *Oh, Dixie. Have you ever been happy? Will you ever be happy?* he wonders.

He reaches in his pocket for a handkerchief, then remembers he hasn't kept a handkerchief since Willie B. died.

Stepping away from him, Dixie leans to wipe her eyes on the hem of her skirt. Sniffing a little, she says, "Did you know Mama has a job?"

"Yes, she told me."

"Your father helped her get it."

"I'm glad," he says, feeling a surge of warmth toward his father.

"She's working for Judge Baker. He's lost three housekeepers in a row. They've all gone to work at the defense plant."

"I hope she likes it."

"She does. She'll be fine if . . ."

"If what?"

"I just hope my daddy never comes back!"

"I know."

"Bobby, you don't know."

"Yes, I do. I heard him one night, the night he left to join the army. He sounded—*it* sounded real bad."

She nods. "If he tries to come back, I won't let him. I'll kill him before he comes in our house again."

"Dixie! You don't mean that!"

"Yes, I do. I mean it." Then, after a minute, she giggles. "But I don't know what I'd kill him with. We don't have a gun. And the only butcher knife we have won't cut butter. I guess I wouldn't kill him."

Bobby laughs.

"Well, he can't come back. That's all." She puts her hand on his cheek and pats it. "I've got to go. I write Jack a letter every night."

"See you."

"Well, good night now," she says, and steps inside and closes the door. He stands a minute and hears her voice and her mother's, like a little duet or something.

Opening his back door he remembers he was going to call

his mother. But it's late and the house his dark. He'll do it tomorrow.

"Bobby!"

"Where are you?"

"In the living room."

Bobby switches on a light inside the living room. His father is sitting in his chair, blinking up at him through red-rimmed eyes.

"At least you're not drunk," he says. "I've been waiting for you to come home. Now go in there and call your mother."

"Dad, it's too late. I'll call her in the morning."

"Go out there and call her. Now!" his father shouts, jumping up and pushing Bobby before him out into the hallway.

"Dad," he protests.

His father lifts the receiver. "Long distance," he says. Then, "Operator, I would like to speak with Mrs. Robert Moore in Washington, D.C. No, I don't have the number. She lives in Georgetown." When he hears the operator ringing the number, he hands Bobby the receiver. "Talk. Talk to your mother!" he commands before wheeling back into the living room.

Trembling with anger, Bobby holds the receiver to his ear. His father has not touched him since he was six or seven. And now he's pushing him! He's crazy!

"Hello."

It's her. It's his mother. He presses the receiver to his ear. Hard. "Mother, you've got to come home."

"Bobby, it's wonderful, so wonderful to hear your voice." She sounds happy and excited.

"Mother, you've got to come home now. Please!"

"Bobby, I can't right now. My work is important. You'll finish school in six weeks or so. You can come up here for the summer. Celia, too!" Her voice has a lilt.

"Mother, Willie B. died. Here. In the kitchen."

His throat closes as he says these words. His mother does not speak. In the silent hum of the telephone he can hear her thinking. Then, "Oh," she breathes softly. "Oh, Bobby."

"You promised her you'd come home if she died in our house," he says. "I heard you tell her that. You promised Willie B."

"I know. I know I did. But I can't come home just now. Bobby, you don't understand. There are so many reasons. Anyway, I can't even think about it until the War is over. Bobby, tell me about Celia. How's your father?"

Hopelessly, he drops the receiver, leaves it dangling and stumbles upstairs to bed.

Chapter 13

· 1 ·

GRACE sits on her gallery to read the letter from John. And the two she has received from Dan Manning. The air is full of the scent of wild plum blossoms and the sound of a mocking-bird perched in the topmost branch of the live oak. John's letter is filled with his concern for her. He urges her to continue doing the things she enjoys—her teaching, her reading, her tennis. *No mention of dancing.* The thought makes her smile. And he warns her against rushing impulsively into friendships. He says that he misses her. Then, the last paragraph:

> *Grace, dear, you know where the house key is. Everything is just as I left it. Do go through Anna's things and take anything you like. There's a mink coat. And an evening dress she bought for the Christmas dance at the club. Never worn, poor thing. The tags still on it.*

Oh, John, she thinks. She crumples up the letter and drops it on the dining room table. She drinks a glass of water. From the gallery she looks down into her garden. She turns and looks across the living room and into the dining room at the crumpled paper in the middle of the table. Small. Innocuous, really.

But it is this that she cannot imagine: herself acquisitive. Going through Anna's things. Picking. Choosing.

Oh, John, it won't do. It just won't do, she thinks.

She walks twice around the block. At home, she tosses the crumpled letter into the wastebasket.

For supper, she puts a potato in the oven, broils a small steak, fixes a green salad. She refuses to think about John's letter.

After supper, she reads Dan Manning's letters. They are full of dreams. They, Dan and Grace, will be married and live on his ranch in New Mexico and ride horses over the red mesas and arroyos into the sunsets, sunsets that are gorgeous beyond belief. He writes, "How do I love thee? Let me count the ways." Then he writes that he loves the way her lips curl trembling just before she smiles; loves the color of her hair that he longs to see unpinned and hanging softly; loves the sound of her voice that, somehow, reminds him of bees in a honey glade; loves her eyes that grow larger, more luminous, when her heart is touched. He will come to her, as the knights of old, and he will kneel before her and ask for her hand in marriage. In bed that night, she reads them again and falls into a sound sleep.

But the next afternoon, another letter. From Dan:

> *I am in the hospital. Nothing serious, but I'll be on crutches for a while. My days in the army are over, I'm afraid. But in another way my life is just beginning. I may be here a couple of months. But as soon as they release me, I am coming to Cold Springs.*

Dan Manning is wounded! Wounded and coming to Cold Springs! But if he's on crutches, his wounds can't be too serious. But she hardly knows what to think about his coming to Cold Springs. She likes Dan Manning. She's thought about him many, many times.

But John is the man she loves.

Driving to school the next morning, she carefully calls forth the night of lovemaking with John. She will not allow it to fade. By the time she sees him, his last letter, meant only to be a generous offer, will have been forgotten. She flips on the radio. Betty Grable is singing "Oh, Give Me Something to Remember You By." *And Dan has my handkerchief.* The thought comes unbidden, and she flips off the radio.

When she turns into the school parking lot on Monday, she hears the sound of sirens. Police cars, their lights flashing, screech to a halt in the street. Astonished, she sits a minute. Frozen. A crowd of students has gathered on the south side of the building. Something has happened. She's been expecting something to happen. The students are pointing, waving, shouting, their faces turned upward, toward a second-story window. Then she sees Mr. Albertson! Mr. Albertson upside down and hanging from the second-story window! Hands hold him there. Hands on his feet, his ankles, his knees. She leaps from her car, runs to the east end door, flies up the stairs and into the room to find what looks to be the football squad, at least four of them, holding Mr. Albertson upside down from the second-story window.

Leaning past Jack Pearce, she grasps Mr. Albertson's belt. "Help me," she says.

As effortlessly as if they were lifting a football, Mr. Albertson is retrieved and carefully placed on his feet. Pale, sweating, breathing heavily, the small man stands there. Slowly, he turns to look directly into each boy's face. When he looks at Jack Pearce, Jack leans forward as if to straighten the teacher's tie or smooth his hair, but Mr. Albertson knocks the hand away.

"What are you doing?" Grace asks. Her eyes flashing, she angrily grasps Joe Mobley's arm. "Steve! Joe, what are you do-ing? Morris! Jack, are you crazy? Bobby, what is all this?"

Steve Schuster looks at Grace, looks down. "We weren't gonna hurt him," he says.

Mr. Albertson takes a deep breath. He smoothes his hair,

straightens his tie with trembling hands, but his voice is firm
when he speaks. "I'll see the four of you in Mr. Lawson's office.
Now," he says. And as an afterthought, he adds, "You, too,
Bobby."

When the boys leave, Mr. Albertson pulls a handkerchief
from his pocket and wipes his forehead. "Whew," he says.

"Are you all right?"

"They scared the hell out of me. Grace, it's a good thing
you came in here. If they hadn't dropped me, I'd have died
from a heart attack." Spent, he sits shakily on his desk.

Now, Miss Speed and Mrs. Crane, and then Miss Dolby
are hurrying into the room as quickly as their high heels will
allow. Dorothy Speed, always calm, always deliberate, is breathless with excitement. "Did you fall? What happened? A dizzy
spell?"

"Those boys didn't push you, did they?" Mrs. Crane says,
disbelief in her voice.

"Are you all right?" Miss Dolby asks.

"I'm OK. Or I will be as soon as those young fools are out
of this school. This was no accident. They were mad. Yesterday,
I told them they would not get credit for algebra this year, and
they would not be graduating with their class. They came to
school this morning 'to show me,' as Joe Mobley put it. They
were drinking. Not a one of them would have been a party to it
if he hadn't been drunk."

"They failed algebra?"

"They cheated. Too lazy to study for a test, they cheated,
and every one of them came up with identical but wrong answers. Arrogant hoodlums!"

"They thought that because of the War—" Mrs. Crane
begins.

"Exactly," says Mr. Albertson.

By the time the tardy bell rings, all five boys have been
expelled and are in the two police cars on their way to the
police station for questioning and, possibly, to face further

charges. Mr. Albertson—slight, balding, his shoulders hunched with age—is at the blackboard explaining an algebra problem to the remainder of his senior algebra class.

· 2 ·

WHEN the sheriff unlocks the cell door, they file in. The fetid, dank smell of the small concrete room overpowers them so that they cough, pull shirts and undershirts up over their noses. The sheriff slams the door and noisily locks it.

"Too bad we only got this one cell open," he says. "But I won't insult that soldier down the hall by putting any of the likes of you in the cell with him."

Bobby hopes the sheriff hasn't noticed him. He can't remember his name, but the sheriff's wife used to be his Sunday school teacher. He turns his face away, but then Pearce calls, "Sir? Oh, sir!"

"What is it?" The sheriff stops, frowns over his shoulder. The frown pulls his black eyebrows together in a thick, straight line across his forehead.

"I'd like to see my lawyer. Please," Pearce adds.

The sheriff grins, wriggling his black mustache. "You won't be seeing anybody tonight."

Uneasily, they watch the broad back of the sheriff move down the short hall, turn the corner and disappear.

"The smell!" Mobley says, and suddenly turning, hand over his mouth, he retches, vomiting into a corner of the bare cell.

"What'd you do that for?" Pearce says.

"Get off his back," Schuster says. "He couldn't help it."

"He could have used that bucket."

"I didn't see it." Mobley says, falling onto a cot, holding his head in his hands.

Bobby stands at the window, looking down on Spruce Street. After a while Schuster comes to stand beside him. They watch as, below, people wait for the light to change. They cross the street. They go into stores and they come out.

"Everything's different now," Bobby says. He takes off his old hat, swats his leg with it and replaces it.

Schuster shrugs broad shoulders. "The sky's the same. Maybe a few more clouds. But nobody's worried about us. They don't care about us now."

"What do you think they'll do to us?" Mobley says, hunched over on the cot, his voice muffled by his hands.

"They'll keep us here for a long time, maybe a year," Morris says. He pulls out a handkerchief and noisily blows his nose.

"Cinco, isn't Judge Baker kin to you?" Jack Pearce asks.

"Sort of. A cousin, or something."

"Couldn't you talk to him?"

"No. I'd rather stay in jail."

"Why not?"

"You heard him," Schuster said. "He won't talk to the judge."

After a while Morris sits with Mobley on the single bunk bed, and Schuster and Pearce sit on the floor, their backs against the wall. Bobby remains at the single window until all the light is gone from the sky. Then, sliding down the wall to sit on the floor, he remembers that Mr. Balderidge had slid down the wall the same way. He wonders if Mr. Balderidge has ever been in jail.

Sometime in the night, Mobley clears his throat and coughs. "I think I'm taking a cold. Would they let me out with pneumonia?"

"No," Morris says.

"Maybe we can think up some story to tell the judge."

"Like what?" Pearce says.

"I don't know. Maybe we could say Albertson fell, and we caught him."

"Maybe we could say he tried to hit Pearce, missed and stumbled." Schuster grins. "Stumbled out the window!"

Then they are laughing, holding their sides, clutching each other, laughing until they have to catch their breath.

Schuster says, "Well, we're in a hell of a mess now. Disgraced."

Sobered by the cold truth, the room fills with despair and silence until, under the burden of it all, they sleep.

As soon as first light comes through the small window above Bobby's head, they begin to stir. They stretch, cough and, one by one, urinate into the bucket in the corner. Mobley gags again, but nothing comes up.

The first one to speak, Morris says, "They won't take criminals."

"What?" Pearce says.

"They won't take criminals. Nobody will."

"Oh, man," Pearce cries, "my dad just about died when me and Dixie got married. My mother said he aged ten years that night. This will just about kill him."

They stare wide-eyed at each other, the thought of not being able to wear a uniform and fight for their country too terrible to bear. After that nobody says anything except, "It's hot," and "Wish somebody would come," and "It stinks like hell in here."

In the middle of the morning the sheriff unlocks the cell, handcuffs them and takes them over to the courthouse. When they come into the room, Bobby sees his father, with all the other fathers, talking to Judge Baker. When Bobby comes in, his father does not look at him. When he does look up, he says, "Take off your hat." Not "Bobby, take off your hat," or "Son, take off your hat." Just "Take off your hat." Then he sees the handcuffs. "Oh," he says, and then his face crumples.

Judge Baker asks each one: "Did you commit bodily assault on Mr. Albertson by hanging him out the window?" And they all say, "Yessir." But when Bobby says, "Yessir," Schuster says, "No, you didn't, Cinco. You didn't lay a hand on Mr. Albertson."

"Bobby Moore?" Judge Baker says.

"I didn't try to help."

Judge Baker nods. "The school has decided, rightly, that you will not be allowed to graduate. You have already been expelled. In addition, you will each be paroled to your fathers for the remainder of the school term. You will have an eight o'clock curfew until the school term ends. At some time during the next weeks, you will each stand before Mr. Albertson and humbly beg his pardon. I do not think he will accept it. But your fathers have said they will see that you do this."

The judge leans back in his chair and looks at them. His eyes narrow; his deep voice fills the room. "I know your fathers," he says. "I know your mothers. What you have done is cowardly. It is despicable. It is dishonorable. You have disappointed your families, your friends and your school. It is up to you to redeem yourselves. You will have to find a way to do this."

As they leave the courtroom, Bobby's father says grimly, "Your mother will be sorely grieved over this."

Bobby does not answer. He knows this will break her heart. And what's worse is that when she hears about it, she will probably come home. Sacrificing herself to come home to live with a man she hates. Thinking this, his heart sinks into a blackness from which there is no escape.

· 3 ·

THE sound of gravel tossed against his window wakes Bobby. He raises the window, leans out. "Schuster?"

"Come on down, Cinco."

Bobby goes downstairs, opens the kitchen door and steps outside. "Schuster, what's up?"

"We're going to Little Rock. We're joining up."

"Joining what?"

"What difference does it make?"

"Man, what time is it?"

"About two, I guess. Come on, Cinco. Grab a few things. Pearce has the car down the street."

"I don't know, Schuster."

"Cinco, come on!" And then, in the cadence of a march, "We few, we happy few, we band of brothers!" he chants.

"For he today that sheds his blood with me shall be my brother," Bobby finishes. Then, "Give me ten minutes," he says.

So. Here they are, these five: Mobley and Morris, who had already planned to join as soon as they graduated; and Pearce, who had been too frightened to join when he eloped with Dixie (and wasn't that courage enough for a while?); and Schuster, who yearns only to redeem himself. And Bobby, terrified one minute nobody will take him and the next sure that somebody will.

When it's good daylight, they stop at the Green Pastures Restaurant. They order ham and eggs and biscuits and gravy. "Eat up, men," Schuster says. "This may be the last good breakfast we'll have for a while."

A black woman brings their orders, moving easily, lightly, in spite of her huge bulk. "You boys been drafted?"

"No, but we're joining the marines."

"Thought so. Your folks know about this?" And in the silence that follows she says, "Thought not. Just can't wait, can you? My boy did the same thing. What you're doing. He ain't coming back."

After that, they eat quietly and leave. But by the time they get to Little Rock, their excitement has reached a feverish pitch. Walking up the steps of the courthouse, "We few, we happy few, we band of brothers!" they shout.

Inside they see the tables, a recruitment officer behind each one.

Suddenly serious, "You guys go ahead," Pearce says. "I'll be back in a minute."

By the time Mobley and Morris have signed the papers, they know Pearce isn't coming back. But then, just as Schuster steps forward, here he is, breathing heavily, grinning. He says, "I called and left a message for Mr. Lawson. I said we were joining the marines."

Bobby is the last. Stepping forward and pulling his hat down, he turns his face to the left.

"You got a crick in your neck, son?"

"Yessir."

"Take off your hat," the recruiting officer says. He gets up and moves around the desk. "Look at me," he says. He holds up a pencil. "Keep your eyes on this," he says, moving the pencil from the left to the right and up and down.

"I can see just fine," Bobby says.

Shaking his head, frowning, the officer says, "You're wasting our time. Son, go on home."

Finally. He has known it would come to this. But he has never let himself think about what would happen when they said, "Son, go on home."

He puts his old fedora back on his head, pulls the brim down low and turns to face the others. "I'll see you, guys. Good luck," he says hoarsely.

"Oh, man," Schuster wails.

Then Bobby is off and running, leaving the four to stand helplessly watching him go. Twenty minutes later, he is out on Highway 270 thumbing a ride up north.

Chapter 14

LIKE wildfire, the news had spread. The boys have redeemed themselves. At least, they have begun their redemption. On April 12, the day President Roosevelt died, four of them had joined the marines. They had driven to Shreveport or, some said, Oklahoma City to join. They would soon be in uniform and fighting in the Pacific. They have sought redemption and found a form of it. All except Bobby. Nobody has seen Bobby in over two weeks.

Mr. Bartlett had brought the news to Grace, finishing with, "And it's a shame. I says to Mrs. Bartlett, 'When those kids ran off, they probably didn't even know the President was dead.' Well, it's a good thing they joined up. They'd have had to leave town if they hadn't. At least now they can come back home with their heads held high *if* they make it through the War. Young Robert Moore went with them, but with that eye and all, a'course they wouldn't take him."

Then he handed her a letter, postmarked Lawton, Oklahoma. From Bobby. No more than a note, really. Retreating from Mr. Bartlett's curious eyes, she goes inside the house to read it:

Dear Mrs. Gillian,
  *I am all right. I'm hitchhiking around Oklahoma. I
don't want my mother to come home to see about me.*
                                   Bobby

She had taken it immediately to his father. Sitting on the settle bench in his entrance hall, she handed it to Robert.

Robert read it and sighed. "He's always been different."

"Yes," she agreed. "Finer than most."

The next week, Robert received a note, postmarked Enid,
Oklahoma:

Dad,
  I don't want Mother to come home because of me. Tell her.
                                   Bobby

Robert had come immediately to Grace's house. Wordlessly,
he handed her the note.

"Robert, you look terrible," she said. "Enid is not that far.
For goodness' sakes!"

"He wanted very much to get into the War. I don't know
what will happen to him now."

"Bobby will be all right. He'll figure it out. Eventually. But
I'm not sure about you. Go to Washington. Go see your wife."

"I don't know. Sometimes, I think I don't even know my
son. He went to Mr. Sandflat's funeral, for god's sake! He didn't
even know Mr. Sandflat."

"Robert, go see your wife," she said gently.

He looked at her for a long minute. "I will." He nodded.
"You're right. That's exactly what I'm going to do."

· 2 ·

OVERNIGHT, the weather turns cold. The wind blowing cold drops of rain. Then it clears. It is almost balmy when Grace steps outside her back door. "Cal," she calls. "Kitty, kitty, kitty. Come here, Cal."

No matter how much she feeds Cal, he proudly brings his kill to her doorstep. Usually, it's a mouse. But in the spring, she often finds bird feathers scattered about. Yesterday, she had found the feathers of a blue jay. "Oh, Cal," she had said reproachfully, as he sat, satisfied, twitching his tail.

This evening, Cal comes empty-handed. Relieved, she sets a saucer of milk on the bottom step and looks up at the moon. It is almost full tonight and as beautiful as if the world were whole again and at peace. Then she sees him, a bundle of misery, in her swing. She knows immediately who it is. She has thought he would come.

Even in the moonlight, he looks tired and dirty. Spent. *Oh, where have you been, Billy Boy?* The song comes unbidden. She walks out to the swing. "Oh, Bobby," she says, and sits beside him.

He doesn't move. Waiting, she hears a dove. In the night the trees are black sculptures, their shadows strong in moonlight.

After a while, Bobby straightens, puts one foot on the ground. Hugging the other leg, he puts his chin on his knee.

"Mrs. Gillian, that speech I learned from *King Lear.* You know, the one that goes:

> *"Come, let's away to prison.*
> *We two alone will sing like birds i' the cage.*
> *When thou dost ask me blessing . . ."*

He stops, swallows and, whispering, finishes:

"I'll kneel down
And ask of thee forgiveness. So we'll live,
And pray, and sing, and tell old tales, and laugh
At gilded butterflies."

Sighing, he says, "When I learned it, I never thought I'd ever be in prison. Not really. But when I was I said it over and over all night long."

"Did the poem help?"

"I don't know. The problem is forgiveness. I don't know what to say to Mr. Albertson. Just to say I'm sorry! That won't help! How can that help?"

"It's a way to begin."

He puts his foot down, runs his fingers through his hair, scratches his head. "And I don't know what will happen to me."

"Are you going to see him tomorrow?"

He shakes his head.

"Where are your glasses?"

"Here." He pulls them out of his jacket pocket.

Grace takes them from him and polishes them with the hem of her dress. "Put them on," she says. "Come inside with me. Lord, you look like a hobo. Come on." She stands. "I'll give you something to eat."

At the table, she sees the circles under his eyes and the light stubble on his chin. As he spoons hot soup into his mouth, at first slowly and then more eagerly, she sees the frayed sleeve of his dirty jacket. And so thin. Always thin, but now bone thin. Lord. She hears the second line of the song: *Oh, where have you been, charmin' Billy?*

He hadn't thought he could eat a bite. He has never liked soup. Not really. But with the hot bread and hot chocolate, the soup tastes good. And going up Mrs. Gillian's stairs, he had noticed his paint job. It still looks nice. He's done a lot on her house. Her yard, too.

Mrs. Gillian puts her elbows on the table. "You are older," she says softly. "Older than when I saw you last."

"I guess."

"Grieving about the War, about the boys Cold Springs has lost. I know you want to be part of it."

"I wanted to get in there. I needed to."

When he finishes the hot chocolate, she pours another cup for him. He holds it in both hands and brings it trembling to his lips.

"They wouldn't take me," he says then. "Nobody would listen when I told them I can see just fine. They just said, 'Son, go home.' "

Tears fill his eyes. Spill over. He wipes them away with a frayed sleeve. Mrs. Gillian doesn't say anything, but a line appears on her forehead. *What a blow. How awful,* her gray eyes say.

He takes a deep breath and exhales. "Going up the steps of the courthouse in Little Rock, we were all together, *men* together, but when they got to me, they said, 'Go home, son.' I took off, hitchhiking. When I got to Oklahoma, I heard about President Roosevelt."

"I felt as if I had lost a member of my family," she says.

"Me, too."

Surprised by the sudden appearance of tears (she had thought she was long past crying about the President's death), she wipes her eyes with a napkin. "Well, look at me," she says. She laces her fingers together, trying to make sense out of chaos. "When the invasion began, President Roosevelt made the most wonderful speech. He told us we were engaged in a mighty endeavor to set free a suffering humanity. I do believe that."

"Well, we've still got Mr. Churchill," Bobby says. "And Mr. Truman's been right there with President Roosevelt."

"I know. Everything will be all right someday. Better anyway." She leans back in the chair. "Look out the window. Still the same old moon."

Cal comes, twines himself around the chair legs, jumps into her lap, purrs loudly.

"Your cat has the loudest motor," Bobby says.

"I know," she chuckles.

After a minute, "My dad's in Washington. He left a note on my bed. I know he's gone up there to get my mother. She doesn't want to come home. I hate it!" He hits his knee with his fist. "I don't want her to come home to see about me."

"There are many reasons we do what we do." Mrs. Gillian goes to the stove, reheats the chocolate and pours herself a cup.

"Yeaw?" Bobby considers the reasons. "Well, she did promise Willie B. she'd come home if Willie B. died in our house."

"That's a reason."

"Yeaw."

"Probably more."

"Maybe."

"Bobby, you can find a way to serve your country."

"No, I can't. Nobody will take me."

"When I went to New York this summer, at every town where the train stopped, women and girls came with coffee and doughnuts. It helped the soldiers."

"Women and girls!" he says scornfully.

"Yes, Bobby," she says firmly. "Women and girls. You'll find a way. But right now you need sleep. You go home and sleep. Come down here in the morning and eat breakfast with me. We'll talk again."

As he leaves, she calls, "We'll have pancakes and sausage. I'm hungry for pancakes."

Bobby does not come for breakfast. Instead, he rings her doorbell late that afternoon. "I saw Mr. Albertson. And I know what I'm gonna do!" He is smiling widely, the old fedora at a jaunty angle.

"What?"

"I'll let you know." He goes down the steps and turns and comes back. "Oh, and Mrs. Gillian, thanks!"

Watching him trot off down the sidewalk, "Oh, Bobby," she whispers, "whatever it is, I hope you're going to be all right."

· 3 ·

BOBBY takes the first empty seat on the midnight bus for Dallas, climbing over a man on the aisle to sit by a window. He's not sure where he'll be sent once his training is over. He's going to ask for Tunisia. He doesn't know where Tunisia is, but it sounds like it's about as far from Cold Springs as anybody could get.

The Red Cross woman told him about the ambulance corps. "Go on over to Dallas and talk to the army. If they won't take you, the British will. They need ambulance drivers all over Western Europe and England and the South Pacific. You might have to go to Canada to join the British army, but they'll take you."

"Are you sure?"

"They've taken both my nephews, and neither one can see to walk across the street without his glasses. They'll take you. Both of them are over there right now, driving ambulances."

Bobby has never been as sure about anything. Being an ambulance driver is what he was born to do. He'll soon be driving an ambulance. He doesn't feel exactly happy, but he feels better than he has in a long time. And sure.

"Did they get you?" the man sitting next to him asks.

"Sir?"

The man, wearing khakis and work boots, has a long white beard and cheerful eyes.

"You been drafted?" he asks.

"No, sir. I'm on my way to Dallas. I'm joining the ambulance corps."

"Whoa now, sonny. I'd rather be a foot soldier. Driving an ambulance. Bound to be risky."

Bobby sits up straight and folds his arms. "They need ambulance drivers. I'm asking for Tunisia."

"Well, good luck, sir," the man says. "Say, I'd like to buy you a meal when we get to Greenville," he says.

Should he accept? Maybe he should wait to accept offers like that until he gets in. Before he can answer the man puts his head back and, immediately, begins to snore.

Bobby has too much to think about to sleep. Mr. Albertson. God! It was hard to go see Mr. Albertson. He had gone at the end of the school day. The halls were empty. He knew Mr. Albertson would be where he always was. And he was. Right there. Bent over his desk, grading papers.

When he came in, the old wooden floor had creaked so loud a deaf man could have heard it. But Mr. Albertson didn't look up. He just kept right on grading papers. And Bobby kept right on standing there, waiting for him to look up. He stood there so long he started counting the hairs on Mr. Albertson's bald head. Then he noticed his collar needed turning. Willie B. could have done it for him. She had turned collars for Bobby's father. Like always, Mr. Albertson's brown suit had chalk dust on it. Willie B. would have made short work of the chalk dust, too. Lord God, he still missed Willie B.

When Bobby felt a cramp in his leg and leaned over to rub it, Mr. Albertson gathered up the papers and lightly tapped them on his desk, straightening them. Looking up through gray, bushy eyebrows, "Bobby Moore," he growled.

"Sir?"

"What have you to say for yourself?"

"I'm sorry."

Mr. Albertson sat and looked at him.

"Being sorry doesn't help, does it?"

"It helps." Then Mr. Albertson sat awhile, looking at Bobby

like he was an algebra problem he couldn't solve. Finally, he said, "You look older, Bobby Moore."

"I should have jumped in there and helped you. I know I should have. I don't know why I didn't."

Mr. Albertson smiled. At least Bobby thought it was a smile.

"If you had, as you say, 'jumped in there,' they might have dropped me. I haven't been as scared since the war."

"The war! Were you in a war?"

Mr. Albertson opened the bottom drawer of his desk and pulled out a picture. "Hell, yes, I was in the war. The first war. I nearly died during the war!"

Bobby looked at the picture and, sure enough, there's this skinny guy in a uniform standing in front of a tire swing in somebody's yard. The guy has lots of hair. But he could tell it was Mr. Albertson.

"Were you in combat?"

"Yes, but what almost killed me was the flu I got on the ship going over. Miserable. Seasick. Crowded. And with the flu. I thought I'd die, and I didn't care if I did."

"Gosh."

"Bobby Moore, Mrs. Gillian told me you were turned down by the armed services. Your friends, God help them, will likely be in the Pacific pretty soon, fighting the Japanese, fighting a war that will have to be fought one island at a time. And I suppose you'd like to be over there with them."

"Yessir, I would."

"Bobby, there's nothing glorious about war."

Mr. Albertson stood up and walked to the window where they had held him upside down. He stood there, looking out. Then he straightened his shoulders and turned around to look at Bobby. "Well, yes, there is one thing," he said softly. "It's your buddies. I've never felt as close, never loved anyone in the same way I loved the men I fought with. I still think about the boys who didn't make it. Sometimes, when I'm at the blackboard, for no reason a face will be there behind the figures on the board or, explaining a problem, I'll hear something a buddy said, *hear his voice saying it.* You don't forget."

While Mr. Albertson was talking, Bobby looked at the picture and then at Mr. Albertson. He looked until the soldier in the picture and the hunched, gray man standing in front of him merged. He wished that he had always seen him like that—a gray-headed, old soldier in a young man's uniform.

Pretty soon, the bus is pulling into Greenville. THE BLACK-EST LAND AND THE WHITEST PEOPLE, the sign at the city limits says. The man beside him gets up. "I'm getting off here, but I'd like to buy you a hamburger. And a drink. What do you want to drink?"

"A Coke, sir."

As the bus pulls out, the man hurriedly hands the hamburger and Coke through the window.

"Thank you, sir."

"Thank you, son. You're a brave man. Good luck to you now."

With the seat beside him empty, Bobby can spread out a little. *You're a brave man,* the man had said. Mrs. Gillian and Mr. Albertson had both seen he was older. A lot had happened to make him older. Willie B. dying and his mother leaving. He had felt like he was a hundred, telling Dixie good-bye.

When he had stopped by, she said, "Bobby, if Jack takes the convertible, maybe you and I could get together after the War." Her brown eyes were enormous behind the glasses.

Remembering the Gypsy Dance, remembering all the times he had been second choice with her, "I'm not sure how things will be after the War ends," he had said.

Her eyes widened. "Well!" she said. Then, hands on her hips, she tapped her saddle oxford in a "Kiss me once and kiss me twice" beat. "Bobby, we can always dance together."

"Sure," he had said.

"And Bobby, we'll always be friends." And then she kissed him. On the mouth.

But it won't be Dixie, when it happens. He's pretty sure about that. When he falls in love, it will be with somebody like . . . well, like Bette Davis.

He wonders what his father will say to his mother. He guesses his father really loves her. *Love.* It's like a great big mystery you never get to the end of. He puts his head back and turns to look at the night. The stars are real, real bright, and the moon is full and bouncing alongside the bus. Keeping up.

And all at once he is visited by the memory of that moonlit night, of Mr. Sandflat jumping for the moon and of Maxine, proudly weeping like some great-hearted goddess out of Virgil. "I want the moon!" she cries. "Jump, Daddy! Jump for the moon!" And Mr. Sandflat, trying with all his might to get the moon for her. It is all there before him—the sweet aromatic smells of meat and chocolate and burning charcoal, the sounds of the animals and the white flowers in the moonlight. The memory remains. Perfect and whole. As if it had happened only yesterday.

Chapter 15

ALL week the town of Cold Springs has been breathless with anticipation. The war in Europe will soon be over. It's just a matter of time now. Days, maybe. Certain their sons will be coming home from Europe (at least for a long leave), farmers cheerfully work sunup to sundown to get the cotton thinned, the beans planted, and mothers work feverishly, turning a garage or a sewing room or a storage room into an extra bedroom. "With all he's been through, he's a man now. He'll need a room of his own," they say. At Chic-les-Dolls, young wives frown into mirrors. "Do you think he would like my hair short? It was longer than this when he left. It was way below my shoulders." Then, made reckless by longing, "Cut it!" they say. Small children, reminded to look at old photographs, ask, "Is that my daddy?" and, incredulously, "Is that baby me? That little baby he's holding? Is that me?" So many changes await the return of the Cold Springs soldiers.

The Texas Flier is on its way back home, its passenger cars filled with children running up and down the aisles, babies crying and mothers consoling them and, here and there, a handful of soldiers, sailors and marines scattered through the coaches.

The civilians look at the men in uniforms with awe and gratitude, wondering what to say, what to ask, what they can do for
men who have given so much, been through so much.

Sergeant Manning is traveling in the second coach. He is
happy. His leg is almost as good as new. In fact, he has not used
his crutch since he boarded the train in New York. But the reason for his happiness is Grace Gillian. He is on his way to see
Grace. She does not yet love him, but he is filled with the hope
that one day she will.

The twenty-two hours he was with her on the train was a
lifetime. He is possessed with her, mad about her. She is always
there, before his eyes. Bending to retrieve a napkin, her white
neck beneath abundant, auburn hair, her clear, cool voice talking to the soldiers. Her hands! A hundred memories of her
hands! Composed in her lap and opening, palms up, as she listened to Private Russell or, hands on her hips, head thrown
back, laughing at something Lieutenant Smith had said.

By the time the train leaves Washington, Sergeant Manning
knows all the children in his coach by name; he has answered
painful questions about the War from his fellow passengers; he
has told the young wives that their husbands would soon be
coming home.

Only the couple who sit in front of him have remained apart.
From the time they boarded the train in Washington, they have
been reserved with each other, distant with their fellow passengers. At first, he had thought they were brother and sister, both
so tall and with similar features. The woman, dark, with thick
black braids around her head and eyes of a shade so blue they
are startling. The man, gray-headed, aware of her every gesture,
his behavior toward her formal, as if to a stranger. Perhaps,
Sergeant Manning tells himself, they are merely acquaintances.

They hardly speak, the man and the woman. "Are you hungry?" the man asks, when the train leaves Baltimore. "Would
you like to have dinner now?"

"You go. Perhaps I'll have something later."

After dinner, the babies sleep and the children grow quiet. The sergeant falls into a deep sleep. Sometime in the night, he is awakened by the man's voice: "Why, then, are you coming home?" The voice is quietly insistent.

"To see my children. But I cannot live with you, Robert. Not anymore." Her voice, softer than his, is calm.

"You know I love you."

"You have owned me. You have not loved me. I did not know this until I tried to help Willie B. And then I knew I was in prison."

"I've changed. I will change."

"Can you? I do not believe it."

"I will try. With all my heart, I will try." Now his voice is raised.

After that the silence is so long, Sergeant Manning believes one or the other of them is asleep. But then, "You may have your own bank account."

"*May* have!" she cries. "My own bank account is a right, not a privilege. I have my own bank account now. My own job!"

"Yes."

The sergeant turns to the window and sees the full moon. *Life is sweet,* he longs to tell them. *Just love each other if you can.* He remembers Grace's smile as she held a book and read. He falls asleep again.

When Robert had appeared at her apartment in George-town, Barbara saw him as a stranger, someone she had never known or cared about. She had opened her door, as she would to any human so obviously in need, and said, "Come in."

He stood in the middle of the small room, his arms at his side, and looked at her. Thinner, she seemed taller. Her hair, as he had seen it countless times, a thick braid down her back. Her face, pale. Her eyes, fringed in long, black lashes, still so astonishingly blue.

"Oh, God, Barbara, I almost went crazy," he said, his voice a deep moan. He pulled her to him, held her tightly.

She was stiff, unyielding. "No. You did not. You will not. But the children have had a terrible time because of me. Because of us."

"Bobby has been expelled. He will not be able to graduate. He's been hitchhiking all over Oklahoma."

"Oklahoma! What happened? Tell me."

He told her all he knew. As she listened, she walked to the desk, lit a cigarette.

"I didn't know you smoked," he said.

"Go on," she said.

He told her about Bobby's expulsion, his drinking, his finding Willie B. dead. He told her about Celia's unhappiness, whether living at home or with the Little Brontës. And as he talked, none of it seemed to matter. What mattered was that he was here with her. In the same room. In the middle of his narration, he stopped. *You have never been so lovely,* he thought.

"Go on," she said. She put the cigarette in an ashtray, stood up, crossed her arms, leaned over and tapped out the cigarette. "Go on," she said again.

"Baker was the judge. He told me Bobby had no part in the assault on Mr. Albertson. But he did nothing to help."

"Where is Bobby now?"

"I don't know. He may be home by now. But he does not want you to come back because of him. He has made that clear."

She picked up the telephone. "Long distance," she said. When the phone began to ring, she counted the rings. When it had rung ten times, she broke the connection and said, "Operator, please ring that number again." After another ten rings, she hung up.

"I am glad you came. I'll call the office and pack. Please. Would you see about the next train right away?"

*   *   *

And now, she asks again: "Where do you think Bobby is? Where could he be?"

"I don't know. The house without you. Who could blame him for leaving!"

"He has to know I love him."

"He knows that. Celia is miserable, moving back and forth between the two houses. Barbara, please come home!"

"I don't know if I can. I truly don't know."

"Oh, God, I've missed you."

"Robert, in many ways I've missed you, too. But I do not think we can live together."

They fall silent as the sergeant, sitting behind them, stands and, slightly limping, heads into the diner for a midnight cup of coffee.

Barbara falls asleep; her head tilts, comes to rest on his shoulder. Robert sits, hardly breathing, so as not to wake her.

Just outside Cincinnati, they go to the dining car together. Robert sees the movement of her hips, the canted way she holds her head, the long stride of her walk. The sergeant sees the longing in the tall man's face.

Dan Manning shaves and changes his uniform. In the dining car he slowly eats a breakfast of scrambled eggs, bacon and coffee, savoring the taste, the smell of it. He glances at the front page, turns quickly to the funnies. Gazing out the train's window, he deliberately conjures up the memory of Grace, of the warmth of her kiss when she said good-bye. He sees her as she had been on the train, waking up, stretching, reaching for his hand. "I dreamed I was taking care of everybody," she had said.

Looking out the window, Barbara sees a child on a tricycle. "Do you remember the Christmas you put Bobby's tricycle on the roof and told him Santa Claus couldn't get it down the chimney?"

He smiles. "It was your idea."

The first time he has smiled. She had forgotten how handsome he is. "And you fell off the roof, trying to get it down," she says.

"And broke four ribs."

She shakes her head. "And the time you took Celia out to the fairgrounds when the circus came."

"And you told her I might buy her an elephant."

"And she cried until the elephant keeper said they needed all their elephants.

"Oh, Robert," she says. "It's just that we are so different. But there are the children. Right now, I want to see them. I cannot promise more."

By the time they cross the Mississippi the next morning, their voices mingle—hers wondering, his pleading.

"I have changed," he says.

"How?"

"Now I know you mean the world to me."

"I want you to understand my world."

"I will learn," he says. "I am learning."

Pulling into Texarkana, the train slows. "We went to Willie B.'s funeral. They sang 'In That Great Gettin' Up Good Mornin','" he says, his voice suddenly husky. "Something happened. I can't explain, but . . . it touched me. The love. The sorrow and joy. Their faith. It was in the music."

She looks into his face, sees tears in his eyes. "Oh, Robert," she says. Turning away she looks out the window, sees cows grazing under giant oaks and cypress trees. She shifts in her seat and turns toward him. "I promised Willie B. I'd come home if she died in our house. I did not forget. I planned to come after the War."

"Bobby's always been different," he says suddenly.

"He's not like you."

"No, he's not. But it's more than that. When Mr. Sandflat died, he went to his funeral."

"I didn't know Bobby knew Mr. Sandflat," she says wonderingly.

Made closer by this mystery of their son, when he reaches for her hand, she is content to let him hold it.

When the train leaves Texarkana, she turns suddenly to the sergeant. "Sergeant, where are you going?"

"To Cold Springs," he grins. "And I need a horse."

They laugh. "That's where we live," the man says, looking at his wife. "Have lived," he adds tentatively.

"A horse?" she says. The sergeant does look familiar. He reminds her of somebody.

"I'm serious," he says. "I've got to find a horse. There's this woman. I fell in love with her just before I shipped out. She's never written me, never answered my letters. But I saw her and I fell in love. She teaches school in Cold Springs. She's an English teacher."

"Grace Gillian," Barbara says.

"How did you know?" the sergeant exclaims.

"My husband loved her once."

Robert Moore's eyes widen; his mouth falls open.

Barbara throws back her head and laughs, a laugh that rings through the coach, causes passengers to turn and smile. "It's all right, Robert," she says. "Who wouldn't love Grace Gillian!"

Robert Moore takes her hand, raises it to his lips. "Not as I've loved you," he says fervently. "Not as I will always love you."

· 2 ·

TWO hours later, Dan Manning watches a woman lead a horse out of a small barn. The barn is old, weathered to a silvery gray. The woman's face is brown and just as weathered. She is a small woman, but the muscles on her arms are surprisingly large, as are her hands. The horse is white and quite old. A scar shaped like a bolt of lightning zigzags across his chest.

The woman says, "Sergeant, I'm in a hurry to get downtown myself. I guess you'll be wanting Old Major for the parade."

"No."

"Well, he'd be fine in a parade. He carried the Colors at the Fort Worth Fat Stock Show a number of times. In his younger days a'course."

The horse stands as the woman, a brush in each hand, begins to groom him. His head is small, the dish well-defined. Dan Manning puts his hand on the horse's muzzle. "Hey, Major," he says. He lifts the upper lip. "Old Major must be over twenty years old."

"Yep. But he's still got good teeth. I feed him up. Lots of grain. But I can't seem to put any weight on him."

"He's got a head like an Arabian's."

"He's got that bloodline. Too bad you're not gonna ride him in the parade. He likes parades and people. Always has."

The woman had noticed the sergeant's slight limp when he got out of the taxi. But except for that, he acted like he didn't have a care in the world. In fact, he had the happiest look about him she'd seen in a long time.

"In a parade, he moves like a young gelding," the woman says hopefully.

The sergeant touches the scar on the horse's chest, sees the rippling effect of tiny muscles recoiling in old memory. "I've got other plans," he says. "That's quite a scar there."

"A storm came on. He took off running. Ran through a barbed wire fence and carried the whole fence about a mile before I could catch him."

"I thought maybe the War."

"No. But I reckon you carry a few scars from the War yourself."

Recoiling as if she has touched a nerve, his mouth tightens, his hand grips Old Major's mane. "I'm limping a little. It'll soon be gone. Tell you what. I'd like to take him out now, bring him back about sundown."

She has just about stopped letting anybody take the horse out. Kids are too likely to run him as soon as they're out of sight. And most don't know a thing about horses. Or care to learn either. But she likes the sergeant. Likes the sure way he touches the horse. He would go easy on Old Major. She can see that.

"Let's get the saddle on," she says. In the tack room, she impulsively takes down the Fat Stock Show gear. Old Major deserves it. And so does the sergeant.

"This is a handsome saddle," he says, tightening the girth. "And this bridle. All the silver. You sure you trust me with all this?" the man says. And now he's smiling a smile that would warm a man in an Amarillo blizzard.

"I do," she says.

She watches proudly as they go down the narrow dirt drive, headed away from the parade toward Pine Street. Old Major high-stepping, flagging his tail, arching his neck; the sergeant sitting tall and easy in the saddle.

"Those two, they ought to be leading the parade," she tells herself, hurrying into the house to get the keys to the pickup.

Chapter 16

· 1 ·

THE Cold Springs High School Band, assembled at East Third and Broad Street, is about to march. A whistle blows. Lines form. Excitement and energy crackle through the sunshine. The drum major blows his whistle, and to the first notes of Sousa's "Washington Post March," he steps out! His baton glitters in the sun; he struts, throws it high, and higher still. Never has his march been as exaggerated, never has he tilted his head so far back and lifted his knees so high. The crowd roars. The brass can scarcely blow their horns because of the wide grins on their faces. The drummers beat a steady *thrum, thrum* of celebration.

The crowd grows more dense.

Germany has surrendered! The war with Germany is over! The battlefields of Europe are silent. Tomorrow, President Truman will remind the nation that the War is not yet won, but, today, all along Broad and Main Streets, soldiers, merchants, housewives and children pour out of shops and schools; farmers jump into pickups, soldiers into jeeps—all hurrying, hurrying into town. Sirens whistle and bells ring out. A chorus of song, "A Mighty Fortress Is Our God," swells from the Methodist church, and from a company of soldiers on Pine and Broad: "Pardon me, boys, is that the Chattanooga Choo-Choo?/Yes,

yes, track 29./Boy, you can give me a shine." The band picks it up. *Doodle-de-doo. Doodle*-de-*doo.* The crowd roars. A huge throng. Shoulder to shoulder. Soldiers grab women, kiss them, whirl them around, turn to find another eager pair of arms, and then, still another. The air is full of exuberance, of joy, of celebration on this day, the seventh of May.

When she heard the sirens, Amelia called. "I'm on my way over. I'll be there in twenty minutes."

"Oh, Amelia, isn't it wonderful? I can't believe it. I still can't believe it!"

"You will when we get downtown. Now, hurry!"

Throwing open her closet door, taking down the first dress her hand touched, she stepped into panties, fastened a bra and slipped blue silk over her head. Buttoning the dress with one hand, she slipped on penny loafers and brushed her hair. She was running down the stairs when she remembered her purse and was turning back to get it when she heard Amelia's car. *Who needs a purse today! Who needs anything today!* she thought exultantly.

And now, Amelia and Grace hurry first to Amelia's church ("I'd have made a good Catholic," Grace tells her) to give thanks to God that the War in Europe is over. The church fills with people, people giving thanks and praying. After Communion (and not raising an eyebrow, Amelia watches Grace take the wafer and the cup) and a hymn, the two women are out again, into streets thronged with people, Amelia saying, "I'm married," before hugging a soldier, and he replying, "I am, too, darling."

"Well, I'm not," Grace says, laughing, before stepping into the arms of a tall, blond giant of a man, and then into the arms of another just as tall, but so thin she feels his rib bones. They hug and laugh and kiss, the old and the young, all in an orgy of innocent joy such as they have never known.

It is Amelia who first sees him. In the late afternoon, she

sees this man on a horse. The afternoon light is behind him so that she has to shade her eyes to be sure that it is a horse and that a man is on its back.

"Look, Grace," she says. "At that man, that soldier, on that old horse."

The sight of the soldier, riding slowly, has gathered a celebratory and curious crowd—some soldiers, a few students, young children, a woman in a pickup truck following carefully. The horse is white and very old. When he comes nearer, they see the man's dark skin, his brown eyes, the cleft in his chin.

"Grace, do you see him? He looks like Cary Grant!"

Grace laughs. "Oh, I see him," she says happily. "And the first time I saw him I thought he looked like Cary Grant."

Now he sees Grace and comes slowly, riding slowly, so that she sees, has all the time in the world to see, the glittering bridle, the burnished saddle leather, her lace handkerchief in the band of his hat.

"You in the cavalry?" a soldier calls good-naturedly. Another calls, "Hey, Sergeant! Where you going on that horse?"

"It's my horse," the small woman says proudly, her truck parked and she out of it by now.

"He's coming this way, Grace. Who in the world is he?"

"He's just a soldier I met on the train." Her voice is vibrant, her face radiant. "A wonderful soldier."

Now he is close—strong hands holding the horse's reins, brown eyes shining in the afternoon sun, a smile that becomes merrier as he reins the horse and prepares to dismount.

"But you don't know him."

"Oh, I do. I know him very well," Grace says, and waits, serenely confident, as he dismounts to kneel clumsily at her feet.

Grace takes his hands in hers and pulls him to his feet.

"Kiss her!" young Barley Timberlake cries.

"Oh, Grace!" Amelia whispers.

The crowd takes up young Barley's cry. "Kiss her!" "Give her a good one, soldier!" "It's been a long, long time."

"Will you marry me?" he says.

"Oh, now, Grace," Amelia begins.

Deaf to all but the sergeant's voice, "I am so happy," Grace tells him. "I am so very happy that you're here."

"I love you, Grace," he says. "And life is sweet. Say you'll marry me."

Hearing the faint sounds of church bells and marching band and singing soldiers, Grace stands perfectly still. Then she puts her hands on her hips and leans toward him. She chuckles. And those who are near enough to hear this, this note of pure, unrestrained joy, break into broad smiles.

The small woman takes the reins. "Sergeant, I'll take Old Major home," she says.

"I'd appreciate it," he says, grinning.

Suddenly serious, he steps closer to Grace, the yearning on his face visible for all the world to see. "I had forgotten how pretty you are. Will you, Grace? Will you marry me?"

"I may," she says softly. "Come. Here's my house. Right here."

"Marry me," he says. "And we'll watch the sunsets, see the mountains, not huge, not like the Rockies, but their colors— purple, blue, amethyst—as the night falls."

He takes her hand. They walk along the sidewalk under giant sycamores, turn up the path to her house. "We'll talk," she says, "and . . ."

"And I'll tell you about the ranch and you'll . . ."

"I'll show you my garden," she says. "The hyacinths in full bloom and the daisies coming on."

And stepping inside, Grace closes the door behind them.

Epilogue

FOUR months later the War was over, and everything was different. Soldiers came home and fell in love all over again with wives and sweethearts. Soldiers came home and found they were no longer in love with women who had become strangers. Under the GI Bill the soldiers went to college, left the farms and sawmills and country towns to become lawyers and engineers and doctors.

Now five years after the War has ended, the houses on the 900 block of Pine Street look very much the same except for the small house across the alley at the end of the block. Repaired and painted a soft sienna color and with pots of begonias along the railing, it has taken on a whimsical, quaint air, somewhat reminiscent of Grace Gillian's house before she sold it.

Dixie still lives in this house. Recently divorced, she has finished Cold Springs Junior College and now drives back and forth to Denton, where she is completing a degree in music. She loves the freedom of the drive, especially on the days when she can put down the top of her convertible (a gift from the Pearces). Then, with the wind in her face, she feels as if she's flying.

The Appleby house has been repainted and repaired. Because John Appleby's young wife, a former WAC, likes to ride, the carriage house has been turned into a small stable. Riding is a passion for Mavis Appleby. In fact, she is seldom off a horse's back, but John takes great pleasure in the ribbons and trophies she wins. The real estate law he practices is not demanding, and he believes he is happy. He does not think about mermaids or about Grace, except on rare occasions such as New Year's Eve when he's had far too much to drink. Then the new people in Grace's house might find him in the swing in their own yard asking if they have ever heard them. Heard the mermaids. Singing.

The Moore house is as well kept as ever. A week after Barbara came home to stay, the Little Brontës forgot they had ever thought of replacing her with Grace. Now that Robert is sublimely happy, Barbara is a paragon of virtue in their eyes.

The surprise of children has repaired their tattered marriage. Barbara had thought her daughter, Celia, would be content to marry and sit by the swimming pool, but she took a degree from the university in three years and will finish law school next year. And Bobby? Although he married a Mexican woman, lives in Mexico and seldom comes home, Bobby has become a legend.

It began with soldiers, some on crutches, traveling through Cold Springs after the War. "A guy I knew was from Cold Springs. Drove an ambulance. *Loved* poetry. He couldn't see worth a damn, but he was absolutely fearless," said a private on crutches. This from a captain: "He'd drive through hell to pick up our wounded, quoting poems, one after another." "We called him Cinco," said a grizzled major. "Quoting Shakespeare and Kipling and who knows who else, he'd drive through minefields, dodge bullets, go anywhere to get a wounded man." When Bobby occasionally visits, he denies the stories. "Some other guy," he says.

Grace Gillian's house has been painted, a more sedate color of gray with white trim. But the town still talks about Dan Manning and about how he came riding on that old white horse to propose to Grace. On his first visit Dan stayed three days, stayed *properly* at Amelia and Ed's house. The morning of the fourth day, he and Grace drove to New Mexico (stopping to repair a flat tire every hundred miles or so) in Grace's car. For a week, they rode by mountain streams, down into canyons, saw rabbits running and kites wheeling in the high skies. She fell slowly (his word, teasing) in love with Dan. By the end of the week, she was madly in love, insanely in love with him, and planning a cactus garden on the ranch.